Blood in the Water

A Sean Kendall Thriller

Seth Sjostrom

wolfprint, LLC
Camas, WA, 98607

For information, contact wolfprintMedia.

Blood in the Water: a thriller / by Seth Sjostrom. - 1st wolfprintMedia digital edition

Paperback
ISBN-13: 978-0-9854389-7-5

1. Sean Kendall (Fictitious character)-Fiction. 2. Terrorism-Ecological-Political-Fiction. 3. Blood Series-Fiction I. Title.

First wolfprintMedia Digital edition 2019.

wolfprintMedia is a trademark of wolfprint, LLC.

For information regarding bulk purchases, please contact wolfprint, LLC, at wolfprint@hotmail.com.

United States of America

Acknowledgements

To my supportive father, Tom Sjostrom. He taught me there are always two sides to every story, encouraging me to research and understand (though not necessarily condone) the motivations of people.

To my wife, Kathi Sjostrom for continued support.

To John Eley who accompanied me on a cold, wet trip to the Olympic Peninsula.

To the Makah Nation for hosting us at their museum.

To Randi Decker for her beautiful cover photo.

One

The fog hung heavy in the air over the Olympic Peninsula. Ecologist Jim Harrison sat on the beach encircling Neah Bay, where the Pacific Ocean and the Strait of Juan de Fuqua met in a cool and often stormy convergence. Despite being mere yards from the water, it was only the sound of the waves lapping against the shoreline that afforded him the knowledge that the ocean was near. Harrison was hopeful that the thick mist would deter the day's proposed hunt. This trip marked the third year in a row that he led the opposition to the Makah Tribe's whale hunting ceremony.

With the exception of a successful and well-publicized hunt in 1999, where a young pilot whale was speared in the waters just beyond the beach he was now sitting, the many groups that opposed the Makah's desire to continue their homage to ancestral whale hunting have kept the tribe's efforts at bay. The courts and the International Whaling Commission had debated granting a reprieve in the ban on whaling for the tribe's annual event. This year, Harrison expected a more massive crowd than ever to participate in the protest. The courts found themselves up against an impending deadline to decide on the long-standing case, and both sides felt that now was the time to make their final stand.

Harrison was deep in thought, enough that he did not hear the footsteps behind him. Then again, each step landed with well-practiced precision that would have allowed a jump on the most sensitive of prey. The mere whoop of a perfectly thrown spear sailing through the air was the only audible warning that the counselor might have had if not for his attention harnessed by the hypnotic pulse of the waves. The cold piece of shale that had been chiseled by hand to adorn the point of the historic weapon punched through Harrison's flesh as easily as a kitchen knife dispensing with a tomato. The startled activist gasped, whirling around to face his assassin. The long shaft of the spear punched clean through his body scraping along the sand as it gorged the wound further, ripping at the sensitive tissue that protected his precious organs.

The activist felt his pulse explode as sheer terror engulfed him. Reduced to instinct, he began running down the beach. He could feel blood streak down his stomach, and with each step that he took, his right lung screamed in pain. Desperately, he searched for solace along the beachfront, but with the morning's dismal visibility, he quickly became disoriented. As well as he knew the area, all sense of direction and rational thought had fled the moment he looked down and saw the spearhead sticking through his chest. The unyielding blood loss caused his blood pressure to plummet, spinning the frightened man increasingly dizzy. In desperation, he tried to scream for help, but no sounds made their way to his lips, just pathetic gasps muffled by the pounding surf.

Harrison stumbled along the sand, finally colliding with a signpost that marked the rules of the recreation area. He hung on the four-by-four wood pole for support, using his ears to scan for continued danger. Even as attentive as he was to his surroundings, the ecologist did not hear his assassin approach. The shadow-less figure crept behind him, and without warning, grasped his full head of hair in strong, gloved hands. Harrison's eyes widened as he focused on the being that stood before him. If it weren't for the blood pounding in his ears, he would have sworn that his heart had stopped beating. The last few moments of his life replayed over and over in his head. His assailant tracked his erratic movements along the beach, sniping him with such stealth and calm. Harrison couldn't believe the Makah would go this far – to murder the voice of the whaling opposition. Now his murderer stood there holding his head up by his thick brown hair, in one fluid motion, his besieger produced a wicked curved blade from its sheath and plunged the steel dagger into his throat.

Silently, Jim Harrison slid down the post that he had clung to and landed headlong into the sand. He lay at the base of the sign in a fetal ball, the spear that seemed to have come from nowhere, flaunted in the air like the sword Excalibur, waiting to be freed. His life bled away as the red syrupy fluid from the sinister gash to his throat mingled with the blood that had escaped from his speared chest. Together the meandering streaks of red made their way down the sandy slope to meet with the froth of the ocean waters. Greedily, the tide lapped at the murderous stain, erasing the evidence of the horror forever.

Away into the fog, as if part of the mist itself, the killer disappeared, an apparition that might have never existed, had the footsteps in the sand not belied his presence. In the faint light of dawn, he left Harrison to slip into inky darkness and away from life.

Two

The single blast of the horn heralded to Tug Gaskill that the freighter carrying him across the Pacific had finally entered into the waters of Japanese authority. That meant his cramped stay on the way to Osaka was coming to its conclusion. The berth that served as the temporary residence for Tug was less than spacious. He was ready for a change. It wasn't so much that he wasn't used to staying in undesirable quarters. He spent plenty of occasions, both in his time in the U.S. military special forces and through his mercenary work in Central and South America, living for weeks in tunnels, cramped ships or even sleeping in trees in the steamy canopy of the jungle. No, on this occasion, Tug was just eager to get his feet on terra firma so that he could begin assembling the details of his next steps - steps that would gain a little retribution along with a great deal of personal security.

He lamented his last mission, one that had afforded far too many loose ends and very nearly his capture. His close brush with a life stay on capital row, he chagrined, all because of the dumb luck of a pair of good-doers that pushed their noses into his business. He admitted, to himself, that the cast of characters he worked with had a hand in the near disaster. It had been his job to lead a group of country bumpkins on a raid to destroy a Seattle convention center that was housing the primary delegates of the Free Trade Conference. All of his crew met their eventual death, which was fine with Tug, but he was winged when one of the do-gooders, a wildlife agent of all people, had confronted him. His determination had allowed him to escape the ambulance, which in all of the chaos of the battle-torn Seattle waterfront, was sent away without an escort, allowing him to meet his rendezvous to safety.

Tug settled in on the freighter as it eased its way out of Puget Sound to its present location, just outside of Osaka, Japan. His primary task now - take out anyone who could identify him from that mission. He had his accountant verify that the senator who hired him had fulfilled his end. One million dollars in offshore accounts awaited the mercenary, and yet, he was deeply dissatisfied. The wildlife agent and his friend needed to be taken care of. Tug was worried that his discontent was merely him being prideful, but he justified his preoccupation as cleaning up potential loose ends. The federal employee, his little pal, and even the Japanese businessman that provided him safe passage out of the country, were complications. The senator and his wimpy aide had more to lose than he did, and he had suspicions that they had more money to toss his way in the near future - enough to allow them to live, for the time being at least.

The mercenary scratched his scruffy chin. He would want to carry out his plans quickly, but he knew that he would have to wait for the dust to settle. As he thought of his options, he knew that he didn't want to let this drag out too long. The risk that someone might be able to finger him was too great. He had ample opportunities to live in the sanctuary of exile, but preferred a life where he could come and go when and where he pleased. No, he would need to take care of any threats that might exist. He looked out at the writing that filled the band surrounding the smokestack of the freighter, H-A-S-E-G-A-W-A. The wealthy Japanese business owner had taken a shine to him. Moreover, he seemed plenty gullible, just the advantage that Tug could capitalize.

In the days following the events that had taken place in Seattle - the tragedy, the drama - Sean Kendall wondered if the romance that sprouted between him and Miranda Shaw was merely an interlude or if it would continue to grow into something more. She had been quite shaken once the reality of her cousin's death set in. Sean's hand in Jeb's death had been too much for the marine biologist to deal with. She left abruptly for her home in Anacortes, and with the exception of a single soft kiss on his cheek, she drove off without a word.

Sean's Greater Swiss Mountain Dog, Sammy, sat beside him and watched as his master tossed rocks into the gurgling waters of the Skagit River. The big dog soaked in the sunshine provided by a departure of the perpetual cloud layer signaling early spring. Most of the snow had melted into the river that was eagerly accepting the small stones launched by Kendall.

Sean must have picked up the phone a dozen times in the last couple of weeks. Each time, he laid it back down, deciding to let the captivating woman have her time to grieve and allow the chips to fall where she, or fate, decided. The two had made plans for him to join her at her home on the Washington coast, but the silence told him that plans would not come to fruition. A bachelor for two years following his divorce, he had become content with his life of solitude, but Miranda had spoiled all of that. He would find himself thinking of her in the oddest of moments. Little things would remind him of the time that they had spent together. It wasn't that he didn't understand; her cousins had been killed either directly or indirectly by his own hands. The events of the short time that they knew each other were intense, crazy - at times, they were downright terrifying.

The attractive marine biologist's entire life had been permanently changed with her family torn apart by the terrorist attack at the convention center in Seattle. The attack her family played a significant role in. No, he couldn't blame her for shrinking into the seclusion of her coastal life; he was just disappointed. She brought out feelings in him that he didn't think would ever resurface after the failure of his first marriage.

The young retiree rubbed his dog's head and reached down for his beer. As the bottle swung up, the wedge of lime slid to the skinny neck of the container towards his lips. Sean gulped the beer and casually tossed the empty bottle over his head onto the soft lawn. The glass clinked as it tapped against the last bottle that Sean launched over his shoulder. He opened the cooler for another, finding it empty. He looked at Sammy, wondering if he gave the command, would his very loyal Swissie know how to fetch more from the well-stocked refrigerator.

A single eyebrow lifted on the large dog as if to answer his question.

"I didn't think so," Sean confirmed.

Three

The beach exploded with reporters, on-lookers, and policemen bustling about in seemingly pointless directions. Yellow tape marked "Crime Scene - Do Not Cross" was strung in a rough square around the beach. Some of the morning's mist had burnt off, but enough clung in the air to keep an eerie, surreal presence around the scene.

Joe Woodfeathers, a detective from the Snohomish tribe, squeezed his way through the growing crowd to join the other policemen that were scouring the beach assisting the forensics team in their search for clues. The Makah tribal police chief had called him in desperation. A murder had taken place on their beach, and they wanted a fellow Native American to assist in the investigation. The local civil authorities had already been summoned, and they were sure that the feds would be sticking their unwanted noses into the incident as well. To make matters worse, the victim had been slain with a traditional Makah whaling spear, and the victim himself, was the leader in opposition to the tribe's renewed attempts to kill a whale during their annual spring potlatch festival. The whole scenario looked to cast a very negative stone against the tribe. Woodfeathers represented their best chance at receiving a fair inquiry.

The detective flashed his credentials and walked up to the site of the speared environmentalist. The body lay slumped onto the sand, his head supporting his torso as it leaned against a signpost. Through his upper back, the shaft of a long spear stuck prominently in the air. Woodfeathers gasped briefly at the sight, collected himself, and proceeded to walk calmly up to the body. He looked up at the other Makah tribal policemen.

"Who was the responding officer?" the Snohomish detective asked.

"I, I was sir," a young tribal policemen responded.

"When did you arrive at the scene?" the detective asked.

"Uh, about an hour and a half ago. My superior called you immediately when he got here," the officer answered.

"This is how you found him?"

"Yessir. It's terrible," came the response.

"Yes. Yes, it is terrible. How long do you figure he was here before you found him?" Woodfeathers continued his questioning.

"I don't know. I got here. He was dead. Just lying there…like that," he said, pointing to the naturalist.

Woodfeathers reached the body and placed his hand on the neck of the hunched-over man. The skin was cool, but not yet cold. He gave the body a slight shake. The dead man's limbs moved slightly. Not like normal, but not with the rigidity of full rigor mortis, either. He looked at his watch, nodded to himself, and began to sweep his eyes across the beach.

"You guys find anything?" the detective asked.

"No, not yet. A bunch of footprints, but they left no identifiable marks," the young Makah tribesman replied.

"Joe Woodfeathers!" a voice called out to the Snohomish detective who was bending over to take a closer look at one of the footprints in the sand.

"Marty, you son of a gun. So, you had them call me in. I'm not exactly in my jurisdiction, you know old friend," Joe said, giving the Makah police chief a hug.

"I needed your help. This doesn't look good for my people, Joe. Especially with all of the media here," Marty Lanook said, his hand following the circle of police tape that kept the throng of onlookers at bay.

"Well, I figure the man has been dead only about three hours or so. One of your hunting spears?" Joe asked, afraid of the answer that he already knew.

"Yes, but not from our hunting party. This one is from the display in the museum," reported the police chief.

"Huh. Well, these prints look like moccasin. Smooth, no tread, nice craftsmanship, really. Have you ID'd the victim?"

"Oh yeah. Jim Harrison. One of the protesters. In fact, the leader of the protesters," Marty replied.

"Man, when you said it didn't look good, you weren't kidding. You know, you aren't going to be able to keep this tribal…" Joe warned his friend.

"I know. But I was hoping that you would stay on to…to make sure that things were done fairly," the police chief said, his voice showing elevated level concern.

"Of course. The locals are en route?" Joe asked as his friend nodded. "Alright, we can keep them out, but I imagine the feds will be here soon enough."

Joe continued surveying the gruesome scene, tracing the footsteps back to where it appeared that the attack had begun. With his eyes, he followed the path of the spear as it met its target. He noticed the half-circle in the sand where the victim, ecologist Jim Harrison, whirled around to face his attacker. He saw the deep impressions in the sand where Harrison pushed off to try and evade a second assault. The trail led directly back to the signpost, where the body still sat slumped over on the beach. One single set of footprints, void of any markings on the sole, plodded after the frightened man.

Blood seeped into the sand, a trail making its way to the shore break, finally diluting in the surf. Joe bent down and inspected the neck wound - a single strike with a curved blade cutting clean through the major arteries and windpipe. He wondered about the weapon, but his thoughts breached with the sound of a helicopter overhead. Pausing, he looked up at the noisy distraction, "Newshounds are here," he mumbled to himself. He looked out at the crowd that was buzzing about the scene, cameras flashing pictures with abandon. He was about to inspect the victim more thoroughly when he noticed that the crowd began to part as though Moses himself had arrived and was summoning the division of the sea.

A series of men in black suits cloaked with dark trench coats made their way through the crowd. Ducking under the yellow tape, they forged a path to the tribal police officers. "FBI, who is in charge here?" one of the men asked, gruffly shoving his badge at the team, inspecting the victim.

"I am. I am the police chief of the Makah tribe. These are my men," Marty Lanook said, pointing to his two deputies and then to Joe, "This is Joe Woodfeathers, detective from the Snohomish reservation."

"Hmm. A little out of your jurisdiction, aren't you Woodfeathers?" the man who appeared to be in charge of the federal agents asked, his voice airing a tone of annoyance.

"I asked detective Woodfeathers to be here as an observer," Marty replied.

"Very well. Just stay out of the way and don't touch anything. Murder is an exemption to rules on reservation jurisdiction, as I am sure you know," the man replied curtly and began giving instructions to the four agents that had trailed him.

The little crew of federal investigators began to set up their staging area. A fold-up table assembled to hold a series of forensic equipment.

"Has anything been removed from the scene?" the lead agent asked.

"No, everything is just as we found it," replied the Makah police chief.

"I want everything inventoried and secured," the FBI agent declared to his team, and turned back to the tribal policemen, "If you gentlemen would like to help, you just keep that audience at bay."

"He's a real charmer," Joe whispered into Marty's ear.

"I am a real charmer, Mr. Woodfeathers, and I have excellent hearing too," the agent called out, his tone never changing from the moment he arrived.

Joe stood back and allowed the agents to do their work. He had seen what he needed to out on the beach. He turned to Marty, "Grab a cup of coffee?"

His friend nodded his head and led Joe to the edge of the tape and into the crowd. "Is everyone accounted for?" Joe asked as they walked along the path leading to Marty's office.

Marty nodded, "Yes. They are all preparing for the celebration. That certainly won't happen today."

"So, tell me, Marty, is there anyone in the tribe who has been in conflict with Harrison?" the detective asked.

"Who hasn't? The guy has been a thorn in the side of the entire reservation. Probably affected the hunters the most. They are the ones who have to deal with his insurgents out on the water. Overall, clashes between the two groups have been primarily made up of verbal sparring back and forth. There have been a few incidents in the water with boats running into each other. Still, as far as physical confrontation between individuals, it has remained fairly civil," the Makah police chief answered.

"Until now," Joe replied.

"Until now…," Marty agreed sullenly.

Senator Timothy Small sat on the balcony of his Washington D.C. office. He watched the traffic on the mall bustle about - the lobbyists, aides and fellow senators and congressmen - like a bunch of rats trying to locate the cheese in a maze desperately. The trick, he surmised, is to control the rats and get them to move in the direction that you want them to. This was a difficult task in this town, but it was one that he had recently begun to understand and manipulate. With the backing of a few affluent colleagues, he had secured his own pied piper to change public perception and policy, or destroy those who would not comply on their own.

He heard the door leading to his office open, "Sir, Mr. Billings has arrived." Jerry Rhinehart, his number one aide, held the door open for the senator to pass through. They both moved into the senator's office and settled into red leather-clad high-back chairs.

"Senator, I don't think I need to tell you the Seattle operation did not exactly go down as we drew it up. Now, I'm here to tell you I expect it to all be cleaned up," the wealthy Texan declared.

"For Pete's sake, Harold, you know me well enough to know that I of all people do not like loose ends. In fact, I've planned for this. I assume you are concerned over our boy, Tug. I made arrangements to keep tabs on him even as he made his hasty departure. I had our weapons conduit, and financier Mr. Hasegawa provide for his transportation. I have been able to receive reports on his whereabouts since he left the port of Seattle six weeks ago," the senator replied.

"Oh, hogwash, Small! A man like Gaskill only lets you receive the information that he wants you to have. Don't be so damned naïve," Billings scoffed at his fellow conspirator, clenching his cigar tightly between his uneven teeth.

"True, but I think even he knows that it would be prudent to lay low for a while. As long as we keep him in our plans, I don't believe he poses any immediate danger," the senator responded calmly.

"Plans? What plans?" the tycoon queried.

"Well, think about it. Despite the attack on the convention center not going off quite as planned, it was largely a success. The effects were felt - we have some folks on the hill running scared and tight-lipped. The downside is the pro-"green movement" has gained some sort of martyrdom from the whole thing. We still have work to do," Small replied.

"You sure continuing to use Tug is the right thing to do?" Rhinehart asked, looking at the other two gentlemen. Seeing Billings shake his head, he knew that he echoed the same concerns.

"It is until we have the right opportunity to take care of him permanently," Small declared, shaking his glass of scotch, watching the shards of ice swirl around the rim.

Sean Kendall reclined in his lawn chair, watching the ripples dance their way down the Skagit River. The hours that past might have improved his aim, but they did little for his mood. He sighted in another stone that he had snatched from the ground by his feet. In a sidearm delivery, he sent the innocent rock hurtling into the cold springtime waters of the swift-running Cascade river.

He looked at his companion, Sammy, who was eagerly trying to get his big tongue to fit into the small neck of one of the beer bottles. Sean couldn't resist but to chuckle at the dog's antics. Sean's deep-seated brooding and contemplation took a temporary backseat to watching the big dog study the bottle intently, batting it inquisitively with his paw.

"Well, pal, if you would have run to the fridge, I'd have given you your own," Sean said, as Sammy looked up at him with frustrated curiosity.

Ultimately, the Swissie gave up on the lime-laced Corona bottles and settled down at his master's feet. Sean was left to his melancholy, ruminating the events of the past few weeks. As he aimed another rock, his eyes caught the little wooden cross by the river on the edge of his property. The small cross fashioned from garden stakes marked the resting place of a wonderful dog that belonged to one of the most intriguing women that he had encountered in his life.

As another stone sailed through the air and into the Skagit River, Sean shrugged his shoulders in acknowledgment that the chips had likely landed where they were going to fall. He was in the heart of the North Cascades, and she was at home in Anacortes. The one call he had found the courage to make to her resulted in a rambling voicemail left unanswered. For Sean, one unreturned call was his limit. Having the ability even to consider entering a relationship after his divorce was enough of a stretch, chasing after a woman who might have unrequited feelings for him was entirely out of the question.

All at once, Sean realized that he spent most of the better part of the day pining over a woman with whom he had only begun to get to know. Shaking his head as though the thoughts of Miranda would just shed off of him, he decided that he had lamented enough and the grand adventure, the fledgling relationship - they were both over.

He stooped over and picked up the half dozen beer bottles that he had strewn on his moss and clover infested lawn, including the one that Sammy was attacking with his tongue. As he headed into the house, pail in hand, he heard his telephone ringing. Instinctively, Sammy picked up his pace.

"It's okay, boy. If it's important, they'll leave a message," Sean told his companion. The telephone was Sean's least favorite of appliances; he would just as soon drive an hour to see someone in person than to talk on the phone for five minutes.

The personal touch served Sean well in his professional career. At times, his personable nature belied his true business grit and acumen, but those that crossed a member of Sean's team quickly learned that he was up to the task. It was this same double-edged sword that propelled him into early retirement, cashing in his lucrative stock portfolio that the blue-chip high tech industry had secured for him.

Swinging his porch door open, he and Sammy entered the kitchen. Sean tossed the bucket of empty bottles onto the counter as he keyed up his voicemail on the loudspeaker. The first message was his friend Adam inviting him over for a barbecue. He and his wife Laura had been trying to keep their friend and quasi-family member busy in the days following the Seattle incident.

Sean chuckled, he didn't like being babied, but he did appreciate their level of concern. What irritated him the most was the uncharacteristic ease of those around him to read his generally closely guarded emotions - and for a one week romance to boot.

He sighed as his voicemail continued with its next message. At first, Sean didn't recognize the voice on the machine. The voice was booming with an intrinsic jovial nature, the slightest twinge of an accent attached to it. His mental filament slowly began to glow. The voice belonged to his friend Joe Woodfeathers, a policeman in the Snohomish tribe along the marshlands of the Washington coast.

The two had teamed up on a search and rescue to find a little girl from the tribe that had gotten swept away in a violent springtime flood a year ago. It was Sean who jumped into the swift-flowing water when her rescue line tangled around her neck and had to be cut loose. Seeing that the rescue boat was not in position to react quickly enough, Sean leaped from the river bank and went after the girl himself. Knife in hand, he quickly split the rope, which was constricting her breathing and towed her to shore by swimming upstream at an angle to the nearest bank where a second rescue line could be safely deployed. The Snohomish people regaled Sean as an honorary tribesman.

Woodfeather's message sounded urgent despite his friend's light-hearted speaking demeanor. The Native American policeman had called Sean to see if he knew the whereabouts of Adam

Raines, the lead Fish and Wildlife agent of the North Cascades National Park.

Sean wondered what was going on to cause Joe to employ an all-points-bulletin for Adam. The young retiree picked up his phone and dialed Adam's cell. After a few rings, Adam's voice crackled through the earpiece, "Hello."

"Adam, its Sean. Where the heck are you? The reception is lousy," Sean asked.

"Been out by Rainy Pass, caught a couple of poachers out there taking elk cows of season, without tags. Worse, they were about to shoot a bull that I have had my eye on all year," Adam replied.

"Ah, the altruistic life of a wildlife agent," Sean laughed, "So if you have been out of cell range, then I assume that you haven't received Joe Woodfeather's message?"

"No, my cell just beeped with coverage, why?" Adam said, his reception improving with each passing mile.

"He called here hoping I'd know where to find you. He didn't say so on the message, but it sounded like it could be important," Sean replied.

"Well, I'll give him a ring, and I tell you what, I'll stop by as I pass by Marblemount and fill you in," Adam said and hung up.

Sean reached down and scratched Sammy behind the ears. In the splendor of the Cascades, he felt relieved to have his faithful companion with him to get through the periods of solitude that turned into episodes of downright lonely. The big dog looked up with his soft brown eyes as if to echo the sentiment.

It wasn't long before Adam was outside Sean's door, and Sammy was issuing a friendly warning bark. Sean swung the door open to reveal his big, sometimes oafish friend standing on his porch. Almost always smiling, Adam reminded Sean of a red-headed Paul Bunyan, a true gentle giant unless you crossed someone he cared about.

"Hey pal, looking good," he grinned, noting his friend's disheveled appearance. Sean was notorious for keeping an immaculate and sharp image, in fact, starkly so for the rough and tumble Cascades.

"Gee, thanks," Sean scoffed and then asked, "Can I get you something?"

"Sure, got any iced tea?" Adam accepted his host's offer. He gazed around the house, noticing that it too was a little out of sorts for Sean's usual level of housekeeping. Finally, his eyes fell on the bucket of empty Corona bottles on the counter. The condensation that was seeping down the side of the galvanized pail told him that the beers had met their end recently. "A little hops and barley for breakfast?"

"Uh, yeah, I guess. Hey, I added the lime for my vitamins," Sean replied weakly as he dug in the refrigerator. Shoving a few items aside, he produced two chilled bottles of iced tea and handed one to Adam.

The wildlife agent studied the bottle label frowning at the contents. "What's this crap? Taurine? Chromium? B-12? I just asked for some iced tea," he spouted.

"Just drink it, it's good for you. Just fancy names for caffeine and vitamins, you'll be all right, big boy," Sean laughed at his friend.

"Hey pal," Adam said, looking at the beer bucket, "You're taking this whole Miranda thing pretty hard, aren't you?"

"What the heck are you talking about? You think I'm sulking about a woman that I'd only just met?" Sean barked.

"Well, yeah, aren't you?" Adam stammered.

"No! Well…she's part of it, but it's just everything. I mean, a few weeks ago, I killed a man, several men. In the process, I nearly got killed myself, more than once. We were neck-deep in a situation where thousands of people could have died. On top of that, this strange woman made me think of feelings that haven't been apart of me since my divorce - oh, not to mention her family was part of the whackos that were trying to kill everybody. By the way, in the process of it all, I was either directly or indirectly involved with the death of her cousin. Why would any of that bother me?" Sean ranted heatedly.

"Alright, alright. Whew! At least it's not about the girl - that would just be way too out of character for you," Adam chided, slugging his best friend in the arm.

"So, what did Joe Woodfeathers want?" Sean demanded impatiently, rubbing his arm where Adam punched him.

Adam laughed at his friend, having gotten under his skin, "Joe wanted my help investigating a murder scene out at the Makah reservation. He said that having a non-native who knew the rules of the BLM and the Department of Interior could be helpful."

"Obviously he was more concerned about someone who knew the rules, not necessarily follows them," Sean grinned, poking at wildlife officer.

"Funny. I was going to ask you if you wanted to come along..." Adam started before Sean cut in.

"To help out Joe, you bet. I'm in!" Sean chimed.

"Well, clean up then, for Pete's sake. If I brought you out there right now, they'd book you just for looking like puke," Adam cajoled and added, "Why don't you grab a few things in case we stay out there. We can drop Sam off with Laura on the way."

Sean merely nodded his head and shuffled down the hallway. Adam looked at the Swissie and then at the stack of unattended dishes piled on the counter. Shrugging his shoulders, he began running hot water in the kitchen sink to tackle the dirty plates, glasses, and silverware for his friend.

Four

I t was early when she received the call. Miranda Shaw was still enjoying her first cup of coffee while staring out at the grey ocean that seemed to have been swallowed up by the insidious mist hanging over the coastal region.

She glanced at the caller ID on her phone and elected to ignore it. She sighed as she took a sip from her mug. The caller was an old friend of hers and she was sure that the call was to "check up on her" - something she did not want to encourage right now. She returned to gazing out of her townhouse window at the gloomy ocean.

The phone rang again. A glimpse of the phone LCD told her that it was the same number. Her friend knew her pretty well and that she would be screening her calls. A second call was their signal that it was important. Reluctantly, she picked up the phone and hit the "Talk" button.

"Hello," her voice sang into the telephone, belying her true melancholic mood.

"Miranda, it's Carrie. Listen, I've got some news for you. God, I hate to be the one to tell you...," the voice on the line sobbed.

"Carrie, what's wrong? Tell me what?" Miranda asked, an all too familiar pit growing in her stomach.

"Miranda, it's Jim. He's dead," Carrie said softly into the phone.

"What? My Jim? How…" Miranda gasped. She felt her body start to shake. Trembling, she placed her sloshing coffee cup on the window sill so that it didn't spill.

"Just this morning. He was at the beach here in Neah Bay…" her friend started.

"That's right! I was supposed to be there. What….how did it happen?" Miranda stammered.

"He was out on the beach, early…oh my gosh, it's just so terrible - he was found dead, with a Makah spear in his chest," Carrie sobbed.

Miranda stared at the phone in shock. It had been a couple of months since she saw Jim last. They were spending a weekend on Whidbey Island, trying to rekindle their waning relationship.

Several months prior, they had "the talk". Having been engaged for two years and not even planned a tentative wedding date, Jim had pushed Miranda for a commitment to their future. With her heart heavy, Miranda handed him his ring back. She suggested that they take some time apart.

The weekend at Whidbey was to be their reconciliation, but Miranda continued to have unsettled feelings deep inside. She refused his offer to re-accept the ring. Jim pledged to keep it until she was ready and gingerly placed it in his pocket. After a mostly uncomfortable ferry ride back to Seattle, they kissed briefly and went their separate ways.

Now she sat staring at the earpiece of the telephone, a rush of nausea welling up in the pit of her stomach. "Miranda? Miranda, are you okay?" Carrie's voice called through the phone.

"Yeah, yeah, I'm fine…I, uh, I have to go," Miranda stuttered into the phone and canceled the line.

Falling into a crumpled ball on her sofa, Miranda sobbed as she thought about Jim. She wasn't sure what she had ultimately wanted from her relationship with him, but she felt horrible about him dying without them being able to understand their feelings. She couldn't believe that he was gone. Charlie, her Labrador, had been killed, her cousins were gone, she was again estranged from her family- life had recently taken an unfriendly toll on her. She suddenly felt alone and powerless. The young marine biologist had always stridden through life with an air of confidence. This latest string of ill fate was just too great, placing a cruel strain on her burden weary soul.

She wiped her tears from her cheeks and decided that she would take control of what little she had. Jumping to her feet, she decided she was going to take a trip to Neah Bay.

Adam's SUV rolled up to a barricade that was being manned by a young Makah man and two county Sheriff's deputies. Leaning out of the window, he addressed one of the officers who stepped forward. "Here to see Detective Joe Woodfeathers," he said, holding out his badge in its black leather casing.

The deputy took the identification and leaned down to his shoulder as he pressed the "talk" button on his radio. A few moments later, the police officer motioned for the barricade to be moved.

Adam guided the truck through the blockade and drove down the paved road that led into the reservation. "From a whale hunt to a manhunt...," Adam grinned.

Sean just rolled his eyes at his friend. He didn't know a lot about the Makah, but he did know that they were a proud people steeped in rich tradition in the northwest. Of course, he knew of their whale hunting ritual and their well-publicized fight to re-engage in them - a notion that he was adamantly opposed. He had full respect for tradition, but some should mature and evolve with the ages. After all, he would reason, people of Nordic descent did not carry out annual festivals of raping and pillaging distant villages, nor did Polynesian tribes celebrate their harvests with virginal sacrifices anymore. It was okay for cultures to develop and civilize while maintaining tradition.

The drive to the Makah tribal headquarters was brief, and Adam found a spot on the side of the road. The parking lot overflowed with police vehicles and blacked-out SUVs.

Inside the building, they were quickly greeted by the cheerful voice of Joe Woodfeathers. "Fellows, over here!" his voice called over the commotion of the investigators, tribesmen, and anti-whaling protesters. He beckoned with his hands, waving them over.

Sean and Adam slithered through the crowd to join the Snohomish police officer. "Adam, this is Marty Lanook, the police chief of the Makah tribe," Joe introduced the native police chief. Turning to Marty, he added, "Adam is a Fish and Wildlife officer in the North Cascades. He and Sean have worked with our tribe on many search and rescues. I thought that Adam's connections could be helpful."

"It is a pleasure to have you two gentlemen assisting us," Marty said, shaking their hands. He spied Sean taking in the décor of the building's interior, "I see that you do not approve of our custom."

Sean was taken aback by the Makah elder's ability to read him so quickly. "I guess I don't. Not that I don't respect your culture..." Sean started, almost feeling apologetic for his opinion.

Marty waved him off, "You do not have to explain. Your opinion is valid, and I do not take offense, and I hope none is given. Please understand, the Makah appreciate and strive to live in harmony and balance with nature. The whale is a gift from the sea, and we do not take the offering lightly. Even before the ban, we did not over hunt, and we always utilize every part of the whale. But then, you didn't come here to be sold on our beliefs nor try to change them. You are a welcome friend."

"Oh, don't mind him, Chief Lanook. Sean doesn't like any kind of hunting," Adam leaned into Marty, whispering loudly in a sarcastic tone. "So why don't you guys tell us what's happened and where things are at."

"We received a call very early this morning, that a beachcomber had found an apparent dead body near our launch site. My first officer to arrive, Cody, located the body slumped over in the sand..." Marty began.

"Can we continue this at the site? I'm kind of a visual person," Adam broke in.

Marty glanced at Joe, unsure of their reception from the federal agents who had shooed them away earlier. Joe nodded casually in response.

"Sure, we can go there," Marty replied.

"Is Cody still around?" the Fish and Wildlife officer asked.

"Yes, instructed him to remain close to the scene," Marty Lanook answered as they strode down the path to the beach.

"So, what about the whale hunt and the celebration?" Adam asked casually.

"We will continue the children's activities as planned. The hunt will be postponed. It would just be in bad form with this morning's incident. I think the evening's events will commence as scheduled, though. You, gentlemen, are welcome to attend. It is a wonderful feast with stories and songs by the fire pit," the Makah police chief offered.

"Perhaps, Chief Lanook. We'll see how things progress today," Adam replied.

"Well, at least allow us to provide accommodations for you. We have some very nice guest rooms in our longhouse. I will have them prepared," Marty said eagerly, not waiting for their approval.

The scene by the body had become even more mob-like as protesters gathered from down the beach and zodiac boats driven in from Neah Bay swarmed offshore. The federal investigators were keeping the immediate area cordoned off as they combed the murder site for any fragment of evidence.

The lead investigator rolled his eyes and sighed audibly as Joe and Marty returned to the area with two more visitors in tow.

He watched as Adam flashed his badge to the attending officer manning the entrance. The officer looked up, a twisted, confused expression washed over his face.

Agent-in-charge John Manning dropped the vial of blood-soaked sample of beach sand that he was looking at and strode haughtily over to the newcomers. "What, we didn't have enough people to destroy this crime scene, you had to bring more in?" Manning bellowed.

"Sir, we have a Fish and Wildlife agent and a civilian," the young officer stated.

"Oh, a Fish and Wildlife agent. Well, this murder investigation case must be about to be wrapped up then. And you are...?" Manning sarcastically spouted to the group and then turned to Sean.

Before Sean could speak, Joe cut in, "When a federal agency intercedes on tribal grounds, we may seek counsel of our choosing to assist in the oversight of the investigation."

"I thought that's what you were for, Mr...Woodchuck, was it?" Manning asked bitingly.

"Woodfeathers. If it is too difficult for you to remember, I'll allow you to call me Detective Joe," the Snohomish tribesman retorted.

"I guess it's of no consequence. Please do as I requested earlier and do not touch anything," Manning snapped, his tone exuded arrogance. "Oh, Police Chief Lanook, please keep all of your hunters nearby, we'll want to begin interviewing them shortly. And can I assume this is the last of your posse?"

"I have told my men to make themselves available, and no, I do not anticipate any more guests," Marty assured the agent.

The men ducked under the police tape. Harrison's body had been thoroughly photographed and lay covered by a bright yellow tarp awaiting extraction by the Clallum County coroner. Sean looked around the scene. The crew of BLM and FBI agents had several dozen yellow flags spotted throughout the area, marking evidence that needed to be recorded.

Sean's eyes followed the trail of yellow markers from the victim's body, down the beach to where the initial attack took place. He noticed the impressions left in the sand. One set, clearly showing the tread pattern of a hiking boot. The other, bearing no distinctive markings, set slightly deeper than the hiking boots.

The men were replaying the apparent scenario when a loud eruption of voices was heard further down the beach. At once, all heads swiveled to locate the commotion.

Out in the surf, two Makah whaling boats propelled into the bay by feverishly stroked paddles. Observers on the beach, both tribesmen and protesters, stood and watched in shock.

Slowly, the murmurs broke out into angry charges from protesters, proclaiming the Makah hunters as murderers. Several members of the anti-whaling group raced for their zodiacs while others began chanting hysterically and lobbing stones and seashells at a band of Makah teenagers that had gathered to watch the event.

The first zodiac hit the breakwater slamming its hull into a wave, sending those aboard scrambling for handholds. The outboard motor whined as it propelled the craft racing across the bay towards the Makah hunting party. The Makah boat, despite its head start, was quickly being overtaken by the gas-powered vessel.

Just as the protest boat closed in, the hump of a pilot whale crested the surface of the gray water. The protest boat turned sharply towards the paddle-powered outrigger of the whale hunters and prepared for a direct collision.

Despite imminent impact, a young Makah hunter raised a spear and sent it rifling towards the water. Moments after the spear's release, the zodiac rammed the wooden Makah boat, sending the team aboard sprawling into the water. The young marksman did not get to see his well-aimed shot strike the intended target.

The zodiac surged forward and circled back to check on the whale. Horrified, they found that they were too late, like oil rising to stain a driveway puddle, a circle of blood in the watermarked the site of the hunter's aim.

Suddenly, one of the protesters pointed to the spear floating a few yards away. Further, in the distance, the hump of the whale breached the surface once more. The spear had only grazed the flesh of the gentle mammal, and with luck, would live out its life with little more damage than a tissue scar. The other members of the zodiac crew joined in a chorus of cheers to celebrate their success.

The celebration was cut short as three Coast Guard boats converged on the scene. Two of the vessels stopped to assist the tribesmen who were treading over to their capsized boat, while the other sped up to the zodiac with their small-arms weapons positioned at the protesters and began reading them their rights for arrest.

The men working the area of the crime scene stood silently observing the entire incident. Tribal Police Chief Lanook immediately placed a call to the tribal council and began walking through the buzzing crowd towards the landing area where the Coast Guard boats headed. A sour expression had crossed his face showing his displeasure in the hunting party.

The sleek Coast Guard skiffs slid onto the sandy shore, and the crews immediately began prodding the parties onto the beach. Each detainee sat cross-legged on the sand, awaiting their instructions. The protest party almost looked pleased with their antics, while the Makah hunters wore expressions of shame. Several members cringed as the tribal elders approached from the longhouses, and police chief Lanook joined them from the beach.

BLM and tribal officers quickly joined the Coast Guardsmen. "What were you thinking?" bellowed Chief Lanook, "Where has the Makah spirit fled to? It certainly does not appear in disobedience to direct orders from your police chief and worse, your tribal chief."

"But Police Chief Lanook, sitting idle is exactly what those people wanted. We could not give in. None of us were pleased by this morning's news, but..." one of the young hunters began.

"You young naïve, you do not know what is best for the tribe. There is a time and a place, and today, was neither," barked Lanook.

One of the hunters opened his mouth to speak, but seeing the stone-faced elders approach, clamped down and sunk his head towards the sand. The group of four elder statesmen looked the scene over. No one in the crowd could read the effect of the tribal leaders, their expressionless countenances offering nothing to reveal their thoughts. The area had become eerily silent as all eyes fell on the four men, even the arrogant federal agents and the boisterous protesters watched in silence.

Sean, too, looked on intently. He found the scene almost more surreal than the taped-off area of the murder scene. The large crowd encircling the two groups that clashed in the bay, the forlorn troop of proud hunters with heads bowed to the sand and the quiet respect demanded from the emotionless leaders, all encased in the persistent gloom of the early spring mist. He noticed that for a moment, even the reporters had forgotten to capture the scene with their flash-happy cameras.

Finally, one of the solemn men addressed the group. Looking at no one in particular, Chief Wanah said, "The grey of the day has been blackened. In this old man's heart, I know that this morning's tragedy did not come by the hand of one of my tribesmen. The antics of our foolish young champions only deepens the shroud of suspicion which has been cast upon us. You hold your heads in shame and properly so. But you are young and this day will pass. I instruct all of you to abide by the tidings of the council and provide the investigators with any and all assistance," the Makah chief declared, his voice booming across the sandy beach. He and the rest of the council looked at the Coast Guard and police officers as if to ask what was to become of the group of young hunters.

"We'll need to collect some information from them. Without the official blessing from the courts, you are held to U.S. law in terms of the International Whaling Moratorium. Without any priors, they will not need to be detained. There'll be some fines handed out, any additional activity could result in formal arrests," one of the Coast Guard officers informed the chief and anyone else listening. The news met with groans from the crowd of anti-whaling spectators.

"I want it known and enforced that everyone here must remain on the reservation or beachfront. There is a murder investigation underway. I want everyone interviewed," lead federal investigator Manning demanded, looking at both groups assembled at the shoreline.

Police chief Lanook nodded his head and began assisting the Coast Guard crewmen in wrangling the necessary information from the Makah hunting party. The protesters who were in the zodiac that chased after the whaling boat did not get off so easily. They were each charged with reckless endangerment and second-degree assault.

As the group of young hunters lined up to provide their information to the authorities, Sean watched them, something suddenly catching his attention. The lean, bronze-skinned hunters all shared a common trait; they were all short in stature. He walked over to the little yellow flags that were marking the footpath of the morning's pursuit. Standing beside them, he took a step. His tall body made a long stride in the sand. His new footprints left impressions longer than those embossed by the hiking boots worn by Jim Harrison. He took note of the stride of the killer. The in-seam length appeared to be very similar to his own.

The others began to take notice of Sean's antics. Agent Manning looked particularly annoyed with him stomping around near the evidence site.

"What the hell are you doing?" the FBI agent barked.

"Well, I was noticing the stride of the suspected killer. I know the attention is on the Makah hunters, but I reason that it couldn't have been one of them," Sean said earnestly.

"Thanks, but I have a team of highly trained investigators, I think we can handle this," Manning declared.

"What is it, Sean?" Detective Woodfeathers asked.

"I was looking at the space between the footsteps and then compared them to the relative heights of the whale hunters. Comparing to my stride, I'd say the victim, Harrison, was a bit shorter than me, whoever chased him was about my size, possibly even taller," Sean pronounced eagerly.

"That's great, junior detective, but strides change depending on gait, now if you would just...," Manning argued, his voice dripping with sarcasm.

"I know, I already determined that. But look here," Sean pointed to the impressions left by Harrison and his pursuer, "You can see that Harrison was running as he came through, his footprint is deep, particularly at the toes. The assailant left soft impressions, with little difference between the heel and toe - he was walking. He must have been confident that Harrison was not going too far, perhaps due to the initial wound."

"Huh, that's not bad," Manning admitted, taking a step as Sean had. Being equally tall, his stride also resembled that of the attacker. He glanced up at the line-up of young tribesmen that were finishing up with the Coast Guard. "I think you might be right. The stride does not match those of the hunting party. We will still want to talk with them, Lanook."

Marty nodded, a twinkle in his eye as he smiled at Sean, relieved that the suspicion hanging over the tribesmen had at least received its first valid rays of doubt.

"Nice work there, Scooby. And they would've gotten away with it if it weren't for those meddling kids...," Adam chided, elbowing his friend.

"Funny. Now, why don't you get to work and figure something out yourself?" Sean elbowed back.

Five

Miranda Shaw pulled her SUV up to the campground entrance. She was instantly met by Clallam County Sheriff's deputies asking to see her ID and ask her business in the area. She produced her driver's license as well as her Pacific Rim Institute ID card. The two deputies conferred over her credentials, and after a warning about what had happened at the nearby beach along with the ensuing investigation, let her through.

Hastily she wheeled her way to the parking area nearest the campsites. A wide array of expensive sport-utility vehicles, beat-up Volkswagen vans, Subaru wagons, and news trucks packed in alongside each other. She hopped out and made her way towards the beach and the makeshift tent city that had assembled under the tall fir trees.

It didn't take long before Miranda ran into some familiar faces. Each greeting her with a look of sympathy. A year ago, she had been at the very same site with Jim. The last that many of them knew, they were still destined to be married - an issue she preferred not to broach with anyone of them.

A particularly friendly face flashed a warm smile at her, he drawled slightly as he gave her a hug, "Miranda, darling, it's so good to see you. I just wish it was under better circumstances."

"Thank you, Brett. I wish circumstances were better, too," Miranda sighed to her old friend.

"Have you seen Carrie yet? She should be coming back from the, well...it's just dreadful," Brett said.

"I know. Would you take me there?" she asked solidly.

"To the mur... uh, the police scene?"

"Yes. I'm not fragile, you know. Brett, how long have you known me, five years? Have you ever known me not to be able to handle myself?" Miranda asked, her voice carrying a steadfast tone.

"Well, no Miranda, of course not. It's just, this is a little bit different," Brett persisted.

Miranda looked up at his kind blue eyes and his thick graying beard. He always reminded her of sort of a middle-age Santa Clause - both in looks and demeanor. He was a very kind and altruistic soul who had a way with both people and animals. He had taken a shine to her and her quiet, room-commanding presence from the first day she sat in his animal behavior class at the University of Washington.

"I appreciate your concern, but I need to do this," she said, giving his hand a gentle squeeze as she offered up a weak smile.

"Not like anyone could ever change your mind, not even Jim," Brett replied and took her arm as he led her down to the beach.

As they walked, he filled Miranda in on the attempted hunt that had taken place despite the morning's tragedy. He also told her of intense media coverage that was following the weekend's events.

They were halfway down the beach when Miranda's friend Carrie caught up to them. Miranda noticed her vibrant red hair from nearly a hundred yards away. They exchanged hugs, and after exhausting a second round of arguing the harm/benefit ratio of Miranda seeing the site, the three of them resumed the short trek to the murder scene.

As they neared the line of yellow tape, Miranda felt her stomach tighten. The crowd of on-lookers and media had dispersed down the beach to view the whaling skirmish, spreading out along the waterfront instead of massed around the crime scene. Still, a large group of forensic investigators remained inside the police tape, making their measurements and ensuring no piece of evidence had been missed.

Miranda's eyes found the trail of little flags that marked each gruesome sign that lent to tell the horrible story. She spied the area of blood where Harrison had first been attacked. Much of the blood had filtered into the sand, but enough was still present to afford her the grim reality of her former fiancé's death.

She gasped and turned away, facing the rolling movement of the bay. She bit down on her lip and called on every ounce of her strength to not allow herself to cry. Both Carrie and Brett took a side of hers to hug.

"Are you okay?" Carrie asked her friend.

Letting go of her lip, she felt anger replace the sadness and shock that had been seeping through her. Miranda spun back towards the crime scene, and defiantly responded, "Yes. I can do this. I'll be fine."

The initial wave of shock passed, and she returned her gaze on the trail of evidence markers. Like so many others that day, she saw the brutal scene unfold from the initial attack to the chase and finally to the signpost that Harrison had clutched to support himself before his life seeped away from his body.

"Like a soldier, he stood up for his fight," Brett said softly.

Miranda watched in silence as the policemen toiled to complete their work. A figure inside the crime scene area caught her attention; she blinked her eyes and gasped in disbelief as her focus became recognition.

The young Makah policeman, Cody, debriefed his chief of police, Snohomish detective Joe Woodfeathers, Sean, and Adam about his arrival on the scene. "As I had approached the beach, there were several protesters present, all of them pretty hysterical.

The on-lookers huddled around the beach sign, and at its base, there was the head protest leader, Jim Harrison lying on the sand with a Makah whaling spear protruding from his back and a slit in his throat."

"Were you able to question any of the people there?" police chief Lanook asked.

"Yeah, as soon as I called for you and I made sure the scene was secure, I asked them what they saw. Unfortunately, they said the beach was empty except for the ecologist," Cody replied.

"Not surprising, as gray as it is now, it was absolutely soupy this morning, couldn't see five feet in front of you," Lanook said.

"Despite shutting down the reservation and the campground, if Sean is right about the killer not being a Makah, they could be long gone," detective Woodfeathers surmised.

"Well, behind every murder is some sort of motive. We know the obvious strife with the tribe, what other possibilities might have there been?" Adam asked.

"Well, we know it had to be premeditated. Someone had gone to the trouble and great risk to steal the whaling gear. They were either making a statement or trying to redirect suspicion onto the tribe," Sean reasoned.

"Makes sense. So, no crime of passion, a piece of driftwood or some other more readily available weapon would have sufficed. I think we need to find out more about Mr. Harrison," Joe stated. He noticed Sean wearing an expression on his face as though he had seen a ghost, "What's wrong?"

Sean didn't answer; instead, he just peeled himself from the group and began walking towards the beach. Over Joe's shoulder, a trio of observers had appeared. In Sean's line of sight, he hardly noticed at first. The fog was rolling back in, so they seemed like featureless silhouettes against the gray backdrop. But as one of them, a female angled enough to afford him a better view. He couldn't be sure, but he swore the woman in the mist was Miranda Shaw.

He took off down the beach after her. The woman and her two friends had abruptly turned back toward where they had appeared from. Sean was just about to break into a run to catch them, when he heard Adam call behind him, "They found someone by the main entrance, let's go!"

Sean paused and looked back towards Adam's voice and returned his gaze to mysterious shadows just as the woman he thought he'd recognized melted into the fog that had consumed Neah Bay.

Rey Chavez drove his rental car down Interstate Five towards Seattle. He was glad that the morning had been so thick with the marine fog; it had allowed him to slip in and out of the woods that surrounded Neah Beach completely unnoticed.

Now he sped towards the sanctuary of the busy northwest city, where a rundown motel would be his anonymous lair while he awaited his next set of instructions. His current employer paid well, and Chavez felt that the big payday was just ahead.

As he sped past the other motorists, he chuckled to himself. Since he left his high profile role in the Mexico City-based cartel three years ago, he had done even more despicable things as a freelancer, and had been paid well to do them. The thing that had plagued him lately is that he was really beginning to enjoy his new occupation.

Taking care of the granola faggot on the beach allowed him to put his own artistic touch on his most recent job. He had hoped his new employer might have some more posts that required his talents and, with it, substantially more money.

He grinned as he turned up the old Santana tune that came on the radio and allowed his thoughts to melt away into guitar rifts and the long stretch of I-5 that would bring him into the "Emerald City".

Jerry Rhinehart hurried along the busy sidewalks of Pennsylvania Avenue. Glad for the protective sleeves that Starbucks used around their coffee cups, he moved at a near jog to bring his boss his morning latte while it was still hot. Unbeknownst to him, he was often the butt of jokes for his all-too-obvious obsessive doting and service for the senator.

Turning into the corridor that led to the first bank of senatorial offices, he licked the milk from his hand that frothed over from one of the lattes and moved down the hall to the door signed "State of Idaho". Backing into the door, he slid into the office of Senator Timothy Small.

The young receptionist, who was usually at the desk just inside the door to the front office, emerged from the senator's private suite. Her slightly flushed cheeks offered a quick smile to Rhinehart as she whisked by, patting creases out of her skirt.

The senator's aide rapped on the door with his highly polished shoe and was greeted with a grunting that he had interpreted as "come in". He pushed through the door and promptly delivered the latte with the exuberance of a Labrador retriever approaching with the morning paper for its master.

"Well, you made good time today," Small declared as he cleared his throat while tucking his shirt inside of his pants.

"Yes, I suppose I did. The coffee shop crowd was light this morning," Rhinehart replied, "Sir, I've been meaning to talk to you about the receptionist."

"She has a name, Rhinehart. It's Tara," Small stated flatly. His aide was known to be a bit arrogant, especially with the rest of the staff.

"Uhm, I believe it is Kara, sir," Rhinehart corrected him.

"Whatever. What did you want to talk about?" Small shrugged.

"I'm not sure she is a good fit here, sir," the aide began.

"Oh, come now, Jerry. Tara is doing a fine job," the senator stated.

"Kara, sir," Rhinehart sighed, his eyes rolling as his mouth contorted when he spoke.

"Right...Kara. Let's just let things stand for now and say I'll keep it under advisement. Now, what is on tap for the day?" Small smiled and redirected his aid. He would soon tire of his rather attractive toy who manned the phones, but that hadn't happened quite yet.

"Well, there is the vote on the treaty to withdraw tariffs on developing countries, which was ratified by the House..." Rhinehart began to roll down the list.

"Damn liberals! That is exactly why our work is so important. If "Seattle" had gone as it was supposed to, that bill would never have gone through. No matter. You know what calls to make. Tell that senator from Oregon that unless he wants his National Park plan pulled from the committee agenda and that sandal-wearing puke from Vermont that his Endangered Species bill to see the light of day, they better get the rest of their tree-hugging buddies to cast a 'no' vote," Small bellowed.

"I have already begun to place some calls, sir," Rhinehart replied dutifully, "Have you put any more thought into the Gaskill situation?"

"Our Japanese co-financier currently has him under careful watch. I still think our best bet is to keep him busy until he either gets himself killed or financially satisfied and retires on some Central American beach. In the meantime, Mr. Hasegawa has asked for an additional favor," Small conceded.

"What is that?" Rhinehart asked.

"We keep tabs in the Northwest. We make sure those friendly to our cause remain positioned that they can respond if situations warrant," Small replied.

"What is he up to? I think we need to lay low," Rhinehart questioned.

"I agree. I think we have a two-way safety valve in pairing up those two in Japan. We can pull the trigger in either direction if necessary," Small flashed a boastful smile. He flexed his fingers together as if he held all of the right cards in the deck.

Hishiro Hasegawa sat in his lavish cherry wood office. Nearly every surface was covered in the dark wood, each piece handcrafted and accented with an ornate honey-colored inlay. Leaning back in his Italian leather chair, he studied his accounts. His business had indeed been profiled as a corporate empire. The company that his grandfather built from a ramshackle warehouse and a single junk that sailed around the Asian-Pacific islands was now, two generations later, one of the most successful freight companies in the world.

Even as Hishiro had taken over from his father five years ago, the company has seen tremendous growth. The company had been a source of pride for the Hasegawa family and certainly for Hishiro. He had inherited the business early when his father had taken ill. Since his entry as the Chairman, Hasegawa Industries had recorded back to back record earnings.

Hishiro loved taking that information to his father's bedside. He had grown the family fortune through real estate acquisitions as well as a few novel trades. As he looked at his financial spreadsheets, he bit his lip. One of those innovative investments was about to tarnish everything that he and his family had worked for, but more importantly, destroy the pride that his ailing father held for him. That was something that he could not let happen.

A few weeks earlier, a Japanese detective was able to trace a Yakusa racketeering and prostitution ring to the young executive. Fortunately for Hishiro, the detective was in an enterprising mood. The detective was convinced that extortion was a brighter prospect than a decoration and a pension that was decades away. The downside was that the amount that the enterprising detective wanted to make the trail to Hasegawa Industries disappear was too large not to throw up red flags to the accounting team. No - he needed the money to disappear.

He sat, staring at the accounts. Every scenario seemed to present as a red flag to anyone scrutinizing the business, especially in Japan. Hishiro realized that his best bet was in America. Then he had an idea. He turned away from the computer screen and reached for the phone to dial the luxury apartment that he owned where Tug Gaskill was holed up.

SIX

Miranda Shaw returned to camp and politely shrugged off her companions. Her thoughts waged war inside of her head. Images from her past flooded her neurons while thoughts of the scene at the beach began to sink in. Jim was actually dead. She shuttered at the vision of the body bag, lying so casually on the sand.

Then her thoughts turned to Sean. The gallant, if impulsive man who defended her in a dark and frankly, seedy bar from a drunken patron who wouldn't take no for an answer. The chivalrous, adventurous, sweet man was everything that Jim wasn't. She developed real feelings for this man, but she couldn't escape the reality that he killed her cousin - justified or not.

She didn't harbor ill feelings for him, quite on the contrary, she felt very warm for him. It was all just a little too weird for her. Now with Jim dead, Sean was not an issue that she wanted to deal with. Yet, here he was at the murder site. Out of nowhere, her warped sense of humor wondered if Sean had anything to do with Jim's death too. She quickly shook that off, realizing that it wasn't amusing.

"Miranda," Carrie called from behind her. She held out a cup of cocoa and peppermint schnapps, "Why don't you join us. It might be better to power through with company."

Miranda nodded and accepted the warm cup. It at least kept her wandering thoughts in check. She quietly followed her friend out to the campfire. The chatter of friends catching up around the crackling of the fire allowed her to put aside her thoughts and slip into a cozy – Peppermint Schnapps – induced mental coma for a little while.

Sean caught up to the group as they hurried up the path towards the entrance of the reservation. A small crowd of Federal agents had gathered around the front door to the Makah Nation Historical Museum. Several agents stood with their handguns drawn in cover position trained on the building.

"What's going on?" Lanook asked.

"We have a suspect inside. One of my men noticed him lurking around as he was about to commence a forensics investigation on the alleged theft of the murder weapons. We thought in case it was one of your people, you would want to be present," Agent Manning reported. He held his hand up in the air and flicked his fingers in the air.

Instantly, his men reacted, pounding up the steps to the museum. As the agents entered, the men out front heard a crash from the rear of the building. Sean was the first to round the side of the museum. A former minor league baseball player, as much as he had lacked in home run power, he was graced with exceptional speed. He saw a figure streaking for the thick growth of trees that led to the road.

Sean raced across the lawn after the figure. His target was cloaked in a tan overcoat, flapping wildly in its wake. Sean crashed through the trees, each step closing the gap until he could dive forward and tackle the man.

Sean's fingertips grazed the figure's shoulders, unable to get a grip. As he neared the ground, he reached out and grabbed a handful of cloth, using the tail of the overcoat to bring the fleeing man down. Hearing the footsteps behind them, the man desperately kicked at Sean to free himself. Catching Sean on the chin, he was able to get up and wriggle away from Sean's grip.

The man turned to run, but only got a few steps before he was face to face with an FBI agent. Spinning the other direction, he found a recovered Sean standing before him. Before the man had time to react, Sean slammed an open palm into his chin, sending the man backward, landing in a crooked prone position.

By now, a crowd of police and agents circled the fallen man, one of them crowded Sean out of the way from further involvement. A uniformed County deputy kneeled next to the man and laced his wrists in steel handcuffs.

Lead Agent Manning walked up through the mass of first responders. "So, what do we have here?" he asked in his usual tone of seeming disconcert and sarcasm.

The deputy who cuffed the man hauled him by his interlocked hands onto his feet. The man looked genuinely frightened as he faced the crowd. He traded gazes with Sean and Agent Manning.

"I, I'm sorry," the nervous and scared man stammered, "I didn't mean to cause any trouble. I just wanted to look for some clues. I know one of these whale-killing bastards murdered Jim Harrison!"

"Well, now, Mr. uhm, what is your name?" Manning asked in an unwaveringly calm voice.

"Kirk Jeffries...," the man responded.

As Sean witnessed the exchange, he almost felt sorry for the man. He stood there with his hands secured behind his back, his khaki pants and tan jacket covered in dark soil and composted fallen leaves and pine needles. Facing the brash interrogation by Agent Manning did not help the disheveled man's affect.

"Okay, Mr. Jeffries, I have a team of highly trained forensic specialists, I'm quite sure that they can handle the investigation without your assistance. Now, why did you think that you were qualified to break and enter the Makah Museum and 'look for clues' moments before running from my agents?" Manning continued his inquisition, each word airing a tone of sarcasm.

"I am a writer. I write articles for several conservation groups. With Indian Affairs here, I was afraid that politics were going to intervene. I hoped that I might compile some evidence myself; it would be a huge break for our groups and my writing. I got spooked when I heard men at the door. When the window wouldn't open, I panicked," Jeffries admitted.

"Well, we'll just have to see how effective you are at cracking this case from jail," Manning offered up a smug smile and then turned toward one of the local officers, "Please book Mr. Jeffries on breaking and entering, interfering with an on-going investigation and resisting arrest."

Jeffries began to protest, but Manning had already turned to head back to the investigation command post, and the reporter knew his appeal to be wasted on deaf ears. As the Clallum County Deputy led him away, the small crowd of on-lookers disbanded.

Sean, Adam, and the two tribal policemen sauntered towards the museum building that the reporter had just fled. Several tribesmen had gathered there to secure the area and were already erecting a protective barrier to the shattered window.

"What was that guy thinking?" Joe asked no one in particular.

"Just a product of being blinded by his cause, that and being a bit overzealous in trying to make a name for himself as a journalist," Sean replied.

"Sean's one of those radicals who enjoys hugging trees," Adam grinned.

"I'm hardly a radical, the group I work for buys land that has ecological value. There is no picketing or hugging any trees. Capitalism for an environmental cause," Sean protested, giving Adam a shove, "You're just upset because I don't go hunting Bambi with you."

"Careful, Adam. He might lay you out the way he did that reporter," laughed Detective Woodfeathers.

Adam rubbed his chin and nodded, "You might be right; he's slight, but mighty. So, let's see what we can find in this museum."

The quartet marched into the Makah Museum and began to examine other points of entry, where the original thief may have gained access to steal the spear and possible murder weapon. All of the doors and windows were in perfect order, with the exception of the rear window that the reporter had tried to escape through.

"No wonder the feds and county cops think the murderer was a Makah. Motive, access to the weapons...it sure doesn't look good," Marty replied solemnly.

The men just nodded and continued to survey the room. Sean spied a similar spear to the one used in the attack on the beach. Marty Lanook pointed out where one was missing, and then he paused at a display case.

"Well, I know the knife that slit Harrison's throat, an adzes dagger is missing. It had a jagged blade that made a very rough and uneven cut. Much like that of the wound on his throat," he pronounced, "I have seen that many times in the preparation of a seal carcass."

The men gathered to the glass case as the Makah police chief pointed to another blade historically used in the ceremony of dissecting the whale and carving out and distributing the useful parts, which in the Makah society consisted of basically the entire whale.

A quick inspection of the case showed that the lock had several scrapes around the keyhole, indicating that it might have been picked. Marty made a note of his findings to share with the FBI Lead Agent.

The four men continued to make a thorough search of the tribal museum. Their efforts failed to yield any more clues to who might have stolen the historic hunting weapons, nor did it give them any indication of how the thief might have entered the museum.

Satisfied that they covered the building to the best of their ability, the four men exited the museum as Police Chief Lanook posted a pair of his men to guard the building.

"You know, Marty, you might just have come to the realization that the killer had some inside help," Joe said, patting his friend on the shoulder.

"I know," Marty sighed. He hoped that that was not the case.

As he looked back at the museum, Sean turned his head with him. He was almost startled when a black crow fluttered its wings above the rooftop and soared overhead towards the nearby trees. Sean noticed that it perched near a skylight that provided natural light into the open main exhibit room of the museum.

"Maybe not," he said thoughtfully.

"Huh? Maybe not what?" asked the tribal police chief.

"It may not have required inside help after all," Sean stated, he pointed up to the roof. "Does that skylight open?"

"Well, yeah. It stays closed most of the time. The elements don't treat some of the more sensitive items very kindly," Lanook replied. "You think the killer could have gotten to the weapons through there?"

Sean, having rappelled off of countless rock faces with Adam, nodded, "It's certainly possible. It is a way in that would avoid discovery from the ground level and might explain why we haven't found evidence of someone breaking in."

"Sean's right, I think it's worth a look," Adam agreed.

Police Chief Lanook quickly requested that one of his men get a ladder. While they waited, Marty Lanook continued to encourage his visitors to stay as their guests that evening. He described the feast and the ancient stories shared around the giant stone fire pit.

It wasn't long before a ladder rested against the rooftop of the museum, and all four men were inspecting the skylight. Detective Woodfeathers quickly spied the scratches in the aluminum flashing of the rooftop window. A pocket tool or a knife had been used to slide through and reach the brass lever locking the window in place. A light tug on the skylight, and it easily popped open, lending access to the museum below.

Adam watched the skylight open with ease and began scanning the rooftop. Walking over to the air conditioning unit that rested a few paces away, he kneeled and examined the footing closest to the open skylight. "The paint on this footing has some rub marks on it. It could've been used as an anchor point to rappel down," he suggested.

"So, we don't have any conclusive evidence, but it does open up the theory that the weapons could have been taken without inside involvement," Joe summarized.

"We should let that Agent Manning know about our findings," grumbled Lanook. "He'll be thrilled that we've meddled in yet another crime scene." Adam chuckled sarcastically.

"It's my crime scene. The division on the beach, he could argue, but theft on the reservation is not a federal jurisdiction," Marty grinned defiantly, his voice airing a lighter note, "You fellas ready for some chow and a beer?"

Seven

As the dark of the evening settled in, an enormous bonfire on the beach was stoked by young Makah men clad in traditional dress. The Makah nation was boiling with activity and excitement. Despite the day's events, there was a festive feel in the air. Dozens of children ran about playing, dressed in their historical garb and wielding hand-carved toys.

Enormous logs were carried out on to the sand and set in rows similar to pews in a church. Behind the expansive fire, several men carried a large stage and set it into place.

All around the reservation, smells of fire-grilled food filled the air. Sean and Adam emerged from the longhouse that they were provided residence. Following a warm shower and change of clothes, their perspective on the hectic day had taken a welcome turn. It was difficult for them not to succumb to the carnival-like atmosphere.

Pulling on his jacket, Sean felt as though it were autumn instead of spring. With the bonfire, the crisp air, and the wonderful smorgasbord of smells, his senses recalled the warm feeling of visiting a pumpkin patch in the days before Halloween as a child. Instead of cider, dumplings, and freshly bailed hay, it was authentic Makah dishes and the thickening mist of the cold Pacific waters. Spring had summoned the return migration of the pilot and sperm whales and was well underway.

They had only made it a few steps before Police Chief Marty Lanook rushed over to greet them. "Your accommodations are good, yes?"

"They are great, Marty. The shower was warm enough to shake off the chill, and I think I caught my second wind," Adam replied, his usual warm, jovial face offered up a genuine smile. Adam's good nature was infectious, and his boisterous demeanor often commanded attention at gatherings and events. Sean couldn't recall a party or social gathering where Adam hadn't eventually made his way to center stage.

"A lot of activity this evening. It looks like spirits are high," Sean said, observing the bustling crowd. Occasionally streaks of children chasing each other around, weaved their way through the grown-ups.

"Yes, this one of our biggest events outside of Makah Days in August," Marty replied.

"Could make it easy for more foul play. We'll have to keep a sharp eye out," Sean said.

"Are you sure you were never a cop?" Adam chided his friend.

"He does seem to have the natural instincts," Marty agreed.

"Ahh! After the stuff I've been through lately, I've just become a little warier," Sean scoffed, though pleased to receive the praise.

"Well, let's get you guys something to eat," the police chief beckoned as he led them over to the log benches and motioned for three plates.

The crowd was quickly gathering around the fire with plates toppling over with food. A young Makah woman balanced three plates in her arms and walked over to the men. She flashed Adam and Sean shy smiles, her glance lingering a bit with Sean.

They thanked her, and she went running back to be greeted by her giggling friends.

"I think my young squaws are quite taken by you two," Marty grinned as they dug into their plates of smoked salmon, traditional game, and locally grown fruits and vegetables.

"Squaws?" Sean asked. "Do you guys really talk like that?"

The police chief laughed as he slapped his thigh, "No. Only when gullible white guys are around!"

Sean rolled his eyes. His attention drifted as he scanned the beach. Beyond the log benches and makeshift stage that centered around the fire, a pair of Makah men stood on either side of the reservation boundaries. They stood guard using a series of torches that were placed in the sand on long poles illuminating the beachfront, allowing the sentries to watch for anyone encroaching the bonfire celebration.

Detective Woodfeathers joined the group. He grinned at his two Caucasian friends. "Enjoying your k'asc'u'u?"

"Yeah, it's pretty good. What did you call it...ka-suu?" Adam replied.

"It is good, what is it?" Sean agreed.

"Seal blubber," Joe answered.

"Seal what?" Sean asked, his eyebrows furrowed.

"You know, seal fat," Joe grinned.

"Ugh, and you guys wonder why I don't ask you to bring the meat to my barbecues!" Sean protested with a wrinkled nose.

Adam paused for a moment and then shrugged, shoveling another generous portion of the Makah delicacy into his mouth. Sean respectfully put his plate down and turned back to the detective. "So anymore word from the charming Special Agent Manning?"

"Well, I filled him in on our discovery of the jimmied skylight. He looked fit to be tied with his forensics team for not finding it first. His team is heading up there now. They'll be working through the night. Really, it seemed to pain him that civilian Sean was the one who thought of it," Woodfeathers grinned.

"Maybe we'll have to give Sean a proper tribal name- 'Eagle Eye'," Marty suggested.

"Maybe 'Stink Eye'. Stink Eye Sean. Yeah, I like that," Adam piped in.

"Funny," Sean shook off his friend's attempt at humor.

"Oh, Manning said one other thing. This case has become so high profile that the BLM's Seattle Division is sending in some higher rank to oversee everything, a Director Beckett somebody," Woodfeathers added as the poking fun of Sean subsided.

Sean and Adam simultaneously whipped their heads around to each other. Adam returned his gaze to Joe, "Stanley Beckett?"

"Yeah, that's it. Regional Director Stanley Beckett. You know him?" Joe asked.

"Yes, you can say that. We have sparred recently. I can't say that he is going to be happy to see me here. Sure as hell, he won't like to see ol' 'Stink Eye' here," Adam motioned his elbow towards Sean.

"I believe that was 'Eagle Eye'," Sean retorted.

Ignoring him, Adam continued, "We'd better have you place a formal request for me to be your counsel, or he will have my tail."

"I'll do that right away," Marty agreed.

"Why don't you send it through Rachel York? She is a friend of mine, and she'll push through whatever you need," Sean added. He was speaking of his friend, who was second in command to Beckett at the regional Department of Interior office that oversaw the BLM, Indian Affairs, and Forest Service in the northwest corner of the United States.

The weathered and worn Makah police chief hustled away to request counsel. In the meantime, it appeared that the evening festivities were about to get underway. Adam reached over and grabbed the remaining seal meat off of Sean's plate. Sean looked up with mild disgust on his face.

"What?" Adam shrugged, "It's protein."

Sean redirected his attention away from the food that his friend enjoyed and towards the stage just beyond the fire. One of the elders that had quietly observed the afternoon's incident on the beach stood on the wooden platform to address the audience. In both languages, he briefly expressed his displeasure in the hunting party. He stressed that the sovereign nation of the Makah should work with the outside authorities, hoping to come to a swift end to the tragic mystery that had befallen on their soil.

Sean noticed that the man speaking expressed little more emotion than the tribal chief had earlier in the day. It was also apparent that the men, women, and children listening held the utmost respect for the speaker and his words. The entire buzz of conversations and activities stopped to lend him their undivided attention.

The speech was about as concise and brief as Sean had ever heard. The elder very quickly and unceremoniously offered the stage to the woman waiting patiently behind him. She was dressed in full historic regalia and cast the audience a suspicious glance. She moved forward as though she were stalking some dangerous animal. As she neared the edge of the stage, she tossed little beads that looked like berries into the fire, causing a burst of flames to rise and crackle. The children gasped as the woman launched into a tale of the 'old times' when the warriors of the Makah Nation fended off ancient mystical beasts from their shoreline villages.

The storyteller's presence was made more magnificent by the ethereal glow from the fire. Her flowing skirt danced along the flames making the Makah elder appear as though she floated from the embers rather than stood behind them. The children listened in earnest as they watched her through wide, unblinking eyes. She talked of how the ancient Thunderbird spirit saved the village from starvation one blustery winter. Swooping over the bay, the mighty spirit plucked a whale from the frigid grey waters of the Pacific and delivered it to the Makah people. The gift of the whale saved the village, and the Makah became the fiercest seafaring hunters in the world.

Leaving the historical stories to the Makah children huddled at the base of the fire pit, Sean decided that he would like to walk around the commons area and see if any more troubling activity might present itself. He could see lights shining from above the museum, telling him that the forensics team was on task collecting evidence from the tampered skylight. The vicinity of the longhouses seemed very innocent, with some tribal members finishing up their dinner duties by dunking dishes in tubs of water and stowing them in their racks.

Walking a path that he had been on earlier, he found himself down by the beach. The cloudy sky did not relinquish a single star, and the moonlight was swallowed up by the seemingly ever-present marine layer. On a whim, he decided to snoop around the protesters' camp, an easy two-mile hike to nearby ShiShi Beach Campground. The well-worn trail was deserted at this late hour, though in the mist consumed darkness, anyone could easily have been lurking just a few yards off the path. Somewhere in the middle of the Makah Potlatch festival and Shi Shi Beach, Sean began wishing he were better equipped. A flashlight would be a welcome tool, never mind a weapon for protection or the eyes, ears, and intimidation of his dog Sammy.

His long stride and usual quick pace got him to a strip along the beach where he could see the soft glow of a campfire. All at once, he was hit with feelings of comfort in seeing civilization on this dreary night, which filled him with uncertainty and apprehension. He knew that he had seen Miranda earlier that day. Was she actually here? And why did the prospect of that seem to bother him so much?

Swallowing hard, he eased himself off of the rock he had been using as a perch and strode towards the encampment. As he closed in on the huddle of tents, he began to hear the murmur of merriment rise above the rhythmic sounds of the surf.

Sean saw a small red dot come towards him through the small sea of tents. It was a young woman. She walked with her arms crossed in front of her chest, keeping her pink sweater close to her body. She looked up and saw Sean.

"Great night for a walk, eh?" she scoffed sarcastically towards Sean.

"Yeah. Summer comes late out here on the coast," Sean agreed.

"I don't know how they can be so lively tonight, but then I guess they didn't all know Jim that well," the young woman sighed as she paused to take a drag on her cigarette.

"You were close?" Sean asked.

"Yes. I was on his staff for the last three years. He was a very kind man...," she trailed off, her mind reflecting on her former associate.

"It was a terrible thing that happened today," Sean said, hoping to keep this young woman talking. She could offer a valuable perspective.

"Absolutely! Those damn savages, barbarians!" she flared in response.

"No doubt it was a Makah? There are no other possibilities?" Sean asked.

"It makes the most sense. He is a ferocious opponent, and he has had the whale killers dead in his sights. When he is locked on...watch out! I mean, he hasn't quite been the same since the big break-up, but I think he always held out for them to get back together. He just thought she needed some time before they got married," the woman said as she bent over to stamp out her cigarette in the coarse sand.

"Is his, uh, would-be fiancé here?" he persisted.

"Miranda? Yeah, she arrived this afternoon. Listen, this has been a long and difficult day, I'm going to go lay down in my tent," the pink sweater-clad young lady said, then held out her hand, "I'm Emily, most people just call me 'Em'."

Sean was stunned at hearing Miranda's name. The fine hairs on the back of his neck rose as a chill rushed up his spine. Numbly, he held out his hand to meet hers and forced a weak smile, "I'm Sean. Thank you for the talk."

"No problem, maybe I'll see you around. Goodnight," she smiled and disappeared among the tents from where she had come.

Sean just stared after her, in disbelief that the woman that he had met and begun to fall for was the murder victim's ex-fiancé. He felt bewildered and foolish. His mind spun aimlessly as he tried to consume these bites of information. He became acutely aware that he needed to remove himself from the Shi Shi beach campground before more people caught him there. He spun to begin the return trail just as a flashlight beam cut through the night from the hedge of tent sites. Quickly and quietly, he melted into the mist of the night.

Miranda cupped the warm mug in her hands. The thickening fog spread a wet chill across the campsite. She and her friend Carrie spent much of the afternoon catching up and swapping stories that reminded them of Jim. As the chill of darkness took hold, they scooted closer to the campfire, using coolers as makeshift benches.

The marine biologist had been careful of her accounts over the past few weeks to be very vague on her details of meeting Sean. She felt the subject matter was somehow disrespectful under the cloud of the day's circumstances. Her close friend Carrie was not as easy as the others to deter. They knew each other too well.

Looking over her shoulder to verify that were indeed alone, Carrie asked in a low voice, "So, what else is going on? You've been pretty aloof prior to me calling about Jim."

"Nothing," Miranda squirmed, "I've just got a lot on my mind lately."

"Miranda, it's me you are talking to. If you want to feed that crap to someone else, that's fine. Heck, today, I don't blame you. But I am disappointed in you if you think it's okay with me," Carrie scolded her friend.

Miranda sighed and looked hard at her. "It's so complicated."

"Try me. Maybe a fresh perspective can lift some of that burden off of your shoulders," Carrie said, her voice upbeat and comforting.

"Well, when I went to visit my relatives, I met a man...," Miranda began.

"Oh, really? So that's what this is about," Carrie replied, a wicked smile crossing her lips.

"Oh, it's much more than that," Miranda admitted.

"Tell me about him," her friend pleaded.

"I met him at a bar - the only bar around for about a sixty-mile radius in the Cascades. Some drunken hunter was hitting on me and wasn't taking no for an answer, Sean - that's his name, came over told the guy to stop, the hunter took offense to it, and all hell broke loose. Sean ended up snapping the guy's arm, and I just kind of used the commotion to sneak out," she filled in her friend.

"You just left?" Carrie asked incredulously.

"Well, yeah. Anyways, I ran into him a couple of days later and thanked him for helping me and apologized for disappearing. I agreed to dinner, and one thing led to another...," Miranda replied.

"So? That's not so bad. You shouldn't feel guilty. You and Jim were broken up," Carrie said.

"I know, there's more to it," Miranda confided, "A lot more." She shifted her weight on the increasingly uncomfortable cooler.

"It turns out my relatives were considerably more backward than I could have ever imagined. You know that terrorist attack in Seattle a couple of weeks ago? My cousins were involved. Sean figured it out and went to stop them. He ended up killing my cousin Jeb. My cousin Daryl kidnapped me, and he died while fighting Sean. It...it's all just too much."

"Miranda, oh my God!" Carrie gasped, "They didn't put any of that in the news, that is incredible. So, what happened to this Sean?"

"He spent twenty-four hours in a grueling debriefing, we all did. We said we'd call...," Miranda continued.

"And he never called," Carrie cut in.

"I never called. He did, he left messages. I just couldn't deal with it," Miranda concluded.

"So, you'll let the hero get away," she got up and gave her friend a hug, "Listen, I don't blame you. You've been through so much. I had no idea. You just worry about yourself. I'm sure your Rambo can take care of himself."

"You want to go for a walk?" Miranda asked, getting up to stretch her legs and return circulation to her numb bottom after sitting on the hard surface of the cooler.

"That's a good idea. They're starting to get rowdy back there anyways," Carrie nodded toward the central fire pit, "Let me grab a flashlight real quick."

The tall redhead dove into her tent and produced a small flashlight to use as they headed through the grove of shelters towards the beach trail. Clearing the short berm that protected the campsites, Carrie's light caught a figure in the mist that was just turning to head down the path. Miranda froze, her left hand gripping the arm of her friend.

"What is it?" Carrie found herself whispering.

"That was him. I swear that was him," Miranda whispered back.

"Who?" Carrie wore a confused look on her face, and then her eyes widened, "Him? Rambo is here?"

"I can't be sure, but I swear that was him," Miranda stated and added, "I thought I saw him down on the beach this afternoon at the crime scene."

"That is why you were acting so funny and bailed like that. But why would he be here? It doesn't make any sense," Carrie said.

"I know. Maybe I'm losing it," Miranda sighed.

"Now that I believe," Carrie giggled, and then a look of horror swept across her face, "You don't think he could have had anything to do with this?"

Miranda shook her head, vehemently, "No, I'm sure there is some explanation for it. What, I have no idea."

"Weird. Must be some kind of kismet or something," Carrie suggested, her eyes glowing wild with the theory.

"I don't know. I think it might just be Sean. He seems to have a habit of being in the right – or wrong place at the right time," Miranda admitted.

"Trouble finds him," Carrie concluded, "He found you. Are you trouble, Miranda?"

"For him, I probably am. I nearly got him killed. And then I wouldn't even return his call. What kind of person does that make me?" Miranda confessed.

"After what it sounds like you had gone through? Human, hon. It makes you human," Carrie said, giving her friend a tight squeeze around the shoulders.

Eight

Tug Gaskill woke up refreshed. The Asian concubine assigned to him had more than served his needs. They endured a hedonistic marathon that touched every corner of the luxury apartment.

He rolled over to find himself alone in bed. It only took him a moment with his head cocked off of the pillow before he could hear the sounds of dishes and pans clanking in the kitchen. Soon the scent of jasmine tea and cooked eggs made its way into the bedroom.

The mercenary stretched out on the thick layers of the featherbed. Despite the warm wafts of breakfast, the smell of debauchery hung in the air. Tug sat up against the headboard as the slender Asian entered the room. She carried a tray of breakfast breads, a plate of eggs over steamed rice, soy sauce, and tea.

Below the tray, her lean brown legs protruded from the short apron that she wore. Her skin glistened just above the square neck of the cooking garment. She flashed Tug a half-smile as she placed the tray over his lap. She leaned over his legs and crawled in the bed beside him. Clawing her way along in a sultry manner.

She pulled a set of chopsticks off of the tray and gently pinched a mouthful of eggs and rice, placing it into Tug's mouth. This decadent service was performed until the tray was empty, and the mercenary was utterly satiated.

The last bite of pastry left a crumb in the corner of Tug's lips. Seeing this, the concubine moved the tray off of the bed and moved in to lick the crumb away gently. Tug pulled her close.

Tug Gaskill slid out of bed and plodded to the bathroom. He walked past the Japanese prostitute, who was fast asleep on the other side of the bed. He flashed a wicked grin to himself; as he watched the woman sleep.

Shuffling across the floor, he turned the crank on the shower and allowed the water to run. He smacked his dry lips, realizing he had a horrible taste in his mouth. Letting the shower run, he decided to grab his toothbrush out of his Dopp bag, still sitting in the living room. Silently pushing the door open, he was surprised to find the bed empty—the impression of his Asian mistress still outlined in the soft mass of the featherbed.

With his years of training and service, his body naturally moved with great stealth. Reaching the bedroom door, he placed his ear to the pale wood. Beyond the door, he heard the sound of a zipper sliding open. Carefully, he turned the knob and pulled the door open just enough to allow his eye to see through the narrow slit.

He was annoyed, but not surprised to see the thin woman slinking across the room, hastily rifling through his canvas bag. Tug gently closed the door and backed away. Walking to the bedroom window, his timing and insight was impeccable. The young concubine had finished snooping through his belongings and stepped out onto the nearby veranda to call in her report.

Speaking softly into her cell phone, the sinewy woman recounted the previous evening, letting the listener know that she had taken excellent care of her guest. She reported finding only clothes, a couple of passports, and a small sundry of light weapons.

Accepting some additional instructions, she hung up the phone and returned to the bedroom.

Tug closed the window and glided back into the bathroom. Feverishly, he began soaping himself up, ensuring his body was thoroughly wet as though he had been in there all along. When he felt that he had consumed the right amount of time for an indulgent hot shower, he shut off the water and reached for his towel.

Nonchalantly, wrapping the towel loosely around his waist, Tug pushed through the door, sliding into the bedroom. The young prostitute was stretched out on the bed in her spot as though she had never left. She looked up at the weathered mercenary and let out a long, inviting purr.

Tug smiled at the woman in the bed and stepped forward. Licking her lips, she flashed a wicked grin and reached towards him. She quickly cast the towel aside and began nuzzling his shoulder, rising to his neck. Grabbing him tight, she pulled him closer.

Knowing her motives were to obscure any thoughts of malfeasance on her part, Tug acted to give into the of the skillful temptress. Suggesting he wanted tea, she dutifully hurried off to the kitchen. Tug quickly dressed and slipped back underneath the covers.

In minutes, the young concubine returned with another tray of food and tea. She brought it next to Tug on the bed and crawled in next to him. Selecting a pair of ebony chopsticks, she began to gather a bite of rice.

Tug waved her off with his hand, "No, let me do it."

Taking the chopsticks in his right hand, he flexed his fingers in the scissor fashion for using the ancient utensils. Without pausing his motion towards the bowl of rice, he flipped the chopsticks from his fingers so that he held them as one would an ice pick, his thumb bracing the untapered end. Arching his swing, his hand darted up towards the obedient hooker, driving the sticks into her throat.

The blunted ends of the ornate eating utensils punched through her carotid artery behind the force of the mercenary's blow. The prostitute's eyes widened with shock in the brief moment that she had to live before the well-trained and efficient killer delivered the piercing stroke. She let out a slight gurgle before slumping back on the headboard of the bed, her head falling limp into her lap.

Tug let go of the chopsticks, still lodged in the concubine's neck, and slid off of the bed. A river of blood cascaded down and began to soak into the luxurious down comforter and fine silk sheets. Indifferently, Tug snatched the bowl of rice and egg off of the bamboo serving tray and retreated to the living room to enjoy the snack the dead girl had prepared.

Snatching another set of chopsticks from the counter, he flopped on the sofa. Flipping on the television, he slid his heels onto the edge of the coffee table. He settled back to enjoy a satellite-fed edition of Sports Center, indifferent to the dead body in the other room.

Nine

Tug searched the living room until he found the prostitute's purse. He quickly zipped it open and spied her tiny cell phone resting on top. Hitting the menu key, he scrolled to 'last called' in the phone's history file. Moments later, the phone was ringing.

"Mushi mushi," the voice called through the earpiece.

"Well, mushi mushi to you, Hishiro," Tug drawled back sarcastically.

"Mr. Gaskill. It is good of you to call. I trust your stay is acceptable?" Hasegawa asked.

"If you mean your little spy-whore, she was a wonderful diversion. An energetic little rabbit, but all good things must come to an end," Tug cooed.

"I don't understand. Is there a problem?" Hasegawa queried.

"Well, let's just say we're gonna need a little extra housecleaning over here. Shouldn't have tried to play me, Hishiro," Tug replied, his voice dripping with annoyance.

"What did you do?" Hasegawa exclaimed, "She was one of my best girls! I just wanted her to keep an eye on you - stay low profile for a while."

"I'm a big boy Hishiro. I've been in this business for a long time. You don't stay alive in my line of work if you don't know what you are doing," Tug contested.

"You are right, Mr. Gaskill. I am sorry for the intrusion. Even I must obey orders from time to time. I hope that our trust is not entirely marred, I was hoping to utilize your services for a personal task of mine," Hasegawa conceded.

"Just so we understand each other. If you snoop on me again, I wouldn't go to bed that night if I were you," Tug warned.

"Yes, of course. You will not be bothered by anyone else while you are in Japan," the Japanese freight magnate assured.

"Now, what is this job that you needed?" Tug asked, his tone morphing abruptly to one of a calm, business-like manner.

"Ah, I see my concubine's actions do not anger you," Hasegawa smiled through the phone.

"I wouldn't push your luck, Hishiro, but business is business," Tug growled.

"Yes, business. It is an easy job for you. I need you to be a liaison for me. I have an issue that perhaps one of your colleagues back in the states might be able to assist me with," Hasegawa replied and proceeded to describe what he needed done.

Sean woke up early. The smell of a smoldering campfire hung heavy in the air. He rolled off of the simple cot provided for him. A few feet away, his friend Adam trumpeted loud snores, still fast asleep.

The former tech manager stood up and looked around the sleeping quarters. The northwest natives called the building a longhouse, a wooden structure built with raw timber as they had for centuries. Each wood piece had been carved and put into place by hand. The interior reminded him of a barn. Little "bedrooms" were cordoned off with waist-high walls like those in a stable. In the center of the room, three fire pits spaced to provide heat for the occupants. In one of the crude rooms, row after row of fish hung to cure.

Sean reached inside his duffle bag and grabbed a bottle of water. Tossing on his jacket, he walked out of the longhouse and strolled towards the beach. He saw little wisps of smoke dance up from the bonfire pit. The area surrounding the pit bathed in surprising warmth. Deciding to take advantage of it to ward off the chill of the early morning mist, he planted himself on one of the logs that had served as seating the night before.

He drained his bottle of water in big gulps as he stared off towards the bay. The shape of fishing boats would occasionally push through the fog and slowly disappear as though they were ghostly apparitions. The tip of Neah Bay served as the main Makah township, as well as a fishing village wrapping around the northern edge of the Olympic National Park.

As Sean listened to the water of the bay lap against the shore, he put his mind to the mystery that unfolded exactly twenty-four hours prior a mere few hundred yards down the beach. The Makah hunters were the obvious suspects. Sean's own opinion about whale hunting initially made that assumption quite palatable. However, there were enough inconsistencies in the evidence trail that made plenty of room for doubt. Who then, would make a reasonable alternate suspect? Someone from within the protest party, Sean surmised.

His mind shifted to the conversation with Harrison's aid. Was it his Miranda that was Harrison's ex-fiancé? That was certainly an unexpected and hardly welcome development. Part of him felt he should about-face and return home. The other part of him was fueled with a sick curiosity that compelled him to find out what was going on and what Miranda's connection was, if any, to this, Jim Harrison.

His mind was so deep in thought that he didn't hear the person step up behind him. He jumped as the rhythmic lull of the surging water was broken by the sound of a deep voice.

"Mr. Kendall," Sean spun to see Special Agent Manning looming over him, "Not worried about being another victim out in this mist?"

Sean noted that his tone was considerably more amicable than it had been the previous day. "No, though I can see how Harrison might have been taken by surprise."

"Sorry about that," Manning offered, "This place sure gets a little thick and gloomy when the fog rolls in."

"Yeah, no kidding," Sean replied, "This place makes you see ghosts at every turn, but masks the real things that are out there."

"Harrison didn't have a chance."

"Especially if he was attacked by someone who knew what they were doing," Manning admitted and quickly switched gears, "By the way, our forensics team has determined that both of your observations from yesterday were accurate. Even at a run, the stride from the hunting party did not match that of the footprints found on the beach. We measured inseams of more than half of the reservation last night. Also, the skylight at the museum was broken into and very recently. No prints, however."

"I'm glad I could provide something useful to your investigation," Sean said sincerely.

"Well, it doesn't rule out a Makah as the killer, but it does broaden our scope," Manning remarked sternly.

"So, what's on tap for today?" Sean asked.

"We'll move over to the protest camp and begin our interrogations there. Find out more about Harrison. Ferret out any jilted lovers, hidden enemies, that sort of thing," Manning replied. "So, what are you out here for, anyway?"

"Just along for the ride. I have worked with Woodfeathers on Search and Rescues in the past. When he called Adam for help, he suggested I tag along," Sean shrugged.

"You former military or police? Your observations are quite astute, and you handled that dumb ass reporter pretty handily," Manning wondered aloud, laughing at recalling Sean laying out the fleeing reporter.

"No, just lucky, I guess. Adam taught me a few things. He's former Special Ops, the things he taught me would have been useful to know back during brawls on the ball field," Sean admitted.

"Where'd you play?" Manning asked, raising his eyebrows with interest.

"Seattle farm system in Tacoma. I played one game in the bigs. Not much need for a soft hitting outfielder these days. Even second basemen are going yard left and right," Sean replied thoughtfully.

"At least you can say you were there," Manning said respectfully, "Hey, for what it's worth, I do appreciate the help so far, but you've got to understand my position. Any interference can undermine my investigation, no matter how well-intended."

"I can understand that," Sean agreed, and shuffled a bit, "There's something I should tell you..."

A shout from beyond the longhouses cut Sean off. "Agent Manning, sir," the voice called. Sean and Manning turned to see one of his men motioning for the lead agent. "We're ready, sir!"

Manning looked back at Sean and dug in the pocket of his jacket, plucking out a business card, "Duty calls. Would you mind calling me if you find out anything else?"

Sean accepted the card that was held out for him, "Of course."

With that, the Special Agent in Charge trudged up the hill towards the fleet of black SUVs that were waiting for him. As Sean watched the agent leave, he saw Adam poke his head out of the longhouse, yawning sleepily. Seeing Sean, the big man sauntered over to the fire pit.

"Man, you'll chum up to anyone," he spat at Sean humorously.

"What? My buddy Manning? He's alright. More or less thanking me for my insight, but he can take it from here," Sean replied.

"Ah, the government rhetoric 'thanks good citizen, but we'd rather do it ourselves, even if we screw it up'," the Fish and Wildlife agent nodded.

"Yeah, I guess that's about right," Sean admitted, his perception of the FBI agent had shifted a bit since the previous day. He brightened and grinned at his friend, "But you never can trust those federal agents, eh."

The wildlife officer grimaced as he held up his hand and flashed his friend "the bird". "So, where was your new pal off to?"

"They are going to start questioning the protest camp," Sean replied.

"Sounds like fun. Let's get Joe and Marty and join them," Adam suggested, a playful smile spreading across his face.

"What about when ol' Regional Director Beckett shows up?" Sean asked.

"He's going to find out about our presence anyway. As long as Rachel was able to slip the request from Marty through, he can't really squawk about much," Adam replied.

On cue, the two tribal policemen were trotting towards them. "Good morning, fellows!" Marty called to them. "Can I take you to breakfast?"

Adam popped out of his seat in an excited rush. "Man, I'm glad you asked. I almost forgot about breakfast," he cried. Not one to miss a meal, Adam gladly accepted the offer for breakfast, and headed to town where their choice of small diners awaited them along the bayfront.

The Neah Bay Marina sat within the inside crescent of Cape Flattery. Across the Strait of Juan de Fuqua, somewhere in the deep mist, lay Vancouver, British Columbia. The town of Neah Bay itself was sleepy, but quaint. A handful of shops and eateries sprinkled amongst the modest homes and the Makah Historical Museum – the crown jewel of the reservation. At the entrance of the harbor sat the Coast Guard Station as one of the larger entities in the little town.

The diner Marty led them to was a new building perched along the marina, replacing a dilapidated structure retrofitted as a hut selling bait and whale watching tours. Sean laughed at the irony of tourists' dollars coming into the reservation for viewing the whales, the same reservation that set out to hunt the amazing creatures down.

Pushing through the screen door, they entered the small restaurant. The smells of steaming coffee and the short-order griddle frying eggs, hash browns, and hotcakes hit them immediately. Adam grinned and rubbed his stomach hungrily.

"Son of a bitch!" a voice growled at them from across the room.

They looked over to see Regional Director Stan Beckett sitting with two other men in dark suits eating breakfast. Adam smiled and walked over to the table with his hand extended, "Beckett, good to see you."

"What the hell are you doing here?" he snarled, ignoring Adam's friendly gesture. Glancing over the wildlife officer's broad shoulder, he looked at Sean with disgust, "And you?"

"I'm glad everything worked out with your job Beckett," Adam chided smugly.

"Not without a review hearing, probation, and a permanent black mark in my file!" the irate man confessed and continued hotly, "Now, I'll ask you again, what are you doing here?"

"I have received orders directing me to attend as an observatory counsel to Makah Police Chief Marty Lanook," Adam replied and introduced the two men.

Reluctantly, he shook Lanook's hand, "I didn't sign off on any request...York!" the Department of Interior Regional Director bellowed after he realized his second-in-command, Sean's friend Rachel, had signed off on the temporary expansion of Adam's jurisdiction.

"Just following proper protocol, sir. Enjoy your breakfast," Adam pulled back from the table and sought a spot for his foursome.

Beckett returned his glare to Sean, "Stay out of trouble and stay out of my way, civilian."

Silently, Sean smiled at the man and walked towards an empty table. "Well, that was fun," he said to the others as they joined him.

"He's charming," Detective Woodfeathers declared.

"You heard about the incident in Seattle? We kind of warned him about a terrorist attack that he refused to follow up. A measly wildlife officer and a nobody civilian helped stop the whole thing. We kind of pissed him off down there," Adam responded.

"I guess so," Woodfeathers agreed and announced to his companions, "Since we've already made friends with everyone, after breakfast, we'll join them at the protest camp."

Ten

Miranda Shaw woke up wearily and crawled out of her sleeping bag. The truth was, she never really fell to sleep at all. The uncomfortable ground, the foreign setting, and the unyielding cascade of thoughts that streamed through her head dashed any hopes of quality rest. Digging through her hastily thrown together duffle bag, she produced a toothbrush and some paste. Exiting the tent, she tended to her morning ritual.

She laughed to herself. Sometimes it was the small things in life that make you feel better - like freshly brushed teeth. Stowing her personal items away, she stretched out in front of her tent, ready to take on the day.

Walking over to the lonely circle that surrounded the still smoldering fire, she passed several tents of snoring inhabitants. In some cases, the scent of stale marijuana smoke hung in the morning air. Miranda conceded that the mix of individuals who participated in these protests was indeed an eclectic one. There were the science-based representatives such as herself, there were the radical hippies and the altruistic, and sometimes naïve college students that were hell-bent on impacting the world.

Leaning back against the trunk of a tall fir tree, Miranda sat patiently, waiting for her friends to awaken and emerge from their tents. Occasionally campers would walk by on their way to find a bathroom spot and wave to her. She was content to listen to the waves lap against the shore in relative solitude. Sadly, she noted that the thick air was every bit as fogged in as the previous morning when Jim was killed, scarcely two miles away.

The visions of Jim being pursued along the water's edge made her shudder. Jim could be arrogant, to be sure, but he was generally a peaceful man. His mouth and legal torts were his way to fight the world, not his physique. Though fit, a physical confrontation was a juxtaposition to Harrison's persona. She slowly began to realize that she was far more disappointed in his passing than truly sad. Her ex-fiancé's death seemed to weigh heavier on her head than her heart.

Miranda's solitude shattered by the sound of powerful vehicles driving to the campsite. Several sets of headlights tried to push their way through the soupy mist. The sounds of doors slamming were followed by teams of dark suit-clad men encroaching on the settlement of tents, most of the newcomers carrying gear or lightweight folding tables.

With remarkable speed and efficiency, the men assembled an interrogation site under a large gazebo that they erected. Phones, recording devices, and rows of laptop computers lined portable tables awaiting their human operators.

When the set up was complete, the fog was broken with three men who, unlike the others, were not laden as they entered the site. Each man wore a long trench coat covering their dark suits. As the men neared, Miranda squirmed in recognition of the one in front – Stanley Beckett. He was the humorless man who was largely dissatisfied with her and her friends' intervention of the Seattle terrorist plot. The marine biologist doubted Beckett would be at all pleased to find her here.

In a wave, she transported back to the terrible incident in Seattle - her mind bounced between the friendship that had begun to blossom with Sean, Adam and Rachel, and the horror of her cousins' involvement and ultimately leading to their subsequent deaths. Turning away from the approaching men, she hoped that she would not be recognized. Dealing with the arrogant Stan Beckett was certainly quite low on her list of desirables. Her wishes dashed almost as soon as they were conceived.

"Well, the gang's all here! Ms. Shaw, is it not?" the obstinate voice of the Western Region Department of Interior Director called out.

"Yes, it is. Hello Mr. Beckett, I didn't recognize you," Miranda lied.

"And what brings you out to this godforsaken party in the rain forest?" Beckett asked.

"You might as well know upfront, Jim was my ex-fiancé. I came out as soon as I heard about his death," Miranda admitted.

"Hmm. Your rogue boyfriend kill him?" Beckett's tactless comment caused Miranda to wince. He continued before she could react to his rhetorical derogation, "No, no – hold that thought. You have just volunteered to be our first witness."

"I'm honored," Miranda facetiously replied.

Begrudgingly, she stood up from her roost by the waning embers and followed the team of black suits under cover of the gazebo. An agent pulled out a chair for her and several more settled into place around her.

A steady and flat affected interrogative assault unfolded upon her: questions covering her relationship with Harrison, what she had done, and where she had been since the Seattle incident - what communication and what she knew of Sean's presence consumed most of the dialogue.

Beckett rolled his eyes upon hearing her explanation of the lack of contact with Sean since she returned to Anacortes. Looking at her as though he were a disapproving father, he pushed on, "So you haven't seen wonder boy since that day at your uncle's ranch?"

"No, I haven't. When you see people, people you are...were...close to killed, it tends to kind of quell any romantic notions," Miranda spat back, unhappy with her personal life coming under review.

"It didn't seem to bother you then," the DOI Director said, an air of arrogance wrapped around his words.

"You are an obnoxious jerk, Mr. Beckett. Would you care to continue this discussion or would you prefer to sit here and lob insults back and forth at each other?" Miranda asked in as polite a tone as she could muster.

Perturbed at being called out, Beckett stiffened and returned to his notes for questioning. "Ms. Shaw, about your relationship with the deceased, did things end awkwardly? Were there hard feelings?"

"I was the one to end it. He was a great guy. I just didn't want to marry him. I certainly had no ill will. As far as I know, and I do...did know him better than most, the only feathers he ruffled were the Makah hunters, non-eco friendly industry, and those he ran up against in the government," she answered calmly.

"Oh, I get it. Another conspiracy theory for you and your friends, eh, Ms. Shaw?" Beckett's voice dripped with sarcasm.

"Cute. I told you before, I am as surprised as you are that they are here," Miranda swore.

"And your boyfriend, Kendall...was he in conflict with your fiancé?"

"They didn't even know each other or about each other. Besides, there was nothing for them to conflict over. I am not Sean's girlfriend, nor was I any longer Jim's fiancé," Miranda replied evenly.

"But they both wanted to be in those roles, didn't they? It sounds like exactly like the sort of stuff that would make two testosterone filled men come into conflict. Did you make them aware of their place...or were you leading them on until you could choose for yourself– kind of keep those strings dangling?" Beckett continued to press.

Chewing her bottom lip to refrain from the outburst he was vying for, Miranda stared directly into the DOI Director's eyes, "For the last time, there were no strings. This isn't about me, Mr. Beckett. I'll be honest with you. Jim was a good man, but he was also good at making enemies– and not with people I have dated, but in his line of work."

"Quite the ecologist– generally a dangerous bunch, aren't they Ms. Shaw?" Beckett laughed.

"Not everybody agreed with his philosophies, yet he was very good at forcing his way. He knew the system and was very adept at using it to his aim. That made him dangerous to many people far more treacherous than you average ecologist," Miranda admitted through pursed lips.

"Hmm," hummed Beckett disbelievingly, he drew his hands up to his lips as if he was taking great care to phrase his next question, "Now, where were you yesterday morning, say around seven?"

"I was at my home in Anacortes, alone," she replied curtly, "As I have said before, I received the phone call about Jim's death and came right out here."

"We'll check your phone records. I assume the person who called you will corroborate that you were on the line in Anacortes?" the DOI director asked.

"Yes, she's here. Carrie Sanders," Miranda smiled grimly at Beckett. Stress and fatigue were setting in and making the interrogation even more taxing and frustrating, but she refused to let her arrogant interviewer see that he was getting to her.

"Perhaps you can go bring her to me," Beckett said, more as a directive than a request. Miranda stood up to leave, and as she neared the edge of the gazebo, he called out purposely, "Ms. Shaw, I'm going to have to ask that you do not leave the area without my explicit consent. You are a suspect in a murder investigation."

"You couldn't make me leave until I find out what happened for myself. You've already shown me how you manage an investigation, Mr. Beckett. I am not entirely impressed," she spat back and turned toward the ocean of tents.

It was not until she was well beyond the eyes and ears of the DOI agents in the shroud of canvas and nylon outposts, did she allow herself to break down. Bursting into tears, she covered her face with her hands. All of the emotions of the past twenty-four hours, the past few weeks - the past year - cascaded on her all at once. Taking refuge behind a small tree, her cathartic outburst lasted only a moment. She sniffed, straightened herself up, and wiped her tear-streaked face with the sleeve of her jacket.

Taking in a deep breath, she collected herself, and made her way to Carrie's tent. She tapped gently on the fabric wall. "Carrie...," she hissed, "Caarrieee!"

Pausing to listen for signs of life, Miranda heard sounds of hasty rustling and low whispering, "It's Miranda!" More indecipherable whispering followed by the sounds of legs shoved through a pair of pants and, finally, the whirring of the tent zipper.

Carrie's head popped out of the doorway as she clumsily exited the tent. Producing a guilty smile, she patted her clothes as if that would rid her of the turbulent sea of wrinkles that had taken hold. "You're up early," she continued smiling.

"I really couldn't sleep much," Miranda sighed, her look casting an air of suspicion at her friend.

"I know. This has been tough on all of us," Carrie admitted compassionately.

"I have been asked to send you over to the crime scene tent that has been set up on the beachhead just beyond the last tent. The feds want to question the protest camp, and they are starting with those who were closest to Jim," Miranda said matter-of-factly.

"Ugh, why don't they leave us alone and concentrate on those Makah barbarians?" Carrie groaned.

Miranda shrugged, "They have to cover all bases, I guess." As she turned to leave, she paused as more rustling erupted in Carrie's tent. She shot a glance at her friend, whose face washed in a guilty scarlet glow. Miranda raised her eyebrows expectantly.

Carrie stood in front of her tent, looking stymied and wriggling in discomfort. A man's voice broke the tension, "You still there, Carrie?"

Miranda's eyes widened in mutual surprise and recognition. The gray hair and beard of Brett Pearson squeezed through the zippered door of the tent. He looked out, stunned to find Miranda still a few feet away. The three of them traded nervous glances at each other in uncomfortable silence that seemed to hang as thick as the soupy ocean air.

Suddenly Miranda smiled, "Good morning, Brett."

"Uhh, good morning Miranda. Carrie and I stayed up late talking...," the distinguished biologist stammered.

Miranda quickly waved him off, suggesting that an explanation was neither warranted nor desired. She eyed Carrie with a single eyebrow raised, "I guess you are due for a second interrogation, my dear." She smiled and quickly shuffled off, absolving them both of further discomfort and embarrassment.

Seeking the solace of her own tent, she flopped on her sleeping bag. Her range of mixed emotions now included a bit of levity. The shock of seeing her friends compromised was as humorous to her as it was surprising. The clique in their world was rather small and exposed, leaving little room for any secret trysts. Miranda's surprise in this pairing mediated by her knowledge of her friend's sophomoric, sorority lifestyle.

Eleven

The two tribal policemen, with Sean and Adam in tow, arrived at the fringe of the protest camp. The path twisting its way through the ocean of tents was easily determined by following the small army of federal agents and press corps. Adam and the reservation officials flashed their IDs and took their place in the procession leading to the forensics and BLM outpost.

Sean vigilantly scanned the area. He knew Miranda was here somewhere. Despite the awkward circumstances leading to their coincidental run-in, his curiosity peaked on her response. How would she react? Did she even know he was there? Sean did not possess a strong virtue of patience for unanswered questions. Whatever the answers might be, he felt he could contend with them better than the unknown.

Approaching the interrogation tent, Sean and Adam were instantly taken aback by a familiar voice. Stanley Beckett froze mid-sentence, breaking off his line of questions with Carrie and rose in response to seeing the two men.

"Well, I'll be damned!" the Regional Department of Interior Director bellowed, "It's true. You two criminals, oh that's right, 'heroes', are here to what, oversee my investigation."

"Beckett," Adam gleefully stood in front of his superior with a sarcastic exuberance, "Happy to be of service, Stan. They still have you in charge of people...human beings...huh!"

Beckett looked around, casting an annoyed countenance, "Why does everyone have such a hard time with that?"

"Glad my tax dollars are still supporting you, sir," Sean took his turn facing Beckett's scrutiny.

Beckett shot Adam a disapproving look, "I'm not sure what you are up to this time Raines, but you better watch your ass. Better yet, just stay the hell out of my way."

The Regional Director pushed his way back under the gazebo. Glancing at Carrie still waiting uncomfortably for him to return, he dismissed her with a casual wave of his hand. Whispering to one of his men, he sat in his chair, pushing a stack of papers aside. A moment later, his agent arrived trailed by Sean. "Mr. Kendall, please have a seat," the weathered Beckett motioned towards the empty seat across from him. "So, let's get this over with quickly. Where were you the morning of Harrison's death?"

"I was at my home in Marblemount. I received a call from Detective Joe Woodfeathers, whom I have assisted on Search and Rescues. I got a hold of Adam, and we headed to the peninsula to assist," Sean replied coolly.

"Ah, yes, you're quite the boy scout. And your area of expertise in criminal investigations is...," Beckett asked sarcastically.

"I did not come on an official capacity," Sean admitted.

"Oh, right, your lover was here. Hey," Beckett exclaimed, clearly enjoying taunting the young retiree, "Wasn't she also the lover of the deceased?" The Regional Director beamed at his interrogatee.

"It appears as such. I have not seen Miranda since she left the Cascades a couple of weeks ago, nor was I familiar with her relationship with Mr. Harrison," Sean's voice remained calm and even despite his interviewer's attempts to rattle him.

"Bull malarkey, Kendall. I've seen your handiwork. You found out that you got played by little Miss Sweet Tart and had granola boy gored," Beckett continued his bullying.

"Right, because my life is as pathetic as yours and I had to hang my hat on the first woman who gave me the time of day. Come on, Beckett, I thought you were smarter than that - not much, but a little...," Sean volleyed.

"Listen here, Kendall, if it were my say, you and your friend Agent Raines would be in jail over the Seattle fiasco. I have had about enough from you," Beckett glowered.

"You mean the fiasco that you could have prevented? You were the one who wouldn't listen to us when we asked for help investigating that poaching ring and again when we discovered that same group was plotting a massacre at the Seattle One World Organization convention," Sean shot back.

"Do I need to remind you that you are a civilian? You have no place in interfering with an official investigation! All you are supposed to do is pick up the phone and call the professionals. Let us handle it, " Beckett snapped.

"Oh, you mean like you? We tried that once. That didn't work out very well," Sean shot back, and tried a different tack, "Look, Beckett, we can sit here and lob insults to each other all day long. We don't have to like each other, but I assume we are after the same thing. I was at home in the Cascades, a good two, three hours away."

Through an icy glare, Beckett studied Sean and the earnest appearance on his face and returned to his questioning, "I assume Agent Raines will corroborate your alibi?"

"Of course, he drove me out here. It is logistically impossible for me to have killed Harrison, driven back to the Cascades, and be picked by Adam anywhere near the timeframe that the events took place. Now, if you would like my perspective on the murder...," Sean started before Beckett cut him off.

"No, I don't want your opinion," Beckett snapped, his face screwed into a look of disgust, "What I want is you nowhere near my investigation. If you step out of line, even once, I will throw your butt in jail!" With his hand out, the DOI director motioned that Sean was free to leave the table and called out, "I'm not done with you, Kendall, don't go far."

Beckett waved Sean off as though casting away a servant and called for another agent to round up Adam and the two tribal American policemen. As the red-faced DOI Director waited, Special Agent-in-Charge Manning made his way through the forensics tent.

"You know, he's been dead-on in a few of his observations and deductions. I wasn't real thrilled with their noses being near my investigation either, but they have been quite helpful," Manning whispered in a low tone to the DOI director.

"You're an idiot, Manning. A crime scene is no place for a civilian. If he interferes at all, and I mean at all, I want him arrested. You certainly cannot go on encouraging this inappropriate disruption of a murder investigation," Beckett snarled at the FBI agent, "Did you know your boy was involved with the victim's lover? I'll bet he had some theories to share with you."

"He what?" Manning's jaw stood agape.

"That's right Manning, so far, you and your boys are doing some excellent detective work. You allowed a suspect to traipse all over this investigation. You be sure he is barred from this area!" Beckett settled smugly back in his chair, awaiting his next party to question.

Looking up and seeing the brawny Fish and Wildlife agent standing in front of him, he grinned slightly, "Agent Raines, I am overriding Assistant Regional Director York's approval for you overseeing this investigation. You are hereby relieved of your duties on this investigation," Beckett coolly told Adam, never taking his eyes off the piece of paper in hands.

Adam glowered furiously at his superior, but before he could speak, Beckett made a shooing motion with his hands, "Get out! And take your little friend with you."

"Beckett, you...," Adam began.

"Uh, uh, aah...careful Raines, I already have your insubordination papers drawn up, give me a reason, I'm just itching to sign them," Beckett snapped, continuing his indignant manner.

Adam opened his mouth to speak, but fighting for control, turned and exited the command post gazebo. Stalking passed the agents controlling access to the tent, he stormed off to find Sean.

Special Agent Manning quickly exited the tent and hustled away as Adam, Joe, and Marty were escorted in. He wore an expression of annoyance as he scanned the area. Locating his target, he moved forward with steadfast urgency.

"Kendall!" he barked at Sean, who was weaving his way towards the beach, "I need a word with you."

Sean stopped and turned toward the FBI agent, "Sure, Manning, what's up?"

"You were holding out on me," Manning began, "You have a connection to the victim. What are you trying to pull?"

"You've been talking to Beckett," Sean sighed, slamming his hands into his pockets, "I know it is difficult to believe, but I just learned of the connection myself. I wanted to sort it all out before I approached you with it."

"And that's what you were doing? Looking for me out on the beach?" Manning asked sarcastically, his eyebrows raised.

"No," Sean scoffed, "But I would have come clean. I don't have anything to lose. I can very clearly be placed about a hundred miles away at the time of Harrison's death - and if anyone thinks that I contracted a hit on a guy, who I didn't know existed, over a woman that I knew for a week, they're crazier than Beckett. Look, he's got a permanent bur under his saddle since we uncovered the Seattle plot that was unfolding right in front of his nose!"

"So that was you, huh?" Manning looked surprised, his entire affect softening, "I guess I should've put two and two together. I've heard about what you did. We owe you a lot of respect and gratitude. A lot more people would have died that day - including some of my fellow agents."

"I don't expect gratitude. I just couldn't stand by and watch innocent people get hurt by a bunch of psychopath terrorists. When we couldn't get people like Beckett to listen, we were forced to jump in there ourselves, it wasn't by design for us to become physically involved in that mess," Sean replied modestly.

"We should all be glad that you did," Manning purported, "But Sean, I need you to be upfront and honest with me."

Sean nodded apologetically, "Sorry about that, as you might have noticed, Beckett and I have not developed a real warm relationship. My interactions with him have not created a trustworthy vibe with federal agents, especially those in charge."

"I guess I can't blame you for that," Manning laughed for a moment and then looked serious, "The word is that Beckett is going to have you guys booted from the crime scene. He can't kick you guys out of the reservation, but he can bar you from any of the investigation sites."

"Thanks for the heads up," Sean nodded.

"You have my card. I am not generally one to entertain the whims of civilians, but I believe you've got solid instincts. If you come up with anything else, I'd like a call," Manning nodded respectfully and hurried off to rejoin his team of investigators.

Sean patted the card in his pocket, turning just in time to see a beaming Adam round the corner. The wildlife agent raised his eyebrows, "Love note?"

"Funny," Sean scowled, "One of us needs to create allies."

"Speaking of allies, have you run into your girl?" Adam asked.

"I assume you mean Miranda. No, I haven't seen her," Sean shrugged.

"Maybe just as well," Adam consoled, "You probably heard, I am officially off the case. Good ol' Beckett, the jerk."

"So, what now? Do we go home?" Sean asked.

"Not just yet. I want to find out how the investigation here in the protest camp goes. We need to be careful though, Beckett will have me transferred to an igloo in the upper Yukon if he catches us," the wildlife officer warned.

"You'd look good in a big parka. I'm sure Laura wouldn't divorce you, or maybe she would...," mocked Sean.

"I'd just as soon stay out of trouble, with Beckett and the misses," Adam grinned and added, "So, I'll let the Makah crew know what we're up to, why don't you go gather your gear, and I'll meet you at the longhouse."

"Will do," Sean agreed as his big friend plundered off.

Spinning towards the path leading back to the Makah village, Sean left the interrogation area of the protest camp. Weaving his way through the perimeter tents and tall fir trees, he nearly ran right into another pedestrian sharing the same path.

His heart jumped as he found himself face to face with Miranda. He opened his mouth, but at first, no words would come out. Finally, a choking, "Miranda!" left his lips.

"Hi Sean," the auburn-haired biologist replied, not affording Sean a detection of emotion, instead sounding as one would with a co-worker, "I'm a little surprised to see you here."

"I'm surprised to see you!"

"What are you doing here? Did you come because..." she began.

"Because Harrison was a...a friend of yours? No. I didn't find that out until the investigation got underway. I was asked to come and help a friend," Sean answered, sensing Miranda's concern.

"So, you know we were engaged..." Miranda assumed.

"Yeah. That tidbit caught me by surprise, about got me arrested for withholding information in a federal investigation," Sean admitted. Looking into her cool blue eyes made his heart swell, he suddenly wanted to dispense with the talk of why they were there and jump to why they hadn't been together. Miranda, though, kept the conversation on track.

"We were over, just so you know," Miranda continued to wear a look that seemed to blend perturbed and suspicious, which to Sean screamed a very frustrating statement of cute and stay away.

"I didn't ask," Sean said defensively.

"I just thought you should know," Miranda stated flatly and then pivoted a step away from Sean and leaning towards the path to the protest camp, "I should be on my way."

The words drove into Sean like sharp icicles to his heart. He wanted to keep her there, regardless of topic or tone, just have her in front of him. Reaching out, he gently grabbed her hand, the feel of her skin, making him feel as though his chest would explode. Just for a moment, as he slipped deep into her hypnotic, intoxicating eyes, he thought he saw a glimmer of similar desire. The moment, real or imagined, was quickly shattered as she pulled her hand away.

"I...I can't. I'm sorry," Miranda swallowed and quickly fled down the path losing herself amongst her friends in the nearby camp.

Sean's heart sunk to his feet, feeling as if those icicles that had impaled him with her words began melting in his veins, seeping painfully cold through his organs. Helplessly, he just watched her dissolve into the sanctuary of the crowd. Cursing as he turned to continue to the Longhouse trail, he felt like he could punch a hole through a tree. Had he known that immersed in the crowd, Miranda Shaw turned her head briefly back towards him. He would have been especially grateful for maintaining his composure.

Twelve

Tug Gaskill dialed the number - an indiscriminate hotel room in the industrial district of Seattle. A gruff voice answered as Tug looked upon the tall skyscrapers of the Japanese city.

"Chavez. Enjoying your lodgings?" Tug asked into the phone.

"Sure, the cockroaches make fine company. What have you got for me?" Rey Chavez snapped impatiently.

"I think you're going to enjoy this one, Rey. It'll provide a big paycheck and maybe a little fun, too. Plus, you'll finally be able to repay that favor you owe me," Tug grinned into the phone.

"If it's so good, why aren't you doing it yourself?" Chavez asked suspiciously.

"Because Rey, I have a nice, fresh target on my back. I still need the embers to die down before I re-engage. But listen, if you don't want to do this, I can get someone else...," Tug began.

"No man, I'm interested, I just haven't known you to turn down big money," Chavez quickly back-peddled.

"It's not going to be easy. Can you assemble a team within the week?" Tug asked.

"A week?" Chavez frowned.

"Sometimes, you need to jump when the field is hot. The requestor has some pressing financial matters that need tending to, it has to be done quickly to avoid undesired scrutiny," Tug replied.

"A week," Chavez replied thoughtfully, "May not be an 'A' crew, but I'll put something together. What are we actually talking about?"

"I have a wealthy Japanese investor who owns a charter cruise out of downtown Portland. He needs you to rob it. You walk away and keep fifteen percent..." Tug started.

"How much is the haul?" Chavez asked eagerly.

"About nine million, it has a sizable vault for his offshore gambling clients. You will have all the access points, minimum resistance, you just need to play it off as hostile and have a solid exit plan," Tug informed him.

"And what is your gain in all this?" Chavez asked.

"A finder's fee - which I'd be willing to kick back to you, if you add in a favor for me," Tug replied thoughtfully.

"A favor?" Chavez called back through the earpiece.

"I might arrange for a victim or two to be on board for you to take care of," Tug cooed into the phone.

"Why not, add a little realism to the heist," Chavez shrugged, "Besides, if this'll make us square, then I'm in," Chavez agreed.

"Take care of this for me and consider us square," Tug confirmed, hanging up the phone.

Hishiro left the board meeting with a dark cloud hanging over his head. Dipping into the company funds had been such a safe and easy exercise for him, but now, with his assets frozen during the Japanese Securities investigation, a couple of holes had been ripped gaping open. His accountants, quite adept at managing the paper trail, had their hands tied before they could make the latest corrections. Having his U. S based cache of funds "stolen" would cover the gaps that his Asian-Pacific books so glaringly had.

The sudden melody of his cell phone jarred him from his thoughts, seeing the caller ID display the code that he had entered for Tug, his spirits rose. He hoped Tug had good news for him.

"Mr. Gaskill, you have news for me?" the shipping magnate asked expectantly.

"I have brokered my man for the second job you requested. We split the pot. I get a fee of say...twenty percent of the takeaway. My man gets fifteen percent, and you get the rest - not to mention the insurance check for the unfortunate incident," Tug laid out the plans.

"He handled the incident in northern Washington, but you trust him on a job this big?" Hasegawa asked.

"Are you kidding me? With all the inside track, this thing is a piece of cake," Tug scoffed, "I wish I were there to do this myself."

"Remember, just the cash receipts and the safe...and clean. It can be rough for a good showing, but dead bodies attract too much attention. The authorities don't care if a rich Japanese man gets robbed, but if a bunch of people die aboard his boat... I have enough problems here at home," Hasegawa stressed.

"Don't worry about it. My guy's a pro. He knows what to do," the mercenary assured him, "After your nice little boat ride, your problems will be over, and I get to start on my much-needed tan."

Thirteen

S ean and Adam remained quiet in the periphery of the
protest campsite, taking great care to stay out of the
way of Beckett and his men. Detective Woodfeathers
and Marty Lanook kept vigil over the FBI-led interrogations,
occasionally sending a Makah deputy to share information of
interest with his two banished friends waiting on the sidelines.

Adam's eyes lit up when a young Makah girl burst through
the bushes carrying two sacks of food. The wildlife officer eagerly
tore into the package to reveal a seal meat sandwich. He didn't
realize how hungry he had become until his senses drank in the
meal before him. Turning to the squeamish Sean, he grinned, "This
one of your little flipper friends?"

Ignoring him, Sean had sunk his teeth into the first bite of
his lunch when a volley of shouts rang through the nearby camp.
He and Adam poked their heads up to try and see through the trees.
The spot they had chosen for cover was too dense with foliage to
afford them much of a view. Putting their lunches down on a
nearby rock, the two men carefully picked their way through the
tree line. Peering cautiously around a large pine, they witnessed the
scene unfolding at the camp.

Sean looked on as two officers held a young Makah boy
who wriggled and twisted in a vain attempt to free himself. Several
protesters gathered around, one shouting a frenetic stream of
accusations. In the outer circle of the crowd, Sean saw the sullen

face of Miranda looking on. A path emerged through the group as the spectators parted to allow Beckett and his procession to make their way through.

The only words that meandered their way successfully to Sean and Adam's ears, were those of the loudest and most animated of the accusers. "We caught him, snooping. He's the murderer!" the protester yelled.

The protester's arms flailed wildly as he spoke. His antics would have appeared menacing, had they not been offset by his teddy bear-like appearance. A grayish beard shrouded his face, his physique softened by years of waning activity and indulgent eating. His persona spoke more like that of a jolly grandfather than the hot temper and contemptuousness he currently displayed. Sean almost laughed at the vision; it was like watching the guy on the oatmeal box, throwing a tantrum. A focused inspection revealed to Sean that this was the same man that had accompanied Miranda to the crime scene the previous afternoon.

As a disgruntled DOI Director Stanley Beckett tried to sort out the details and elicit lucid feedback from the man, Marty and Joe joined the fray. Marty looked visibly upset at the confrontation and appeared to protest as the tribal boy was placed in handcuffs. Beckett quickly rattled off commands to his men. The mix of DOI, FBI, and county officers scurried off to comply.

Reading the body language, Sean and Adam had a pretty good idea what had happened - Beckett had a suspect. Without warning, a figure oozed out of the shadows, taking the two men by surprise. Startled, Adam reached for his handgun, but quickly recognized the figure as one of Lanook's men.

The young tribal policeman grinned, "You do not have a successful hunt if you alert your prey."

"I'll remember that the next time I'm hunting a Federal agent and his friend," Sean retorted, "They are arresting the Makah boy?"

"Yes, for questioning, but the accusations are not true. He was just curious. He didn't murder Mr. Harrison," the officer protested and then went on, "But Detective Woodfeathers would like to meet you down the road. Just past the museum, there is a little pullout on the left. It provides access to the beach. He says he will be there in ten minutes. Now I must go. Chief Lanook will need my help."

Sean and Adam thanked the tribal officer as he slipped into the foliage as quietly as he appeared. "Man, I didn't know the Makah were ninjas. We could have used that kid back in Special Ops," Adam laughed.

"He's lucky you didn't shoot him," Sean relied scowling.

"We're lucky that a Makah hunter didn't want us dead," Adam countered grimly.

"Sir, I am concerned about this Tug Gaskill thing," senatorial aide Jerry Rhinehart warned his boss of the last seven years.

The two men were enjoying the early afternoon sunshine on the veranda of Senator Small's Capitol Hill office. Rhinehart did indeed wear an expression of concern on his face.

Small shot his right-hand man a perturbed look, "What do you propose I do about it?"

"We should have him eliminated," Rhinehart pleaded.

"And how would you suggest we accomplish that? One of the most dangerous men to turn merc out of Special Forces? It's like throwing rocks at a bee's nest – at some point, you just piss them off, and they come after you. No, Jerry, we sit tight and use him to our advantage, and when the time is right, we terminate his contract. If we keep giving him a paycheck, he'll be alright," Small consoled the aide.

"So how do we keep him in check?" Rhinehart asked.

"We keep him in our employ," Small replied, "You have that number that Hasegawa gave you?"

The aide nodded and sifted through his coded contact list. He looked at his boss, who motioned toward the phone and leaned back in his chair. Moments later, the tone of the ringing line greeted them through the speakerphone.

"Gaskill," Tug's voice acknowledged.

"Tug, this is Jerry Rhinehart. I wanted to ensure that you had arrived in Osaka safely and that Hasegawa has accommodated you sufficiently," Rhinehart spoke into the phone under his boss' guidance.

"Yeah, it's a regular vacation. I appreciate your concern," Tug spat sarcastically, "Now what the hell do you want?"

"Well, we...uh, I wanted to maintain contact to ensure future arrangements," Rhinehart stammered, he felt like the former Special Ops soldier evaluated every word he uttered.

"I'm a little busy right now, do you have something specific for me?" the curt reply showing the mercenary's growing impatience.

"Oh, well, no. We have some plans coming up, and we just wanted to be sure you would be... " the senatorial aide began.

"If you want to know what my plans are, just ask me," Tug responded hotly.

"What are your plans, Tug?" Rhinehart asked, his voice carrying a vexed tone, belying his concern and annoyance.

"None of your damn business," Tug snapped coldly.

Rhinehart felt a chill seep down his spine as he heard Tug's words over the loudspeaker.

"I don't work for you, Rhinehart, or your boss Senator Small. I work for myself. If I like a contract, I take it. I do not need to be babysat. Frankly, it pisses me off. From now on, you may reach me through my messaging service. If I elect to call you back, you will hear from me. But Rhinehart...and Senator Small, if you're listening, and I assume you are, don't piss me off," the speakerphone buzzed as the line clicked off.

"Wake a sleeping dog...," Small said, disconnecting his side of the call.

"We should take care of him, sir," urged Rhinehart.

"Maybe, but not right now. He may prove useful yet again," Small replied, scratching his chin.

"Is that wise, sir? The things that man is capable of...using him for another assignment...it leaves this office vulnerable," Rhinehart resisted.

"Nonsense. We have kept our noses clean. All of the backing has been from outside sources. There are no trails that would lead to us. We're fine, Jerry. Have another drink, and when it comes to handling men like Tug Gaskill, you leave that to me," Small smiled at his more youthful protégé and picked up the latest sub-committee dossier on the development of trade relations through the One World Organization.

The senator from Idaho had strong desires to disenfranchise the United States from the rest of the world. He felt the bleeding heart liberals were allowing poorer nations to suck America's prosperity dry. He had made it his life's work to remove the world's lazy lips from the teats of the United States, as he often referred. To him, political structures like the United Nations and the World Trade Organization were anti-American deluge sapping away the American way of life. In his way were politicians like Senator Johnson of Oregon and his nemesis – President Marshall, each keeping America's connection with those organizations alive.

He reflected on the risks of working with such characters as Tug Gaskill. Smiling into his swirling glass of cognac as he stared at the White House just beyond the green lawn of the mall, he assured himself that it was well worth it.

Miranda watched in silence as the agents led the young Makah hunter through the maze of tents and into the back of a waiting Clallam County Sheriff's car. Somehow bearing witness to the arrest did not feel resolute. It didn't make the pain that she had cast in Jim Harrison's final months of life go away.

Seeing the look of fear mixed wash away, the defiance on the young boy's face left her with a surprisingly sympathetic view on the scene. Despite the years of arguing against the Makah's hunting practices, Miranda saw sincerity in the detainee's pleas.

Across the crowd, she saw Sean and Adam, just as they melted into the dense tree line of the adjacent forest. Once more, Miranda felt the pangs of confusion in her heart and head over Sean Kendall. It was such a strange coincidence that they were both in the remote Makah territory of the upper Olympic Peninsula. She thought that she had convinced herself to move on. Put her brief interlude with the charming man into perspective as just that – an interlude. Seeing him again, looking deep into his eyes made her question whether or not she was okay with that decision. Why had their paths crossed so closely?

Shaking the questions from her head, she resolved to pack her things and return to her home in Anacortes. There was nothing she could do for her old friend and ex-fiancé here. The authorities had their suspect in custody, and out of respect, the Makah tribal council had called off the season's hunt. Miranda told herself that it was time she got her life back together. Mourning Jim or cousin Jeb, wishing her family was intact, pining for the man that had killed her cousins was not healthy. No, she was going to wash away the past and return order to her life. Charming and handsome as Kendall was, his place was a memory in her heart.

The scream of tires capped with a blood-chilling yelp. Running to see what had happened, Sean was afraid that he recognized that inhuman cry. His fears were confirmed as he saw a young Makah boy dart into the street and fall to his knees behind the front bumper of a car that sat cockeyed in the middle of the road.

Coming to the boy's side, Sean saw the motionless brown lump of fur next to him. The driver of the car approached, a bureau agent who was navigating the black sedan through the rough, narrow Makah Village streets. The trench coat cloaked man ranted about the incident, not being his fault and to hurry and drag the animal off the road. Ignoring him, Sean turned to Adam, "Grab the first aid kit from Agent Kindhearted there and tell him to shut the heck up!"

Adam looked at him with a quizzical glance and scoffed, "What are you going to do, give him mouth to mouth?"

Slipping his fingers under the dog's armpit, Sean searched for a pulse. Not detecting one, he delivered several quick chest compressions into the animal's side and then clamping the muzzle shut, Sean gave a series of breaths into the dog's snout.

Adam stared at his friend in puzzled amazement, "I guess he is giving the dog mouth to mouth. That's the craziest thing I have ever seen...and I've seen some stuff." Proceeding to ask the agent to produce his medical kit from the trunk of the black cruiser, he called back to Sean, "I'm not kissing you after that!"

At first, the agent denied Adam's request citing agency guidelines regarding equipment. Adam squared up his tall, muscular body, "Just get me the medkit! I'm pretty sure the bureau frowns on mowing down kid's puppies, too!"

That piece of logic sent the agent scurrying to the trunk, producing a small nylon case which he tossed to the Fish and Wildlife agent. When the two men returned to the front of the agent's car, they found that Sean had revived the scraggly brown dog.

In a very calm voice, Sean asked the boy, "Can you comfort him and hold him still? We need to check him over real good, and if he squirms, he can hurt himself worse."

The boy eagerly nodded his head and began gently stroking the dog and softly cooing to him. Sean carefully and thoroughly began running his hands over the dog, feeling for signs of broken bones or other injuries. When his inspection was complete, he had identified only a single broken bone in the dog's front left leg.

Taking a roll of gauze from the medical kit, Sean began to wrap the hound's injured leg. Following a thorough taping, ensuring there were no loose ends for the dog to chew on, he looked to the boy, "Is there a vet on the reservation?"

"No, sir. The closest one is in Sequim, over forty-five minutes away," the boy replied.

"Well, this will have to do, I guess. When you get home, spray something the dog doesn't like on the bandage, like hot sauce or something, that'll help keep him from chewing on it. Keep him calm and quiet for a while, and watch him closely. If he acts strange or sick, take him to, uh, take him to the town doctor," Sean instructed.

The boy nodded, his big brown eyes damp with tears. Giving Sean a quick hug before returning to his pet. "You did good kid," Sean said, mussing the boy's hair and then announced, "Hey, I bet Agent Speedy here'll help you get him home."

The agent started to protest, but after taking the stern glares from both Sean and Adam, he threw his hands up and scooped the dog up and put both the boy and the animal in his backseat. As the car drove away, Adam patted Sean's shoulder, "Nice work Dr. Dolittle. My only recommendation was to shoot the poor thing and put it out of its misery. But you, you got in there and...hey, you need a breath mint after that? I mean, you had a dog's nose in your mouth! Very heroic, very weird."

Sean just smiled and shook his head. He wasn't sure how serious the dog was hurt, but he hoped he had given the boy's pet a chance. "Shoot him, huh?" Sean glanced at his friend, "I'll remember that the next time you need a bandage."

"Well, hopefully, that isn't anytime soon, come on, Joe should be parked over there," Adam pointed through a stand of cedar trees.

Adam and Sean pushed through the branches of the low growth that lined the twisting reservation road. Curious about the arrest, they were hoping their friend would have details. Joe Woodfeathers was already waiting for them in his truck.

"I guess you fellas don't need me to recap what went down out there. Marty is pretty distraught over the feds taking in the kid. He's got his men trying to reverse the circumstantial evidence. He believes strongly that the boy just got his nose stuck where it didn't belong," the detective said.

"And what do you think?" Sean asked.

"I think it doesn't look good. I guess the kid had been seen around the camp, and he has no alibi for the morning Harrison was killed," Woodfeathers responded grimly.

"He had access to the museum weapons?" Sean queried.

"Yes, all of the hunters do. It gets worse, the detective confessed grimly, "They found the missing knife on him. He claims he found it in the bottom of the creek he was collecting crawfish in, but that seems too coincidental for the FBI men."

"You're right; it doesn't look good. What are you going to do?" Sean asked.

"We will continue to try and corroborate his story back at the reservation. You guys want to stick around a bit?"

"With the hunt off, the protest camp is going to disassemble. I imagine you and Marty can handle things there. I thought maybe we would look into our departed Mr. Harrison a bit. It sounds like he has ruffled a lot of feathers in his work. Maybe we can flush out some more suspects," Adam suggested.

"Couldn't hurt. Take some heat off the Makah boy if you find anything," Joe agreed.

"A trip to Portland?" Sean asked, his eyebrows raised.

"Harrison's office would be a reasonable starting point," Adam admitted.

"Then I wish you two good luck. We appreciate your help, I know it means a lot to Marty," Detective Woodfeathers said and nodded indicating towards the passenger door, "Hop in, I'll drive you back to your truck."

The two men readily accepted and climbed into the cab as the Snohomish detective called ahead to have their things prepared.

Sean gazed absently out of the window as the thickly forested reservation sped passed. The haze that had begun rolling in off of the Pacific waters made the scene that much more surreal. The thickening fog marching along the sand appeared as though an army of ghosts were making their way onshore. It was easy for Sean to imagine an assassin oozing silently through the thick air and taking his victim by surprise. If the assailant was experienced, Jim Harrison didn't stand a chance.

Fourteen

Rey Chavez took the morning to drive down the I-5 corridor to reestablish his base in Portland, just across the Columbia River into Oregon. He chose the Palms Hotel, a once-popular choice in North Portland for families, now a derelict hotel that had become more accustomed to hourly visits and overnight stays for travelers more concerned with discretion than amenities and accouterments. Here he could pay in cash, and as long as the bill was paid in advance, come and go unmolested.

The location provided him a limitless number of avenues to enter and leave the downtown area. Light rail, walking bridges, automobile traffic, and even boats could ferry him across the Willamette River, which split the city and his intended target. Deciding to collect some preliminary data, he hopped on the light rail train, noting the stops, routes, and schedules of each platform.

With the exception of a single college student, Rey had the car to himself. He sat near the rear doors, taking in the scenery of the Portland cityscape. In true northwest fashion, the views transitioned from sketchy neighborhoods to those reclaimed and cleaned up by investors to excellent microbreweries hiding between industrial buildings and finally across the river and into the bustling city center.

Jumping off of the light rail train, Chavez started on a particular course that he had plotted, assuming it was the quickest route to the objective. Again, he took care to note any locations that might create delays or trouble spots either getting in or out of the Portland vicinity.

He found that despite cumbersome traffic, the city's tree-lined streets were reasonably easy to navigate and quite pedestrian-friendly. The brisk spring walk took him to his destination in a short time; the Riverplace Marina nestled on the western shore of the Clackamas River in the heart of downtown Portland. He cocked his head up, taking in all ninety-six feet of the Nagaremono – a gleaming motor yacht with the upper staterooms converted into a magnificent ballroom.

Methodically, he inspected the access points and security of the docks, finding most traffic freely coming and going with very little notice. The staffed crew attended to their duties with barely a glance to passersby or deliveries made to the vessel. He quickly realized why the free-spirited city ranked as one of the friendliest to terrorists – their staunch push for tolerance left them vulnerable to characters that seemed out of place. Portland was a community that welcomed out-of-place as a lifestyle.

Satisfied with his precursory glance at the objective, the former Mexican Special Forces turned cartel operative left the docks for the Third Street station of the light rail and dialed the number for Tug Gaskill. He was instructed to locate a web address where he would find additional details. Finding a nearby Starbuck's, he slipped into a chair nestled into an empty table. Flipping on his smartphone, he searched his entries. Within moments, he had located the site and entered in the encrypted code he had been furnished.

Several files populated the folder: a detailed schematics of the boat, a document listing two internal employees who were trustworthy and loyal to Hasegawa as well as exit plans for Chavez and his team. Chavez chuckled, Tug was always detail-oriented. Closing the screen, he started for the hotel. He had a long night of studying ahead of him.

Behind him, Chavez noticed a shadow creeping alongside. As he passed an alley, the shadow reached out and touched him. Spinning to face the unknown assailant, he saw a shaggy, heavily bearded man staring at him through dark shrouded eyes. Poised to react, he was surprised when the man yanked away his tablet computer and began hobbling down the alley. Taking glances at passersby, who scarcely looked up from their lattes or cellphones, the mercenary darted after the vagrant.

Sloshing through puddles in the alley that was scarcely used for more than storing garbage dumpsters, he quickly caught up to the thief. The pale blues eyes of the vagrant grew wide as the menacing face of Rey Chavez glared at him. Immediately, he dispatched the laptop back into his possession.

The vagabond shrank back in fear, trembling under the fierce visage of Chavez. He thrust his hands in front of his face as a feeble means of protection. His pursuer cast a glance towards the sidewalk, and by the time his gaze returned to the would-be thief, the mercenary's palm plunged outward, connecting with the vagrant's face, driving the fragile pieces of bone and cartilage of his nose into the hobo's brain. Without a sound, the vagabond dropped wearily to the soggy concrete of the dank alleyway.

Tucking the laptop under his arm, Rey Chavez strode out of the alley. Mixing into the crowd, he left the waterfront, and the alley, safely in the distance.

Sean and Adam found Jim Harrison's office nestled in the affluent Portland suburb of Lake Oswego. The stately building was fronted with a dramatic facade of rock and cedar that melted into a gurgling creek with several metal-crafted salmon leaping among copper reeds and river grass.

Sean shot Adam a disapproving glance, "Nice place for a supposed altruistic non-profit guy."

"Hitting too close to home, greeny?" Adam raised his eyebrows.

"Hey, when have you ever seen me in socks and sandals?" Sean glared at his friend. For years, Sean had volunteered his time and money for a group called the Conservancy. His last project for the organization was to purchase an eagle nesting and salmon spawning habitat in the North Cascades. It was during that project when he met Adam almost two years ago.

"Yeech, I just pictured your scrawny legs running around with Birkenstocks and gray hiking socks - not good," the wildlife officer twisted his face in a sour expression.

"Thank you for your fashion moment, can we go in and get to business?"

Pushing forward, Sean marched through the entrance doors and into the reception area. The nicely appointed room overflowed with flower bouquets surrounding a framed eleven-by-twenty-four picture of Jim Harrison. Sean leaned in closer to study the photo. It was his first time to be able to see an example of the man from when he was alive. He found Harrison to be nice looking enough of a man - a few years older than Sean, fit, attired in a fashion that seemed to be an amalgamation of hippie and yuppie. Taking another look around the office, Sean reasoned the deceased naturalist had done quite well for himself. The office was richly appointed with expensive furnishings and bronze sculptures depicting wildlife in their natural habitat.

His observations were broken up by a young woman careening around the corner, carrying another vase of flowers to add to the colorful jungle that had already taken over the small room.

"May I help you?" the girl asked, setting the flowers down next to the others and pushing her glasses back up on the bridge of her nose.

Behind the gold wireframe and lenses, Sean found that he was looking at an attractive young woman. Her blonde hair was pulled back in a loose ponytail, the lenses of her glasses magnifying her freckled cheeks and pale blue eyes.

Trying to work his charm into the scene, Adam thought quickly for something to break the ice. Smiling, he looked at the growing floral display in front of them and joked, "Well, if I were selling allergy meds, I'd say I was in the right place..."

Whatever slight smile the young woman wore instantly melted away into a stern, disapproving glare. "We lost someone extraordinary this week, any jokes you have on the subject are not appreciated," she snapped, her face twisting in obvious disgust.

Sean quickly stepped forward to try and salvage their entry into Harrison's office, "I'm sorry about my partner's inappropriate stab at humor, he always says stupid things when he gets around an attractive woman."

Putting her hands into the air, still wearing the dour affect, she conceded softly, "It's okay. This has been a really difficult week."

"I imagine it has been," Sean replied in a soothing tone, "I'm sorry for us to intrude on your day. I'm Sean Kendall, we're with the Conservancy Group, I know what an important figure Jim was to all of our efforts, that our members would want an immediate eulogy that properly paid tribute to him."

Reaching and grabbing Sean's hands, she smiled, "That is so sweet. That would mean a lot to all of us. Sorry I snapped, all of this has made me a bit edgy. My name is Katie. I'm an intern here. Jim really treated me like...like...."

"A daughter?" Adam offered.

"Oh, no. We were more like, well, special. Let me go get the press kit for you," Katie excused herself and stepped into the back.

When the door shut, Sean shot Adam a glance, "Nice. Make light of the guy's death."

"What? That's a lot of flowers!" Adam protested, shrugging off his friend's disapproval.

Sean just shook his head in silence as he waited for Katie to return. The perky intern emerged through the door promptly and handed him a pre-packaged press kit.

Sean smiled as he took the envelope from the girl and hesitated as he turned to leave the office, "Say, Katie, would it be possible to spend a little time here? It's one thing to receive a fact sheet of someone of Harrison's stature, but I think he's deserving of a write-up that really speaks to the emotional impact that he had on those around him."

Katie wore a confused expression on her face for a moment, re-taking stock of the two men who stood before her. Flattening her lips, she relented, "Well, I guess it will be okay. I'm not sure what you'll get out of it, there's no one here today, and I'm busy trying to handle the press kits and media releases."

Holding the door open, she continued, "There is a library down this hall to the left. There are plenty of news articles and personal mementos in there, including things from Jim."

"Thank you, Katie. I'm sure it will help me gather enough to do him justice," Sean replied, following her into the hallway.

As Adam filtered in behind them, the intern paused and snapped, "Please keep to the library, we had a break-in earlier this week, as if we didn't have enough to deal with!"

Sean and Adam's heads snapped towards each other in unison at this news. Sean looked at Katie with curiosity, "A break-in?"

"Yeah, just a prank or something. Nothing was taken, probably disappointed they broke into a non-profit - we don't have much of value. They came in through Jim's office and then turned around and left without really disturbing anything else," Katie shrugged and stressed, "I have to get things finished."

The two men watched her bounce down the hallway to return to her duties. "A break-in, huh? What might be of value in an environmental activist's office worth breaking into - or even lead to murder?" Sean asked the rhetorical question as they stuck their heads out of the library room to ensure their host continued on her way.

"Information," Adam replied, watching the intern disappear into her office. Breaking into a wide grin, he continued, "Wow, Sean, you were really working her. I was half expecting you to ask her out on a date?"

"You mean as opposed to cracking dead guy jokes? You know the saying, you catch more flies with honey," Sean defended his approach, "We are, after all, behind the locked doors."

"Yes, we are." Adam admitted and then opined. "She seems pretty broken up over this guy."

"The dearly departed? I'd say they were an item," Sean replied.

"The intern and Harrison?"

"Yeah. Judging by her reaction, they've been seeing each other, though, perhaps not publicly," the young retiree observed.

"Hmm. The old dog getting frisky with the young fox. That a boy, Harrison," Adam beamed.

Sean shook his head in mild disgust, "You are remarkably eloquent."

Inside the room they were directed to, they were greeted with a series of hip-high bookshelves stuffed with a variety of hard and paperback books, bound notebooks, and magazine collections. Above each bookcase, dozens of black and white eight by tens lined the walls. The two men leaned in to view the photos. Most were shots taken with magnificent backdrops of mountains, rivers, and forest views. Most included Harrison as the subject, and a few featured the intern who let them in.

Several photos stirred peculiar feelings inside Sean. He studied the prints, keying on scenes which included Miranda. Shots of her backpacking, helping work parties, and leaning against the railing of a boat, were all accompanied by Harrison's arm slung around her shoulders or smiling face hovering nearby. Something in the man's smug grin annoyed Sean.

"Man, this guy really liked himself!" Adam exclaimed, noting Harrison's predominance among the memorabilia.

"Hmmmph," came the only reply Sean felt worthy to muster, keeping his attention on the task of mentally cataloging the items in the room.

Adam picked up a magazine that fanned out among the others on the top of a bookcase. It had none other than Harrison on the cover. "I don't even know the guy, and I'm getting sick of seeing his mug."

"Check out the articles and see if they mention any conflicts that he was embroiled in. Especially large corporations or a political figure...or even the Makah Indian nation," Sean suggested as he opened up the press kit he had been handed.

The first few sheets included basic information detailing Harrison's background and his significant accomplishments. The activist was born in Massachusetts to a family that owned a large food products company. He interned at his father's plant, implementing a major recycling initiative that ended up saving the company hundreds of thousands of dollars before taking off for Berkeley and graduating with an environmental law degree.

Harrison quickly garnered a reputation for his vicious assaults on powerful corporations, reeling in millions of dollars for various environmental groups. Ultimately, he established his own foundation to take on legal battles for all sorts of "green-minded" causes.

Sean plopped the information sheets on the table in front of him, succumbed to the realization that he was dealing with a bonafide left-wing hero. The remaining items in the packet consisted of press photos of Harrison shaking hands with various presidents, standing in front of a bulldozer somewhere in the wilderness, and kneeling on top of a cliff with the sun setting in the background.

He flipped the photos across the table at Adam, "More photos for you. Maybe you can put them on the wall next to your collection of Teen Beat posters."

Adam looked up from his stack of magazines, shooting a humorous look at his friend. "Funny. I'm sure I can find a cozy picture of Miranda for you in all this mess," Adam stopped short and sighed, "Sorry, buddy. That was out of line. Just poking fun."

Sean waved his friend's apology off, "So what have you found?"

"I've got two piles going. General articles that don't have any adversarial dirt in them and then this nice thick stack chock full of big corporations, politicians, and even countries he has butted up against. This guy's a real boy scout, like you... a real pain in the butt though, too – again, like you," Adam thumbed the stack of magazines in front of him.

"Any of particular interest?"

"Well, nothing real current. And I would bet he met his early demise over something he was more recently working on," the Fish and Wildlife officer mused.

"So, we need to get into his private files. We need to try and figure out what whoever broke in was after," Sean concluded.

Adam grinned, "That we do, my boy. Suppose the door is unlocked?"

"No, I gave the handle a twist as we walked by," Sean admitted.

"Well, I can get it open, but it's not going to look real good if our favorite intern comes wheeling around the corner. We're going to need a distraction..."

Fifteen

Grumbling to himself, Sean ambled down the hallway in search of Katie, the intern. He found a room with light spilling out into the corridor. Craning his neck, he stuck his head in the doorway, "Katie?"

The young girl engrossed in her computer screen startled at the intrusion. She held her hand to her chest as she steadied herself as she looked up at Sean.

"I'm sorry to bother you, I was just hoping you might have a few minutes to talk," Sean cooed in a soft voice.

"I suppose I could take a break. Sit down, please," the intern held out her manicured fingers to gesture to the chair across from her. "I was just finishing up invitations for a memorial dinner. One of the dinner cruises in town was nice enough to offer their space and service."

"That's very generous of them," Sean replied.

"Yes, it is. Jim has a lot of supporters from a variety of walks of life. He has done a lot of good for this world."

"So I have been reading," Sean pointed his thumb over his shoulder towards the library he had just come from, "What had he been working on recently?"

The blonde intern shifted in her seat and studied Sean before she responded, "Jim was doing a lot with whales. Of course, the annual fight with the Makah's..." her voice trailed to a squeak as she choked and brought her fingers to her lips, "I'm sorry, it's just... those bastards…"

"It's quite alright. What happened on the peninsula was a tragedy," Sean consoled.

"Anyways, where was I?" Katie cleared her throat and continued, "So, like I was saying, he was doing a lot with whales. The Makah issue, some disputes over the International Whaling Moratorium, and some big secret project he thought would have a major impact. If you ask me, he had taken on the focus to try and get his girlfriend back."

"Girlfriend?" Sean prodded, knowing the answer.

"Yeah, Miranda. Nice enough, girl, but she dissed him already. He should've just let it go," Katie replied.

Before Sean could ask her another question, an abrupt and alarming clatter sounded from down the hallway. Sean and Katie jumped to their feet and sprang out of the office to investigate the noise. Watching as the young intern darted down the hall, Sean groaned, having a good idea who was behind the ruckus.

As soon as Sean disappeared, Adam set to work on the lock to Harrison's private office. Slipping his credit card through the slot between the doorjamb and the door itself, he maneuvered the card up and down until he heard the satisfying click that he was seeking.

The door opened up to one of the most lavish offices that Adam had ever seen. A stately maple desk dominated the room, accented by a line of matching barrister's bookcases. A full-sized leather sofa sat beneath a large window and next to a rock water fountain, which Adam figured to be a smaller version of the one at the building entrance.

Casting his gaze around the room, he noticed a whole new stock of pictures of Harrison. "Figures," he scoffed to himself. Leaning in, he saw photos of the activist with politicians, wild animals, and low and behold, Miranda and Katie.

Chuckling to himself, he turned his attention to Harrison's desk. Sliding into the buttery leather of the manager's chair and stabbed at the power button of the burl wood-sheathed laptop resting on top of the maple surface. As he waited for the system to come alive, his eyes wandered around the room.

His gaze flitted from object to object as his fingers fumbled with the locked drawer of the desk. He stopped suddenly in his survey of the room as his eyes rotated back to the leather sofa. A patch of pink cloth stuck out from the back folds of the cushion.

Adam rose from the chair to investigate. He reached forward towards the silky material and gave it a tug. The cloth snagged on the innards of the couch. Adam examined his prize closer – a pair of silk panties that had slipped behind the cushions. Giving the undergarment a final yank, the silky clue sprang free from its hold, taking flight over Adam's head.

The Federal officer watched helplessly as the woman's underwear sailed across the room and landed on a sconce on the far wall. The frosted globe teetered on its perch and what seemed like slow motion to Adam, fell to the ground in a horrible crash.

The sound of smashing glass rang an alarm throughout the office. Adam rushed to dispose of the panty evidence, taking care to avoid the shards of splintered glass. About the time he had the suspect item in his grasp, the furious face of Katie-the-intern stood in the doorway.

Adam looked up, sheepishly at the woman, "This doesn't look good."

"What in the world hell is going on in here?" screamed the hysterical intern.

"I heard a noise and came to investigate?" Adam lobbed up.

"Get out!" Katie screamed and seeing Sean join them added, "Both of you, get out before I call the police!"

"Ma'am, I am the police," Adam informed, flashing Katie his badge, "Federal Agent."

"I don't give a moment's care who you are. You don't come back without a warrant," she replied, ushering the men down the hallway. Sean and Adam began to protest, but ultimately complied and followed her to the door where she held it open without looking at either of the men.

Adam paused on his way and held up the panties that he realized were still in his hand, "I guess these are yours."

Katie snatched the garments from the outstretched hands and melted back into the office, allowing the door to slam behind her. Sean shot Adam a look. "What has gotten into you today?" he laughed despite himself.

"That was serious investigative work," Adam grinned.

"And what did you uncover in your efforts?"

"I confirmed that the old dog was indeed making hay with the young pup," Adam laughed.

Sean stared, unblinking at his friend, shaking his head.

Miranda arrived at her bayfront home in Anacortes, grabbing her stack of mail on her way through the door. Dropping her bag by her bedroom door, she sat on her window seat and pawed through the pile of envelopes. Tossing the usual a sundry of junk mail aside, she paused on a piece of hand-addressed stationery.

Tearing the envelope open, she freed a card from its sleeve. It was an invitation to a memorial service for Jim. The service was to be held on a dinner cruise sailing out of Portland. Sighing, she reluctantly gave way to the idea that putting him to rest as quickly as possible was the best way to move on.

Looking at the unpacked bag at her bedroom door, she knew she might as well dump it out and start repacking it all over again. She snatched her phone off of its cradle and dialed her friend Carrie to see if they might carpool together. The experience at the reservation did little to improve her fragile psyche, and she couldn't argue that the moral support for the wake would do her good.

The sole picture of Jim that she kept up after their break-up stood vigil on her mantle. The photo seemed to act as a sentry to her life, guarding against progress. As the phone rang in her earpiece, she walked across the room and removed the picture from its duty, placing it neatly inside a drawer. Feeling a wash of sadness, she turned her focus to the voice calling "hello" on the phone line.

Sixteen

R ey Chavez' crew pulled their grey catering van into the parking lot of the Riverplace Marina. Dressed in chef and wait staff garb, they unloaded their crates and transported them down the gangway onto the one hundred and twenty-foot luxury yacht. They had an hour before their guests would arrive, and Chavez wanted the team to be firmly in place.

Throughout the cruiser, Chavez took careful stock, noting every detail he had studied from the plans Tug had emailed him. Pleased that the electronic schematics translated correctly with the actual vessel, he accounted for every entry and communication point - crucial areas that would be part of the initial phase of the plan. Controlling the guests and cutting off the outside world would be stressed as the priority.

When his review was complete, he assembled his men for final assignments. Each would be integrated with the yacht's actual crew. Chavez carefully matched the boat duty with the strategic need of the heist. One by one, he had men assigned to the boat's captain, the kitchen staff, the guest coordinators as well as the boat's functional crew. Satisfied that every man understood his detail, he integrated with the boat's crew using Hasegawa's loyalists as Tug had aforementioned.

The ship's first mate and Hasegawa's personal cook had been discreetly assigned to assist Chavez. The security staff was left in the dark to add an air of realism to the heist. Chavez had urged Hasegawa to leave as many elements on the boat in the dark as possible.

The crew scattered to carry out their respective duties. Those attached to kitchen and wait staff detail grumbled about their tasks, but did as instructed. Two men were sent to the kitchen and were quickly handed duties in the washroom. Two more integrated with the wait staff in the ballroom, busily setting place settings for the guests of the environmental attorney's wake. The gaming tables had all been converted for dining, draped with long white linens as an army of florists placed flowers on each table.

The remaining men assimilated with the ship's staff, performing their preparatory tasks to ready the yacht for its cruise. Whether polishing the gleaming rail of the promenade deck or spot swabbing the teak walkway leading to the ballroom, each man had a commanding view of a strategic point.

Chavez, himself, shadowed the first mate that was in charge of the evening's overall success, acting as one of the Foundation's hired event planners. They studied the tide tables, monitored weather reports, and inspected the crew's preparations for the evening.

Reviewing the guest list, the mercenary took note of a name that jumped out at him– a figure who would likely prove useful in his ruse. Handing the list back, Chavez followed the first mate to the executive suite, where they arranged the room to host a high-stakes Texas Hold'em match that would be held simultaneously with the memorial cruise. Chavez had been pre-warned that several wealthy northwest players would be in attendance, and that while they were fair game in the heist, they were not to be harmed.

The Nagaremono was nearing readiness, with little more needed than guests to arrive and drinks to be served. The yacht was a novel investment for Hasegawa, who had added several pleasure ships to his fleet of freighters to add another source of money flow. The northwest had seen wild success of the Tribal casinos, a venture Hasegawa had creatively found a way to capitalize. The investment allowed for an easy way to launder money from his less savory enterprise as well as lent an avenue to impress his affluent customers by taking them offshore for gambling cruises. Unfortunately for Hishiro, his own pension for high stakes gambling had created evenings where he had lost more in cards than the entire house had won in the main gaming hall. Still, his offshore enterprise had become a cash cow for him, feeding into the risk-addicted culture of the U. S.

Chavez made a note of the critical invitees that he was instructed to eliminate in the process of the pseudo-larceny. Miranda Shaw and Senator Rick Johnson- two individuals who had pissed off Tug and his employers. He had been instructed to leave the gamers relatively unharmed, but the attendees of the tree-hugger's party were all pretty much fair game.

The review of the plan's details was broken up by the arrival of one of Jim Harrison's contacts from the foundation, Ms. Katie Schuler. Saito Moto - the first mate, and Chavez were called to the gangway entry to greet the young woman. Grumbling under his breath, Chavez assumed his role and followed the spry Japanese man to meet the guests.

"Ms. Schuler, it is a pleasure to have you aboard. My apprentice and I are at your full disposal," Moto declared.

"Thank you. The staff and I are very appreciative of the owner's offer to host us. He must have been a big supporter of Jim's work," Katie said graciously.

"Yes, ma'am. My employer had a keen interest in the Foundation,"

Moto smiled as he helped the intern onto the cruiser.

"My, this boat is beautiful!" Katie exclaimed as she took in the ship's accouterments. Elegant draperies lined the windows of the ballroom, their lush velvet a rich scarlet. The multi-colored wood inlay flooring was polished to a high shine allowing the lights to highlight the intricate pattern of a nautical star in the center of the room. The ceiling was equally impressive with carved warriors protruding from the crown molding, keeping vigil over the room.

"May we get you something to drink, ma'am?" Moto asked.

"A glass of white wine would be lovely," Katie forced a faint smile, "I have a load of items in my car - flowers, pictures and stuff..."

"You parked in the lot just above?" Chavez asked as the girl nodded, "Don't worry about that. We'll take care of that for you."

"That would be great. Mine's the hybrid parked right next to the stairs," Katie smiled, handing Chavez the keys.

Rey gave his men a nod indicating for them to follow him out to the parking lot. The eight men fell in behind their leader and hustled up the gangway. When he was satisfied that they were out of earshot from the boat and the parking lot was empty, he began laying out some last-minute details.

"Alright, the security is thin, but to make this look good, they must be dealt with. I want you to wait on my signal. In the course of the evening, I will drop a glass. That will be your cue to snap into action. Desmond and Lou, you take out the security detail. Once they are neutralized, Desmond will return to the ballroom while Lou mans the security center," Chavez instructed as the two men nodded.

"Smitty, Cortez and Naches, you three lockdown the ballroom tight. Make sure all access points are secure. I'll set up point in the captain's stateroom just off the galley. Desmond, when you return, you will guard the boardroom where the card game'll be going down," the mercenary continued, "The rest of you, maintain the perimeter, so that we can lock down quickly."

"What do we do now?" Rocco asked.

"Now?" Chavez wrinkled his face, "We deliver flowers."

Hishiro Hasegawa had grown increasingly concerned with the heist of his own establishment, not appearing believable. He thought of a way to add authenticity to the scheme. Instructing Chavez to plant him amidst the hostages might further remove him from appearing involved. Add in a few bruises, and he had himself a very sweet alibi. He knew if he wasn't able to pull this plan off - the plane, the personal driver, the condo - were all luxuries that would be in dire jeopardy.

His jet landed at the Portland International Airport as scheduled, and his driver was waiting for him just outside the hangar. Hasegawa missed the days before heightened airport security when his car would pull up on the tarmac right where the plane would be parked. This was an especially yearned for luxury in Portland, where rain was the staple weather for several months out of the year.

Arriving just before rush hour, the shipping magnate made it to the downtown area in reasonable time. He wanted time to stop at his Pearl District condo to freshen up before heading to the boat. The flight path for a private jet from Japan to Portland was one with numerous refueling stops along the way. To Hasegawa, it was all a burden well worth the price. Still, he was a man who managed his image carefully. He could not show up to his cabal appearing disheveled. No, the boat would wait a few minutes for him to freshen up.

The boat, a one hundred and twenty-foot cruiser that he had purchased two years prior which served to provide a medium for legal offshore gambling, was berthed right in downtown Portland. Hasegawa enjoyed flaunting his vessel in front of the authorities, keeping his enterprise firmly butted up against the finite legal boundaries. For a year, the feds would shadow his boat, planting operatives in anticipation of a slip up that they could finally indict him. The crew of the Nagaremono managed the cruises with precision, as soon as the stern would cross the imaginary line into international waters; the first hand would be dealt. Every detail was run with immaculate control, ensuring that the feds receive no fodder.

Eventually, the strict regimen of the crew's adherence to the legal limits, the law enforcement agencies lost interest in the gambling excursions, limiting their scrutiny to a few random checks throughout the year. Whatever level of surveillance lofted towards the Japanese businessman's activities, he had his men prepared in response to it.

Hasegawa sighed as the car swung onto Front Avenue towards the Marina, if only he controlled his personal life as well as he managed his businesses, he wouldn't have had to resort to this bold plan to bail himself out. Shaking his head, he succumbed to the reconciliation that by the next day, he would have the money to funnel back into his corporate books back in Japan, and he could shake the authorities off of his back once more.

After beating their hasty retreat away from Harrison's office and the furious intern, Sean and Adam regrouped in the safer confines of the U.S. Fish and Wildlife SUV. "Wow, that was fun!" Adam exclaimed.

"What part exactly? Offending the woman, getting busted stealing her panties or the overall experience?" Sean asked sarcastically.

"I guess I'd have to say pretty much the whole thing," Adam chuckled as his friend groaned in disgust at him, "Aw come on...it was kind of funny."

"So, what now? We never did find out what his secret project was..." Sean scratched his head deep in thought.

"Unless that secret project was a five-foot-four blonde..."

Laughing, Sean added, "No, there was something else going on. Katie mentioned Harrison was mixed up in something with whales."

"He had a pretty nice place for a philanthropic environmentalist - I'd have imagined something a little more stark, but his placed was decked out," Adam mused, "Maybe he was involved in some shady politics. That would explain all the nice stuff."

"Could be. It would certainly pose a solid motive for murder," Sean agreed.

"We need to get back in there. Now, who do we know that could get us access to get in there?" Adam turned to his passenger, wearing a mischievous grin.

Sean instantly began shaking his head, vehemently, "Oh no. I'm not going to call her. No way..."

"No, Sean. I can't believe you are even asking me. Just go back home and return to being the charming guy living in the woods, enjoying his early retirement. I would think you'd be done playing cops and robbers after everything that has happened," Miranda's reply came back stern and steady.

The words stung as they filtered through the earpiece to Sean, making him cringe as though a child being scolded by a parent. It was the even, icy tone that chilled Sean the most. "I understand where you are coming from. I had no idea that the guy...Harrison was your ex-fiancé."

"Yes. Jim and I were engaged. Look, I just want this to be over," Miranda maintained, "And it is a little weird for you to be poking around in what...what was my past."

"I just want to get to the truth, Miranda. This has nothing to do with you...or me...or us," Sean assured.

"They got the guy at the reservation, just let it go, Sean," Miranda pleaded.

"But what if they didn't? A kid's life is hung on the authorities being right over some pretty circumstantial experience. Is that what Jim would want? He seemed better than that to me," Sean contested, knowing he probably lobbed a cheap shot.

"What do you want?" Miranda sighed.

"We just want in his office to see what he was working on."

"Fine, I'll set it up," Miranda relented and quickly added, "On one condition. You keep me in the loop on what you find. If it's nothing, you leave it alone. For good."

"It's a deal. How would you like me to reach you?"

"I'll have my cell. I'm in Portland, myself. There is a memorial for Jim on some dinner boat. I figured it would be better to attend it with his friends and co-workers than the funeral with his family," Miranda replied.

"I really appreciate this, Miranda," Sean said.

"I'll call one of my friends and have them meet you there this afternoon. Just stay out of trouble, okay?"

"I can promise that I will try," Sean grinned, hanging up the phone. Closing the call, he leaned back in his seat. Despite the scolding, it felt unusually good to hear her voice. Once they had worked their way through the discomfort, tinges of the warmth that Miranda exudes began to seep through.

"See buddy, that wasn't so bad," Adam patted Sean on the shoulder. He quickly returned his gaze to the road as his glib remark met with a humorless glare.

Seventeen

The ride back to the Resources Defense Foundation was a quiet one. Adam contemplated what an environmental litigator would be digging into that would get him killed. Considering Harrison's success against so many large businesses, there could be an extensive list of influential people waiting in line that might applaud him being deceased.

Sean, on the other hand, was lamenting a much different concern. His conversation with Miranda caused a stir of feelings in him that continued to take him by surprise each time he spoke to her. He wondered if their relationship would ever get another chance.

The SUV swung into the Resources Defense Foundation parking lot, snapping Sean out of his thoughts. Standing outside of the office, was the man Sean had seen with Miranda at the crime scene near the Makah Reservation. A dark, well-tailored suit hung on the man's thin shoulders instead of the down vest draped over flannel as Sean had first seen him. The man's salt and pepper beard opened up into a bright smile.

"Hullo there," the man beamed, extending his arm out to welcome the two men, "I'm Brett Daniels. Miranda asked me to stop by on my way to the wake to let you fellas in. Any friend of Miranda's is a friend of mine."

Sean and Adam shook the man's hand as they followed him back into the building. Brett continued as he unlocked the door to the back offices, "Not sure what you'll find. They caught the little menace that killed Jim, think you're wasting your time."

"Just looking into some loose ends. Know anything about the last project Harrison was working on?" Sean asked.

"Nope. Jim was real tight-lipped over that one. Why do you ask? Think it may have something to do with his murder?"

"Maybe. We just want to check it out," Sean shrugged.

"Just an angry, unevolved culture up there if you ask me," Brett offered up his opinion as he opened up Harrison's office. Adam and Sean smiled quietly at the man's comments, not willing to join the debate.

Brett turned to the men, holding the door wide for them, "I need to scoot, so the boat doesn't take off without me. Miranda says you're trustworthy; I'm going to hold you to that. Just lock up when you're finished and snap off the lights if you would."

Sean and Adam nodded as the jovial naturalist ambled down the hallway. Sean quickly made his way to Harrison's computer desk, his shoes crunching over glass remnants of the sconce that were missed from the hasty vacuuming that must have taken place after their departure. Sliding into the supple leather chair, he turned on the monitor only to be met instantly with a password secured gateway.

He looked up at Adam, who was pawing through the lateral files underneath the bookcase, "Did you get anywhere with this the last time that we were here?"

"No, unfortunately, I was distracted by the, uh, undergarment mishap," the Fish and Wildlife officer admitted, "You know, I can never remember my passwords. I usually have them scribbled down somewhere nearby."

Sean nodded his head silently as he began searching through the desk drawers. Unloading the contents of each, he flipped through notebooks and day planners, scouring every scrap of paper - all efforts exercised in vain. As he stuffed the items back into their respective drawers, a calculator missed its mark and tumbled to his feet. Bending over, Sean patted blindly at the ground to recover the errant device. The calculator eluded his fingers lying just out of reach directly under his chair.

Grumbling, Sean got to his knees and stooped to snatch the calculator from its hiding place. Straightening up, he paused as his eyes caught a little flap of yellow paper curling down from the underside of the chair. Tossing the calculator back on the desk, he reached back and grabbed the yellow slip from its perch.

Holding it up, Sean studied his find. It was a little two by two Post-It with the text "MS6445" scribbled on it. Sean easily recognized the code - Miranda Shaw and the last four digits of her cell phone.

Plopping back in the seat of the office chair, he whirled back to the computer and punched the code into the patiently waiting box. He was instantly met with the Microsoft jingle and Harrison's desktop homepage. Sean's heart sank as he found the entire documents folder empty.

"We're too late!" he cursed loudly, "His folders have all been wiped out!"

"The break-in," Adam sighed and then brightened, "Harrison seems like he would've been an anal kind of guy, he probably has a back-up somewhere."

Sean nodded and relented to a renewed search, this time for some type of media for copying files. As he began fumbling back through the desk contents, he noticed a black and white photo of Harrison and Miranda on top of a mountain, to Sean, it looked like the south end of the crater wall on Mount Saint Helens.

He picked it up for a closer inspection. As he grabbed the picture frame, his fingers ran across a small bump about the size of a pen cap. Flipping the photo over, he found a tiny USB card taped to the cardboard backing. Eagerly, he snatched the card from its perch and spun around, slamming it into the computer's receptacle.

"I think I have it!" Sean exclaimed, staring at the screen. He was pleased at how organized the befallen environmental lawyer was, his electronic files were neatly ordered and easy to comb through. It didn't take long before one file jumped out at the de facto sleuth.

Clicking the mouse on the folder icon labeled "HASEGAWA", he was met with a barrage of recent files. Online news clips, harbor master reports, police reports - both from the US and Japan, lawsuits, bank records, and a prospectus of Hasegawa Holdings Corp. Among the cavalcade of documents, he found one labeled "Hasegawa Letter 2-20".

Opening the letter, his eyes quickly scanned the contents. It was dated just a little over two weeks ago. The message was abrupt and to the point - warning Hasegawa to discontinue his fishing fleet's whaling practices just outside of the boundary of the U.S.- International waters. Harrison went on to advise Hasegawa that if he did not adhere to the request, that a very nasty public investigation and a lawsuit would ensue, and he assured the freight magnate that that would not be in his best interest.

Sean looked over to Adam, who was stretched out on the leather sofa thumbing through a stack of files he had piled up on his belly. "I wonder if that is how Harrison has such nice stuff in his office."

"What's that?" Adam asked, peering over a file folder.

"He has an extensive file on, believe it or not, our old pal Hasegawa. It sounds like he was threatening Hasegawa with turning loose some harmful information that he had," Sean replied from behind the thin, flat-screen monitor.

"Hmm, so maybe our greenie hero was pulling a Robin Hood by extorting the rich and feeding the organization. Extortion can be an excellent motive for murder," Adam mused, "Does it say what the information was that Harrison had on him?"

"No, it just alludes to linking accounts that are hidden entities with ties to Hasegawa Holdings."

Sean burrowed back into the computer. Filtering through dozens of files, he searched for something that might enlighten him to what Harrison had uncovered. Clicking on the record titled "Hasegawa Connected Accounts".

A surprisingly lengthy list filled the screen, businesses connected by either solid or dotted lines. Sean assumed the different lines delineated between direct and indirect links. Leaning in, he sifted through the list, one company at a time.

The compilation began with Hasegawa Holdings Corporation and listed the various Hasegawa freight and fishing fleets, each connected with solid lines. Entry after entry, Sean read an endless variety of trading companies, warehouses, and logistic firms littered the page noted with both direct and indirect annotations. The further down the list, the more dotted lines connected the many holdings under the Hasegawa reign. Here, Sean saw a mix of office buildings, restaurants, and offshore casinos scattered throughout the entire Pacific Rim, especially in Japan and the U.S.

An icon noting a web link resided next to several of the holdings. Sean ran the pointer over to the links and systematically ran through the attachments. The freight companies turned up a slew of investigations that filed against the group, including smuggling charges for transporting illegal animal parts, weapons, and even people. Few charges ever stuck, those that did amount to fines but no criminal indictments.

Likewise, the fishing fleets had been under fire for their collateral massacres of dolphins and other sea life caught in their nets while their whaling fleet had clashed with protestors around the globe. Sean could undoubtedly see why Harrison would take an interest in the Japanese tycoon.

Sinking back into the buttery caress of the office chair, Sean mulled over the information that he had uncovered. Scanning the entries trying to create a link, he touched his fingers to his lips as his hands formed a little teepee.

Adam, looking up from his stack of information, laughed at his friend, "Uh oh, he's thinking!"

"Man, this guy was into a lot of stuff," Sean replied.

"Harrison?"

"No, Hasegawa. He didn't own a business, he ruled an empire," Sean remarked as his eyes again were cast upon the computer screen, "Shipping, night clubs, casinos...a few legal indiscretions, but not much has been able to stick."

Deciding to take the information with him, he transferred the data from Harrison's PC to his handheld. "Come up with anything?"

"Files full of our good lawyer's heroics, but nothing too useful. I think the Hasegawa thing is it. He is certainly setting up like someone who stood to lose a lot if Harrison pushed his findings, no doubt enough to provoke a wealthy man to drastic measures. He had the resources and the connections. He did finance a terrorist assault - allegedly - killing one slimy naturalist attorney is small potatoes for him," Adam surmised.

"I think you're right. Let's put things back and get out of here," Sean suggested. "We need to come up with a plan on what to do next."

The Captain's Room at the Riverplace Marina rang with the sounds of ice clinking to the bottom of crystal glasses as the small collection of high rollers came together. Each fancying themselves the top of the food chain amongst northwest high stakes gamblers. Their host had yet to make his entrance as they waited to board the boat. In the meantime, the bartender toiled to keep their drinks full as the air filled with hearty boasts.

Each invitee carried with them a special invitation and half a million dollars in Swiss Bank Treasury notes. By the time their host added his share into the pot, there would be several million to be won that evening.

Just as the next round of beverages graced their hands and the conversations escalated in grandiosity, Hishiro Hasegawa stepped into the room. The crowd hushed and turned with highball glasses in the air to offer a hearty welcome to their host as the bartender promptly delivered a snifter of Courvoisier.

Hishiro beamed at the attention provided him from some of the most notorious gamblers and crime family heads on the west coast. Taking stock of the group, each of them millionaires many times over, he knew regardless of how the cards were dealt, each of them adding to the pot that would be lining the Japanese magnate's pocket. Hoisting his snifter in response to his guests, he smiled - one toast, one drink before the evening would commence.

Miranda parked her SUV in the Riverplace parking lot and found the walkway for the boat. Jim loved being on the water, making Miranda feel that this was the perfect way to pay tribute to his life. She followed the meandering concrete path as it snaked its way past the shops and restaurants of the downtown marina.

The pulleys on the sailing masts of docked boats tolled mariner songs as the breeze tugged at their rigging. The sounds stirred warmth in Miranda. She loved life along the water so much. Nearing the wooden dock that led to the Nagaremono, the marine biologist recognized a familiar face hustling down the floating sidewalk towards the gangway. "Brett!" she called, watching the man stop so abruptly that he nearly lost his balance.

Red-faced, the man spun around to face the siren who called to him. "Miranda!" he grinned as he held his arms wide to receive a hug from his friend, "You nearly sent me into the Willamette! I'll tell you this is a river that I would rather float on top of than in."

Miranda giggled as she hugged Brett, "Why such a hurry?"

"Oh, you know me, I hate to be late. After stopping at the office to help let in your friends, I was afraid to miss the boat."

"You always were the early bird. So, no issues with Sean and Adam?"

"Forsakes, no. On your word, I just left them to their search and asked them to lock up when they were done," Brett replied.

"Thank you, Brett," Miranda smiled. "And let's keep their visit between you and me of now."

"Sure thing Miranda," Brett assured.

Miranda turned her attention on the boat before her. A short ramp led from the dock up to the dinner boat. Two crewmen flanked either side of the gangway to assist guests up the initial step. One was diligently checking the guest list to ensure attendees were properly accounted for.

Inside the vessel, Miranda and Brett were led into the main ballroom, where several tables were draped with fine linens and adorned with flower centerpieces offset by framed photos of the late Jim Harrison. At the front of the room, an easel supported a large, gold-framed portrait of the environmental lawyer.

Katie, the intern from the Foundation's office, was frantically running around the room lighting candles. Brett, true to form, rushed to help her.

Miranda found a little spot at a table near the back of the room. In days past, she would have been thrust to the forefront of this group. Today, she felt unusually like an outsider. Her purse stowed atop a place setting, she walked to the outer deck of the boat and quietly watched the procession of attendees make their way up the gangway.

Streaming down the wooden dock, members of the Foundation, local activists, and a myriad of ranking political figures came to pay their respects. Leaning on the boat's railing, Miranda looked on as she enjoyed the slow movement brought on by the wake of a passing ski boat. A glance at her watch told her they were due to shove off, yet she hadn't seen her friend Carrie among the arriving passengers.

Deciding to wait another minute before she called to check up on her friend, who was notoriously late, she kept her vigil overlooking the docks. The setting sun cast a glare on the dark waters of the Willamette River, forcing her to squint tightly.

Miranda's daydreaming was rudely broken up by a clanging near the boat's stern, causing her to jump. Leaning over the railing, she looked toward the rear of the yacht, scowling at her irritation at being startled, she saw a second gangway lowered into place.

Casting her gaze back towards the docks, she saw several impeccably attired men make their way to the newly readied boat entrance. An Asian man appeared to be at the center of attention. The man looked familiar, but through the glare cast by the late day sun, she couldn't be sure. Her focus was suddenly displaced as she caught the comical image of a frantic strawberry blonde hurrying down the dock flapping her arms desperately at the crew on the boat. The sounds of the bow plank being prepared for stowage alerted Miranda as to why her chronically late friend appeared as though she were trying to take flight. The boat was readying to depart.

Miranda chuckled as Carrie raced the final steps to the replaced boat ramp. Walking over to meet her, Miranda looked at her watch and let out a precocious giggle, "Now that's the Carrie I know. I thought you were going to have to leap to get on."

The Foundation naturalist leaned back as she gave Miranda a once-over, as she ignored her friend's teasing, "You always did look great in black. Just sorry it's the color of the evening."

"We need to come up with better reasons to get together," Miranda agreed through pursed lips.

"Come on, let's get in there and get this thing going before Katie takes over," Carrie grabbed her by the hand and drug her into the ballroom.

Eighteen

As soon as the last member of Hishiro Hasegawa's group had the soles of his shoes on deck, the planks hoisted, the lines drawn. The twin diesel chugged in ascending rhythm as they labored to churn the propellers and motivate the big boat away from its berth. The quintet of card players followed their purser to the lavishly appointed executive quarters of the yacht.

Two attendants were immediately at the group's side greeting the men, hanging up jackets and relaying drink and cigar orders to the bartender waiting in the corner. In the center of the room, a large round table surrounded by five leather captain's chairs. Each chair had bare legs and arms crafted of rich mahogany, flowing into the deep tones of the dark stained table. Their contrasting vanilla hued leather matched the light wood inlay of the mariner star that adorned the center of the table.

Hasegawa sat at the northern point of the star, his back to the large picture windows that made up the entire outer wall of the room. A snifter of cognac was placed in front of him as a hand-wrapped Cuban cigar was snipped, and a gold butane lighter with its blue flame held steady for the magnate to puff his stogy to life.

The other members of the party had taken their places at the table and waited as the purser brought a deck of cards to the host. Carefully, the attendant unwrapped the cellophane around the cards and handed them to Hasegawa. Silently, the shipping heir cut the deck and slid the pile to his left for the first deal of the evening.

Before the first card was spun face down to one of the competitors, the opening bid of one thousand dollars was called as five chips landed in the center of the inlay star piling up into a fat fifty-k pot. Hasegawa leaned back and grinned behind his cigar-smoke filled haze; the games had begun.

The ballroom had filled up and rapidly grew into a steady buzz of conversations, some lighthearted as people reconnected and some sad as they shared in reflections of their lost friend. Several Foundation members came up to Miranda with hugs and hellos, most having not seen her for months. Her heart swelled warmly with the wealth of well wishes and caring that came her way. Each hug, handshake and smile reminded her how good these people were and how much respect she had garnered over the years.

Despite how quickly she slipped into an old feeling of comfort and acceptance with this group, she resisted Carrie's attempts to get her to join the Foundation crew that was assembling at the front of the room. Sans Miranda; Brett, Carrie and Katie stood at the front of the wake attendees.

Brett clanged a butter knife loudly against the crystal rim of a wine glass to attract the attention of the audience. Heads turned his direction as the roar of voices faded into respectful silence. "On behalf of Carrie, Katie, and myself - and the entire Foundation, we would like to thank you for joining us to reflect...no, to celebrate the life of a fine man, Jim Harrison."

The attendees joined in a chorus of agreement and cheers before giving the floor to Carrie. "I just want to parrot what Brett said. Jim was a revolutionary in environmental law, and his loss will be felt, very deeply, by all of us."

Almost before the group could respond to Carrie's words, Katie broke into her soliloquy, "Jim meant so much to all of us.

We all need to do our part to ensure his legacy goes on. He lived to make this world a better place. He died protecting what he believed in. He died protecting what we all believed - a healthy planet for all living things and a body to watch over those who could not defend themselves from greed and destruction.

I, too, would like to thank Governor Roberts, Senator Johnson, Brett, and Carrie, and of course, the Foundation supporter who so generously offered the use of this beautiful boat to celebrate the life and the spirit of our dear, beloved, Jim Harrison." As the girl finished her last triumphant word, she surprised herself by breaking down into a torrent of tears.

A murmur of sympathy rose throughout the audience. A glance told anyone who looked that she was not alone - several heads were slumped in shaky hands as mourners gave into the reality of the occasion. Carrie held the weeping intern in her arms in an attempt at consolation. With Brett's assistance, she escorted Katie to their table.

Miranda was almost shocked that she was not crying herself. Instead, the marine biologist's mind was analyzing the scene. Her eyes kept trying to tell her something, but she could not figure out what. Miranda knew something was out of place, but whatever that thing was remained elusive to her.

Sitting back, she succumbed to quietly sipping at her glass of wine, observing the antics of the room. It slowly came clear to her that there were two diverse sets of wait staff. Half were the ultimate in professional servers. They scurried about, fluidly caring to the needs of the room. The other half stood around, more often than not. When they were active, they appeared lost and fumbling. They seemed to station themselves around the room, forming a sort of strategic perimeter.

Scoffing to herself, Miranda looked deep into the burgundy liquid in her glass. Shaking her head, she told herself that she had spent far too much time dealing with conspiracies and criminal organizations. She needed to relax. Refilling her wine glass, she walked to the outer deck of the boat.

Stepping out into the crisp night air, she soaked in the breeze and spray of the boat as it slipped through the current of the Columbia River. Watching the wake of the powerful yacht, she was surprised at the speed at which it traveled for a dinner cruise. Most of the river dining excursions she had been on were gentle floats that eased down the Willamette towards Lake Oswego and turned back to downtown. The invitation did mention this being a more extended cruise. Shrugging, she leaned back against the deck rail and succumbed to turning her suspicious mind off and enjoying being on the water, one of her favorite pastimes.

Sean and Adam sat in the riverfront brewery, reviewing the inventory of facts they had compiled as they waited for their pints to be delivered. From his pocket, Sean retrieved the tiny device that he had used to extract the data from Harrison's computer. Numerous files linking activities and bank account transactions littered the screen. Harrison had followed the path of multi-layered accounts to Hasegawa's corporate empire. To find out what the environmental attorney had found, Sean knew he would have to root out the same trail. Considering the volume of information he had to sift through, he knew it could be a very long night.

Lifting his arms out of the way, Sean made room for the waitress to place to frosty mugs of draft beer on the table in front of him. The tan froth atop the amber liquid trailed down one side of the glass, slowly sliding down to pool on top of the cardboard coaster on which the beer rested. He thanked her and hoisted his chilly mug in the air, "It's gonna be a long night partner."

Adam smiled as he raised his glass in the air, "I'm sure the tap will stay running. Let's see what we've got."

Sean paused to take a sip of his beer as he slid his tiny computer around so Adam could see the screen. "Looks like invoices for events and purchases that have been tied to various accounts. The invoices are vague 'Services Rendered' type entries with a numerical code that says where the money is coming from. Harrison put in his own flags as to what he traced the invoices to -

a myriad of things like political donations, boats, and equipment for his whaling fleet and mostly clearances of just 'cash'. Undoubtedly so there was no record of payment for less savory expenses. As for the accounts, they are a rats' nest of stacked corporations that ultimately end in either anonymous offshore accounts or to Hasegawa Holdings."

"That's great and all, but it doesn't sound like Harrison had anything concrete. A bunch of layered accounts and secret offshore dealings might arouse suspicion, but I certainly don't see anything damning," Adam said, frowning after gulping his beer.

"Well, this is interesting," Sean hummed over his beer mug, "Harrison has highlighted the paper trail of Hasegawa's movements during the course of the Seattle terror attack. He has air traffic records, credit card activity, and undisclosed bank transactions in some fairly hefty amounts."

"We know he was there, but so what? He's a big-time gambler, we know he was likely into illegal hunting with the McKenzie brothers…," Adam shrugged.

"Maybe he blames Hasegawa for threatening Miranda," Sean surmised.

"Possible, I still just don't see anything viable enough for anyone to use against him."

"There's gotta be something in here worthwhile for Hasegawa to want him killed," Sean said, his head buried in the screen, "We find it, we find the killer."

The stream of eulogies brought an array of tears and occasional moments of levity as the group in the dinner boat's ballroom honored the life and work of Jim Harrison. The boat's crew hastily brought out the first course and labored to keep the wine glasses full. The surreal luxury of dining while cruising down the river, mixed with the flood of emotions, lulled many of the diners to the brink of intoxication.

Rey Chavez looked impatiently around the room. If he had to listen to one more story about the full-of-himself sissy naturalist, that he was now more glad than ever to have run through with a spear and finished off with a slice to the throat, he was going to open fire on the entire crowd The mercenary grinned as he thought of the curved blade of that wicked knife, wishing he had kept that little souvenir instead of planting it as evidence.

Chavez left the room. The sight of his men serving those snotty sycophants was making him sick. He took a glance at his watch - they still had two hours before they left the mouth of the Columbia and entered the tumultuous waters of the North Pacific. In his mind, he ran through the plan. He wondered if they could successfully accelerate their time table. The plans for taking a run into international waters had already been filed with the harbormasters as well as the Coast Guard - their cruising path was expected. That and this was a course that the Nagaremono ran numerous times each week. Communications would be completely knocked out, as long as his crew implemented their duties as prescribed, this cruise would look like any other as seen from the shore.

Chavez' escape route had already been put in place the moment he stepped on the mega yacht. In fact, he had woven in several layers of escape in case anything went wrong. He tapped his fingers against the rail as he mulled the scenario.

"What the hell..," the mercenary muttered under his breath. From inside his server's smock, he released his hefty Desert Eagle handgun from its holster and checked the chamber for a round. Satisfied, he looked through the porthole window in the swinging door that separated the galley from the ballroom. To his man stationed at the entrance to the hall from the outer deck, he gave a quick signal with the flick of his wrist. The man nodded and whirled out of the ballroom and onto the deck.

Edgar Noches, a former tactical officer for one of Mexico's most lethal cartels, knew that his first job might be the most crucial. He had to make sure that the outer decks were cleared, and all guests and employees of the boat were corralled inside the ballroom.

Remaining faithful to his role as an attendant, he swept the decks letting passengers know that they were requested back to the ballroom for a special announcement. Most nodded their heads and left their perches along the rail to return to the room as requested. Some stopped to take a final drag of their cigarettes before tamping them out in nearby ashtrays and then proceeded back to the ballroom.

Noches kept a keen eye on all of them before moving on to the next group of loiterers. As one tipsy woman moved from the safety of the rail, she slipped to the teakwood decking of the Nagaremono. Rolling his eyes, Edgar stooped over to help pull her up and guide her in the direction of the ballroom. He groaned as he found the reason for the woman's fall evidenced on his shoe. She had been vomiting over the side of the boat while leaning on the rail. Her aim, weakened by half a dozen glasses of Cabernet, left the contents of her stomach spilled on the wooden floor of the deck. Grumbling, he pulled a handkerchief from his pocket and began smearing the pile off of his shoes. Throughout the episode, he missed seeing the young woman enter the deck side restroom that he had checked moments ago. Oblivious to his error, he continued with his task along the deck.

Nineteen

Miranda feared the long wait she had endured the last time she used the ballroom restroom. All the while, she had been forced to stand in line next to the talkative and arrogant Katie. The intern babbled loudly about how lucky Miranda had been to have been "Jim's girl" and if she had had the opportunity, she wouldn't have messed it up. She had heard the rumors of the young intern having a crush on Jim. Carrie had kept her up to date on all of the gossip from the Foundation office. Each comment made from the bouncy tart followed with a knowing smirk, and a glance shot Miranda's way.

Sneaking past the crowd that was filtering back into the ballroom, Miranda side-stepped her way towards the restroom she had spied on one of the dockside strolls. While being around so many familiar and supportive faces had made the evening more enjoyable and cathartic than she had assumed it would be, she could only deal with it all in small doses. The trip to the out of the way restroom offered her the respite that her mind required.

Stepping out into the night air, she gulped in a huge breath that she let out slowly. She had been prepared coming into the wake for it to be an emotional ride. She found having to answer questions about the relationship and enduring Katie's rants were far more stressful than coming to terms with Jim's passing. While her ex-fiancé had issues, there was a lot of celebration of his life shared, which she felt was a fitting tribute. Hearing the stories of the positive things Jim did for the world, Miranda knew that he left his mark on the world.

Outside the ladies' room, the deck had been cleared. Noches had encouraged all of the attendees that had been deck side to return to the ballroom in the center of the boat. From his pocket, he fished out his earpiece and positioned it gently into place.

"Noches reporting. Deck side sweep is successful, all members are inside," the hired paramilitary man spoke into the air, seemingly to no one.

The small assault team, each with a similar earpiece in place, heard him loud and clear. Rey Chavez, all too happy to shed his service staff smock, cast off the white jacket revealing his thin body, clad in all black jeans and turtle neck, with two sidearms and a cellular phone attached to his waist. Tossing a crystal goblet over his shoulder, letting it arch high in the air and shatter on the banquet room floor, Chavez commanded, "Let's go to work, boys!"

In unison, the well-trained commando team snapped into action. From under aprons, stainless steel terrines, and chaffing dishes, as well as employing strategically placed serving carts, the team produced weapons of every shape and size. Most of the mercenary squad strapped a handgun to their side and wielded a semi-automatic Steyhr or H&K assault rifle. Fluidly, each member slid into position as those guests sober enough to be aware of their surroundings began letting out panicked shrieks.

To quell chaos and rampage, Chavez stood on the main stage and grabbed the microphone from the podium. "Ladies and gentlemen, this is your new captain speaking. The Nagaremono in which you are riding aboard now belongs to my crew and me. I assure you that if you stay in your seats and comply with our instructions, you stand a decent chance of surviving. I also assure you that if you in any way try to become a hero or ignore our requests, my very efficient crew will make the last few moments of your life exceptionally painful."

To prove his point, the mercenary released his grip on the microphone allowing it to slam to the floor with a bang. Grabbing the collar of the unwitting closest mourner, he hauled him out of his seat. Holding the wobbly-kneed man by his shirt, Chavez slammed his knee into the man's stomach and dropped him to the floor.

"I don't want anyone to get hurt, but hear me right now, we are deadly serious," the mercenary snapped. Swiveling his head around the room, he spent a moment glaring into the eyes of anyone who dared look his way.

With all of the passengers and crew reigned into one of three areas - the bridge, the ballroom, and the executive suite - access points to each manned with an assault rifle-readied guard. Two of Chavez' men ushered the remaining members of Hasegawa's staff out of the kitchen and into the ballroom with the guests of the wake. At the same time, assault team members secured the bridge, forcing the captain and crew onto a cushioned bench in the back of the pilothouse. A man named Stone Jeffries, a former Navy boat pilot took control of the vessel while a partner trained his weapon at the three legitimate crewmen of the Nagaremono. Very quietly, two more men hovered outside of the executive suite, ensuring its occupants, too, held in place.

Chavez had every assault team member not responsible for guarding an access point, relieving the boat's guests and official crew of phones, watches, mace, and any other personal item that could be used as a weapon or communication device. Most of the shocked passengers complied, as Chavez ordered, digging in their pockets for any item that the assault team found objectionable.

As the collectors of contraband made their way around the ballroom, an inebriated man lurched out of his chair, lunging at one of Chavez' men. Ignoring the pleas of his tablemates, he tried fighting off the nearest terrorist. In a single, deft move, Felix Cortez, one of Chavez' top enforcers and a former sergeant in the

Mexican army, answered the impetuous man by slamming the butt of his assault rifle into the young man's face. The impact of fiberglass and steel met the man's chin with a horrifying crack, sending him sprawling onto the floor in a motionless, blood-spattered heap. The wake attendees joined in a chorus of terrified shrieks, many falling into their seats, faces buried in their hands, frightened tears soaking their palms.

"I thought I made myself clear. People, this might be a good time to notice what happens if there are any more heroes in this group. Frankly, I'm a little surprised that Cortez didn't just kill … eh, what's his name?" Chavez paused, looking at the woman closest to the resister's seat.

Quivering, the woman responded in a weak whisper, "Don."

"Don. Let's just say for those of you who survive, you'll be attending a lot more of these dead guy dinners if you're all as stupid as Don," Chavez called out to the diners.

Quietly, the patrons were searched one by one by Chavez' men. Cell phones, PDAs, pocket computers, cans of mace, and any other questionable item deposited into a big tub brought out from the kitchen.

Frank, "Franky" to his friends and associates, was not feeling very smiled upon by lady luck this trip. Already down half a million dollars, he decided he needed to step out and collect himself. Scooting his chair back, he snatched his lit cigar from its perch and placed it between his clenched teeth as he excused himself from the table. A quick walk around the deck would hopefully refresh him and ensure that he would be ready to test his luck once again.

The rest of the card players took the brief respite to have their drinks refreshed and swapped their advice on which Cohiba or Cuaba to light up next. Their attention snapped when Franky opened the door. The short, stocky Italian froze abruptly in the doorway as the barrel tip of the Steyhr assault rifle was positioned at his forehead.

"Sorry, sir, you're going to have to remain inside," the man at the other end of the gun stated flatly.

"What's the meaning of this? Do you know who I am?" Franky shouted, glaring at the gun in his face.

"Frank Caputo, heir to the alleged Mafia frontman Gino Caputo. Regardless, I will shoot you if you do not move your short, fat ass back into the room!" the gunman ordered, shoving the nose of the powerful weapon into the pinstriped, silk jacketed shoulder of the poker player.

Caputo shrank back into the room with the rest of the card players. Hishiro stood up to address the gunmen, "Gentleman, the Nagaremono is my boat. What is it you are after; let's make this as civil and painless as possible."

"We are not interested in your help, what we are interested in is all of you shutting the hell up!" the man waving the Steyhr shouted, looking down at the pile of cash on the table, he motioned with his head for his partner to gather up large kitty.

One of the two attendants working the suite for Hasegawa slowly slipped his nine-millimeter handgun from its perch in the small of his back. With one of the gunmen intent on the game table loot, he thought it the opportune time to turn the tables on the situation. Cautiously, he slid the gun out of its sheath and around his waist. Eyeing the assault weapon-wielding member of the pairing, he drew the handgun up to take a shot.

The attendant froze in surprised horror as the gunman stuffing cash in his pockets had kept a keen awareness of the room and calmly squeezed off a round from his own silenced handgun, landing a steaming pellet of steel between the attendant's eyes. The server melted to the floor as a red dot emerged on his forehead, followed by a slow, seeping trickle of blood.

Swinging his gun in the direction of the bartender, the gunman asked, "You want to try and be a hero?" The middle-aged

Japanese man behind the bar shook his head wearily. The color drained from his round face.

"Why don't you drag your carcass out here with these fine folks, be easier to keep an eye on you," the mercenary with the assault rifle growled, a scowl on his face giving away his irritation for being blindsided by the would-be hero.

Doing as he instructed, the bartender slid a chair over to the game table and joined the men he had been serving. The man with the handgun studied Hasegawa, "This is your boat, right rich guy? I think you might be of particular use to us. Get your fat butt up. You're coming with me," as he turned to leave, he motioned to his partner, "If anyone so much as scratches an itch, you shoot them." Closing the door behind him, he nudged the Japanese freight magnate down the corridor.

Miranda studied herself in the mirror, questioning whether this whole evening had been cathartic or just taxing. Sighing, she remembered the cruise was a long one, and they would not be returning to the docks in Portland for hours. This reality set in, she straightened up and determined to make the best of the evening, enjoying her time with her friends.

Stepping out on the deck, she thought it a bit odd that no one had elected to remain outside to enjoy the evening, whatever the announcement was, it must have been holding the crowd's attention. Moving swiftly towards the french doors of the ballroom, she came to a halt as she noticed the image of a figure's shadow in front of the doors through the frosted glass. Not wanting to hit the person as she entered, she paused with her hand on the door, ready to push it forward ever so slightly to nudge the individual out of the way. Before she continued, the shadow moved, rotating their body, as they did so, the shadow revealing that it was holding something in its hands, an assault weapon!

Miranda backed away from the door, her heart racing. What was going on? Before she could think of an appropriate reaction, the sound of footsteps began coming from the corridor that led to the boat's stern, an area that had been marked "off-limits" for the guests of the wake - the area that Miranda had witnessed the group of men board via the second catwalk.

Spinning her head around for a place to duck into, she quickly slipped back into the women's restroom. Leaving the door cracked, she saw two men approach. The first was the Asian man that she had thought that she recognized. Behind him, was a man dressed in all black. In his hand was a gun aimed directly at the Asian tycoon's back!

Urging the first man on, the gunman herded his victim down the hall. Miranda's mind reeled wildly, her heart pounded with a fury in her chest. She had to call for help. Digging her phone out of her purse, she pounded the numbers 9-1-1. Waiting expectantly for a helpful voice, she glanced at the screen. No bars greeted her eyes. Groaning, she looked around the room. Maybe she could get better reception outside.

Cautiously, she pushed the restroom door open, revealing a once again, empty deck. Slipping out of the doorway, she danced lightly across the teakwood deck, looking for an appropriate place to try her phone again. Spying a set of stairs leading to the top deck of the boat, she hurried up the steel steps, ducking behind a waist-high wall on the landing. Her phone offered up a single, weak bar of reception.

Miranda fumbled with the buttons on the tiny cell phone as she heard footsteps again on the deck below her. The footfalls paused near the stairs that led to her precarious perch. Holding her breath, she waited in desperation as she prayed that whoever was down below continued along their way. Letting out a brief sigh of relief, Miranda was elated when the sound of a lighter's lid slamming shut, and the footsteps sounded again, making their way towards the stern.

"Hello? Hello?" Sean called into his phone, only to receive silence in return. About to hit the 'end' button on the keypad, he noticed the caller's identification on the screen. It was Miranda.

Sean continued to stare at the LCD quizzically when a voice finally emerged from the tiny speaker. "Sean?" Miranda's whispering voice held an air of desperation.

"Yeah, it's me. What's going on?"

"I, I was trying to call 911, but they put me on hold," Miranda replied, scrolling down her phone list, she landed on the one person who might know how to handle the events she was about to describe.

"911? Is someone hurt?"

"I don't know. I don't know what's going on. There are men with guns," Miranda whispered, her voice shaky.

"Guns? What are you talking about? Where are you... " Sean started, but held up when he heard Miranda gasp on the other end.

"Oh, my God!" Miranda reactively covered her mouth with the fingertips of her free hand, "I think it is Hasegawa!"

"Hasegawa?" Sean frowned, "He is involved!"

"Involved? What are you talking about?"

"Harrison had been investigating him. I think he may have even been extorting him with some of the information he had uncovered," Sean replied.

"What? Jim would never...," Miranda started to defend her ex-fiancé.

"Never mind that right now. Where are you?" Sean asked urgently, getting the conversation back on track.

"We've been cruising for about two and a half hours. I'd say we were halfway between St. Helens and Astoria. I'm not really sure," Miranda guessed, trying to make out any landmarks along the terrain of the riverbanks.

"Have any shots been fired?"

"No, at least I haven't heard any. They pretty much corralled everyone into the ballroom. I just happened to have slipped into the ladies room when they were herding everyone off of the deck. I almost walked right into a man holding some kind of rifle when I returned," Miranda filled Sean in.

"What the heck is Hasegawa up to?" Sean scowled.

"I'm not sure he's up to anything. When I saw him go by, he was escorted with a gun in his back."

Sean leaned back in his booth to allow the news to sink in and try to make sense of the information he was just given in conjunction with what he and Adam had turned up. With the Hasegawa connection, he thought for sure the terrorist supporter had something up his sleeve. Someone holding a gun to his back was not the picture of the scenario he had in his mind.

"Are you in a safe spot? Can you hold on until I can get help to you?" Sean asked.

"I don't know. I'm up on the...hang on...," Miranda whispered.

Sean listened to the silence for what seemed an agonizingly long time. Over the phone's sensitive digital speaker, he could hear rustling, presumably Miranda changing her position. Finally, he heard a gasp and then unfamiliar voices, "We've got a stowaway!" one of the voices called.

"Damn it, Noches, how did you miss her?"

"Aw man, she's got a cell phone!" a second voice groaned.

"No!" Sean heard Miranda shriek as more rustling was heard through the line before she let out a weak gasp, "Help...Sean...."

The young retiree stared in horror at his phone as the line went dead. A feeling of infuriating helplessness catalyzed to boiling rage.

Adam looked across the table at him, a questioning frown taking over his face, "What's up?"

"I think Miranda has just been held hostage."

"What?" Adam exclaimed.

"Hasegawa's on the boat. It appears a group of men are holding the whole thing captive," Sean replied, his mind working over time.

"We need to call it in. I'll call local, you call Rachel and see if she can ante up some federal assistance," Adam said, already pushing the buttons on his phone.

Sean cycled through his cell phone's database and found Rachel York. Rachel, now the assistant regional director for the Department of Interior, had become good friends with Sean during his stint as a lobbyist in Seattle. The tone of the ringing phone played through Sean's earpiece.

"Hello?" a stern yet sultry voice answered.

"Rachel, it's Sean," he began.

"I thought you might be calling. It sounds like you and Adam have been busy pissing off Beckett again," the voice smiled through the phone. Beckett, the DOI director that oversaw the investigation at the Makah Reservation, was Rachel's supervisor.

"Yeah, we have been. Listen, this is even more serious. Miranda was attending the memorial for the guy who was murdered on the peninsula. Some group of men overtook the boat they were on and are holding them hostage," Sean informed his old friend, "And, get this, Hasegawa is aboard the boat!"

"What? Oh my ...how...," Rachel exclaimed, "Do you suppose Hasegawa set it up?"

"That's what I thought, but Miranda said he was being prodded at gunpoint, too."

"Sounds like someone trying to clean up a mess," Rachel mused, "Have you called it into the local authorities?"

"Adam is right now," Sean replied.

"Are you still in contact with Miranda?"

"No, they grabbed her while we were on the line," Sean informed her grimly.

"Oh Sean, I'm sorry," Rachel soothed, "I have a friend in the FBI down in Portland. I'll give him a call and see if I can't swing a favor. I'll call you right back."

As Sean hung up the phone, he felt his stomach tighten and fought to keep the room from spinning. His ears picked up Adam finishing his call. "Well?"

"They are going to alert the Longview and Astoria police departments as well as the Coast Guard. Being a hostage situation on a river straddling two state lines, I imagine they'll bring in the FBI as well," the Fish and Wildlife agent replied.

Before Sean could ask another question, his cell began buzzing at his side. "Hello?"

"Sean, it's Rachel, I have a helicopter headed your way. There is a parking garage in John's Landing next to the Water Tower Shopping Center. Can you be there in fifteen minutes?" the voice said on the other end.

"We'll be there in ten," Sean replied, nodding to Adam to start up his truck, "Thanks, Rachel."

"No problem. But Sean, stay out of trouble," Rachel pleaded.

"You know me," came the terse reply.

"I know, that's why I worry."

Twenty

Miranda grimaced in terror when she looked up to see the man in all black standing over her. The man quickly snatched away the phone and struck her hard in the face with his other hand. "Puta!" the man spat at her as he pocketed the phone.

Wiping her lip, a smear of blood-stained Miranda's hand. Leaning back as far as she could, she wasn't able to avoid the hand coming back, grabbing her by the arm and forcibly making her stand up. The man's grip painful around her thin bicep, she refused to show that it hurt. Roughly, she was led down the steel steps to the deck below.

"I think you'll be the first one to die, lady," the man sneered as he escorted Miranda forward until they reached the ballroom. Flinging the door open, he shoved Miranda past the guard and into the room.

Heads spun as the mourners turned hostages, gasped at seeing Miranda man-handled into rejoining the group. From across the room, Chavez witnessed the intrusion and came over to find out what was going on. Edgar Noches whispered in the heist leader's ear about finding Miranda talking on the phone.

"I see. And do you have any idea what she was talking about or with whom?" Chavez whispered back.

"I don't know who, but I'm pretty sure it was a call for help," Noches reported, his voice declaring his concern.

"Give me the phone," Chavez ordered with his hand extended.

Complying, the mercenary handed over the cell phone he had confiscated. The team leader studied the phone, searching the call history. Finding a single number dialed since the cruise began, he pressed the "call" button.

The phone rang twice before a hopeful voice answered, "Miranda?"

"Ah, so that is our little stowaway's name," Chavez smiled into the phone, "It seems she has found herself causing a little mischief."

"What have you done with her?" Sean growled into the phone.

"I hope I am not talking to a hero. Tell me, do you like this Miranda girl? She is rather…attractive after all?"

"Who are you? What do you want with those people?" Sean demanded.

"Rule number one, boy. I ask the questions, you answer them. Do we understand each other?" Chavez snarled, "Now, if you do like her, you will do all the things I say. If you do not, her pretty brains will be splattered all over the fine mahogany on this here boat!"

"Fine, I get it. You're the boss," Sean mumbled, trying to keep his voice from trembling under his curtain of anger.

"That's a good boy. Now, since you have undoubtedly notified the authorities, you will call them to let them know I have well more than enough bullets to imbed one in each one of these traveler's heads. If anyone should try anything, they will be responsible for the resulting massacre," the mercenary sneered into the phone and added condescendingly, "Now, if you can behave yourself and do exactly as I instruct, you just might get to see your girlfriend again."

Ending the call abruptly, Chavez pressed the transmit button that signaled to his wireless earpiece. "Engine room, full speed."

His man in the pilothouse called back an "Aye, aye" as the boat's engines began to churn faster. Chavez looked ahead towards the western horizon. The passage through the Clatsop Spit that guarded the entrance from the Columbia River to the fierce waters of the North Pacific would tell the tale deciding his imminent death or greatest conquest. Either way, Chavez reasoned to himself, he was going to die a rich man.

Twenty One

The Bell Jet Ranger helicopter cut through the dusk sky with cyclonic ferocity. Instinctively, Sean ducked as the aircraft came to rest on the concrete rooftop of the parking garage. A door opened up, and a solemn-faced man waved the two over.

Sean and Adam exchanged glances and complied, rushing under the rotating blades and climbed into the rear of the helicopter.

The instant Sean and Adam were inside, the rotors lifted the vehicle back into the air. The man who waved them in promptly provided headsets to allow them to converse through the noise of the powerful engine tearing through the air.

"I'm agent Dawkins. Our pilot is agent Rivers. I understand you know Rachel York. I kind of owe her one as she helped cut through some red tape on a case I was working on," the agent said, introducing himself and his partner, "So you want to tell me what's going on?"

Sean relayed his conversations with Miranda and her captor, carefully expressing his concerns over any overt actions. Respectfully, he asked the bureau agent what the rescue plan was.

"Well, we are going to drop the bird in Astoria. I assume the boat is heading for the ocean and international waters, as their log records indicate. Over the past few minutes, they have increased their cruising speed, probably to try and get ahead of anyone setting up a welcome party," the FBI agent called over the headset.

"I don't think so," Sean replied unconvinced.

"What's that?" the agent asked, looking back at Sean with a frown.

"I said I don't think so. They have to know the Coast Guard will be waiting for them. Besides, they have a boatload of leverage - literally. I think they have a schedule to keep," Sean replied.

"Like a rendezvous?"

"Maybe...," Sean said watching out the window as the helicopter skirted the hills of the Coastal Range and followed the meandering flow of the Columbia River.

Chavez left the ballroom in the hands of his men and made his way back to the bridge, where Hasegawa was being held along with the crew of the boat. The man who guarded the room gave way and opened one of the large French doors. The squad leader was met with unwelcome stares from the captain and the attendants.

The former Mexican cartel enforcer smiled at the group, "Sorry to break up your little card game. Probably wouldn't be that much fun without the pile of cash that my men are...keeping safe."

"Enough of this foolishness! What is it that you want?" Hasegawa demanded tersely.

"Ah, Hishiro Hasegawa...just the man I came to see," Chavez cooed and held his hand out towards the door, signifying his intention to have the shipping magnate follow him out into the hallway.

Reluctantly, a furrow-browed Hasegawa rose to meet Chavez' bequest. Before he could reach the hallway, his captor turned to face him. With snake-like quickness, Chavez' hand darted from his side, striking Hasegawa hard on the cheek. The open-handed slap resonated loudly through the executive suite.

"Don't make demands at me. I am in charge here!" Chavez scolded Hishiro sharply.

The Japanese heir winced briefly to the blow but quickly straightened up. Thinking to himself, he felt this Chavez guy was carrying out his role convincingly. Staring straight ahead, he moved into the hallway, the mercenary prodding him along roughly.

The jostling continued until they reached the pilothouse where Hasegawa was forced into a chair. The boat captain and first mate looked on, impressed at Hishiro's level of calm that he was displaying in the face of the siege.

"Now, if you would dispense with your codes, please," Chavez requested as he sat back comfortably in the soft leather chair.

"What codes?" Hishiro asked belligerently.

His hands folded neatly on his lap, causing his fingers to form a pyramid, Chavez stared indifferently at the multi-millionaire. Finally, he gave the slightest nod to one of his men.

Without a moment's hesitation, the butt of an assault weapon leveled into Hasegawa's gut. The tycoon fell out of the chair and onto the floor as he expelled the contents of his lungs. Despite knowing that the mercenary was merely playing out his own devised ruse, Hishiro glared at the assault leader with a brief shot of anger.

"Might as well speak up, you are going to tell me. It's up to you as to when and how difficult this needs to be," Chavez informed the man as he returned to his upright position. Warily, the Japanese tycoon played his role with Chavez. He was alarmed by the twist of Chavez demanding his account codes – a part of the plan he was unwilling to comply. Still, they had to put on a show. His bruised body was certainly convinced that he was a victim.

Hasegawa knew the plan called for law enforcement intervention at some point in the cruise to lend credibility to the heist. He just hoped milking the process didn't prove too painful for him.

The ballroom stifled under a heavy cloud of fear, discomfort, and occasional bouts of drunken belligerence. The now mixed group of mourners and boat staff corralled in a bunch on the floor. She glanced at her friend Carrie, who fidgeted uncomfortably. Knowing her friend all too well, Miranda sensed trouble as Carrie shifted from her cross-legged sitting position.

Carrie, with reddening eyes matching the crimson of her fiery hair, had decided she had about enough. Finding the nearest guard, she stood up and approached him. The moment she rose from her spot, all eyes in the room, along with several assault weapon muzzles, turned their attention to her. Miranda gulped, silently praying for her friend to sit down or for some divine force to intervene.

"Hey you, handsome...," Carrie called out as she staggered towards the armed man by the door.

"Lady, sit your butt back down!" the man commanded, his voice displaying more annoyance than threatening tone.

"Wait, wait. Listen, I need to see the big guy...," she stammered.

"What you need, is to sit your rear end back down!" reiterated the man, an increased level of sternness in his voice.

"Now you listen here, my daddy is a very important man, he can help all of this go away," Carrie continued her rant.

The gun-toting mercenary began moving towards the inebriated woman, "I don't care if your daddy is the President of the United States. You need to get back to your seat!" The assault team member shoved Carrie back, knocking her to the floor.

She wore a twisted, confused look on her face, as she pointed with an outstretched finger to two gentlemen at opposing tables, "No, daddy's a CEO at a software company, but he's a US Senator…and over there – he's the governor." Placing her finger to her lips, she slurred in a whisper, "They don't like each other

BLOOD IN THE WATER / 155

much, shhh. Anyways, you mess with him, and you'll have the entire navy up your…!"

Miranda cringed at her friend's alcohol-induced poor judgment. Quickly, she hopped up to intercede. "You have to forgive her, your idea to wine the group into easy submission worked a little too well with her, I would say," she said apologetically, hoping to occupy their minds away from Governor Roberts and Senator Johnson as she hustled to Carrie's side.

The man's attention turned from Carrie to this new distraction, "Ah, the dumb broad with the cellphone. Just can't keep your nose where it belongs," he scolded as he whipped around the back of his hand, striking Miranda in the face. The impact sent her once more sprawling to the floor, blood dripping from her lip.

Screaming incoherently, Carrie dove for the man's leg, chomping down on his calf with her teeth. The mercenary kicked his leg away, catching Carrie in the head. Two men closest to the assaulted women began to rise in their defense until two shots from a guard on the opposite side of the room imbedded into the floor next to them.

"Enough!" Noches, the mercenary who fired his weapon, shouted, "The next person who moves will be shot! Are we clear?"

The dead air of silence and frozen bodies indicated the group's acceptance of his claim. "Now, Raul, take those two women and lock them in the kitchen storage pantry. If either of them gives you any trouble, put a bullet in them."

Raul nodded and ceased rubbing his sore leg and prodded Carrie and Miranda up to their feet. As the trio shuffled along to the kitchen, Noches turned to Governor Roberts and Senator Johnson, "You two come with me."

The very angry and embarrassed Raul silently shoved the two women into the dry-storage pantry and swung the heavy door shut. He found its padlock resting on the stainless steel shelving just outside the door and fastened it in place.

Inside the room, Miranda cleared space on a lower shelf for Carrie to lie on and took stock of their situation. The room was a simple ten-by-ten square, completely lined with shelves. Her initial survey noted large bags of flour, sugar, and rice and a sundry of large tubs full of mayonnaise and sauces, but nothing useful to provide a means out of the improvised cell.

Sighing, she looked at Carrie, whose wild hair flowed over a bag of flour she was using for a pillow. Carrie flashed a goofy grin at Miranda as if to thank her for her care. Slowly the smile vanished and melted into a confused frown. Pushing her head forward, she lurched into a torrent of spewed vomit and rolled back to her flour sack pillow succumbing to wine-induced somnolence.

Her face wrinkled in disgust, Miranda shrank back from her friend's maelstrom of bile. Grabbing an apron off of a nearby shelf, she held it to her face as a chemical shield and slumped onto a rack she had cleared for herself. Her mind surged with fraught and despair, trying desperately to think of a way out.

Sean was amazed at the speed and agility of the helicopter as it maneuvered along the Columbia River channel. Passing dozens of barges transporting goods to and from the Port of Portland, he quickly recognized the different wake pattern standing out from the other vessels. The boat that they were approaching was moving at a much faster speed than the others on the river.

Through the in-flight headsets, the pilot stated, "There's our objective, the Nagaremono."

The field agent who waved Sean and Adam on board, trained a powerful pair of binoculars on the swift-moving yacht, "Decks are clear...looks like a half-dozen heads in the bridge."

Sean and Adam pushed their noses up to the window to observe the boat. If they hadn't received the call from Miranda, they would never suspect anything sinister was taking place aboard the cruiser. Despite moving at an above-average clip, there were no visible signs of the ordeal that was taking place within its interior.

Through the headphones, Sean could hear the FBI agent try to communicate with the yacht through its registered frequencies. The agent turned back to face his two passengers, "Communications on the boat are down."

The matter-of-fact tone told Sean that this was an expected development. What he did not expect, was his cell phone to begin buzzing at his side. Holding it up, he read the caller-ID announce that it was Miranda's phone ringing him.

Agent Dawkins saw Sean with the phone and shook his head. Pointing to the rotors above their heads, he signaled that there was no way Sean would be able to hear over the whirring blades. He also flashed that they would be landing in minutes, allowing Sean to try his cellphone then.

Sean's heart raced. He squirmed in his seat, wanting to already be on the ground. Did Miranda avoid being captured? Was that her on the phone? His anticipation heightened as the powerful helicopter sped along and finally began its descent.

On the ground below, Sean could see a blaze of flashing lights. Emergency vehicles and police cars filled a parking lot in the small, coastal town of Astoria. The helicopter made a direct line for a clear piece of asphalt, a large circle left by the battalion of vehicles for the pilot to land.

As soon as the skids hit the asphalt, Sean had the door popped open and was out of his seat. Hitting the "send" button on the cell phone, he waited, hoping to hear Miranda's voice on the other end.

"Ah, our young hero, I'm glad you returned my call," Sean winced at the voice, not being Miranda's. Sean put the small phone on speaker for Adam and Agent Dawkins, who came running over to join him.

"I'm no hero," Sean stated flatly. He could feel his pulse pound behind his temples.

"Glad to hear that. That means we just might have an amicable relationship and your lady friend, as well as the rest of the passengers, might just make it out of this alive," the male voice said, Sean, picking up the faintest hint of a Latino accent. The man continued, "I assume you are responsible for the government bird that flew overhead?"

Sean just glared at the phone, not offering a response. The voice on the line went on, "I also assume that there is a welcoming party for us up ahead. The helicopter touched down somewhere in Astoria, and the Coast Guard is no doubt clogging the channel. No matter. Here's the deal, Mister...Kendall, I believe the call screen said, you are now personally responsible for our safe passage. If anyone tries to stop us or board our boat, passengers will die. I think you'll find me quite liberal with that penalty."

Dawkins grabbed the phone from Sean, "This is Agent Stephen Dawkins with the Federal Bureau of Investigation. I am taking charge of this case. I will be your contact moving...."

"No, I don't think so, greyman! I make the rules, and I have selected my contact!" Chavez shouted into the phone at Dawkins.

"You have to be reasonable. Kendall is a civilian. I will be in a much better position to see that your needs are met," Dawkins persisted.

"Call him my interpreter, then. His little girlfriend called him, so by default, he is now a part of this. If I hear anyone else's voice on this line, I will kill a passenger," the mercenary declared.

Sean looked to Agent Dawkins for the next step. Dawkins looked around for something to write on. By then, a large crowd of law enforcement personnel had gathered around the three men. A second helicopter had landed, and several men jumped out, ducking slightly under the pressure of the blades. Sean sensed that one of them was the agent in charge, by the way, his entourage catered to him. The newcomers made a bee-line for him and Dawkins.

"Who's talking to the perpetrator?" the man in the traditional dark suit demanded. A local field agent pointed to Sean and Dawkins. "Who are these civilians? Get them into the interrogation quarantine and get a tap on that phone!"

Lining through the crowd, he strode over to Sean, Adam, and Dawkins and snatched the phone from Sean. "This is Michael Montgomery, Area Director out of Portland for the FBI..." he growled into the phone.

The high-ranking federal agent was abruptly cut off by the sound of gunfire on the other end. Chavez' voice crackled over the tiny speaker, "I said no one's voice other than Kendall's. Damn you government types are thick-headed. That one was on you Mr. 'Area Director'. Let's see...you took the life of First Mate Sakimoto. Very sad, I am afraid you made me a man of my word. My first demand is obvious, the boat passes through and into deep water unharassed. Anything I see that I don't like will result in the immediate death of one of these fine people."

With that statement, Sean's phone fell silent. The crowd had become equally quiet, trying to come to terms with the apparent ferocity of the terrorist aboard the Nagaremono.

Area Director Montgomery broke the silence. "So, who the hell are you?" he said, casting a look of disdain at Sean and Adam.

"I have a friend on board. She got word to me before they found her," Sean said flatly, not in the mood for a bureaucrat's inquiry.

Adam stepped up, beaming, "Adam Raines, Fish and Wildlife."

A quizzical look washed across Montgomery's already perturbed face, "Freaking Fish and Wildlife? Unless it is a boat full of misplaced squirrels, I'd say you're a little out of your jurisdiction, pal."

Adam just smiled, "Why does everyone always react that way?"

"Since you are the chosen one, here is the deal. You will have one of my agents on you at all times. When your phone rings, it will be tapped into our command vehicle parked right over there," Montgomery said, pointing towards a dark blue van littered with antennas and satellite dishes, turning his attention to Adam, "Fish and Wildlife, you stay out of the way. Go count roadkill or something." The area director marched over to the van with the antennas.

Agent Dawkins saw another vehicle of interest and motioned for Sean and Adam to follow. As they walked up, Sean noticed the large LCD screen mounted on the side of the van. On the display was a feed from one of the Portland news channels that had a helicopter hovering above the Nagaremono.

The boat remained as placid as it had when Sean had flown over minutes ago. They watched as the yacht powered its way towards the mouth of the Columbia River, where they now stood.

"Probably twenty minutes away," Dawkins calculated, noting a landmark he had recalled from the flight over.

The news station helicopter zoomed their camera to the window of the pilothouse. Through the tinted windows, they could barely make out shapes inside the captain's bridge. Several men could be seen standing in the room, but their details were not clear.

"How long has that chopper been there filming?" Sean asked.

"I don't know, I saw the first images when you were on the phone," Dawkins shrugged.

"Can you guys clear up the picture?" Sean asked.

"Sure, let's step into the truck," the FBI agent held out his hand for the two to climb in the back of the communications van.

Inside, they were greeted with a bank of television screens, computers, recording equipment, and a host of other surveillance and communication equipment. Adam swiveled his head around and let out a soft whistle, "Man, this is place is a geeks Santa wish list dream."

"Yeah," Dawkins agreed, but added, "Just don't touch anything."

Tapping the young field tech on the shoulder, the agent asked him to replay the last several minutes of footage from the news copter. In seconds, the men were leaning over the flat-screen monitor watching the coverage of the yacht. The news cameraman combed the boat from stern to bow, slowly keying in and zooming in on the reflective windows that surrounded its midsection and then finally the pilothouse. In the lower right-hand corner of the screen, the time of capture was displayed.

As the camera panned and zoomed in on the pilothouse windows, Sean could make out the shadows he had seen from the large outside screen. "There!" he pointed at the image on the monitor, "Can you zoom in right there?"

"Sure," the field tech replied and began clicking on the pointer, locking in on the windows of the enclosed bridge. Slowly, the screen was filled with a shadowy figure that appeared to have a hand to the side of his head.

"Clean it up a bit," Dawkins muttered as he leaned closer into the monitor.

Again, the field tech began tapping away on the devices under the screen, bringing the shadowy figure into clear focus through the complicated filters of the software. The figure revealed itself to be a medium-built Hispanic man talking on a cell phone. Each man did a mental survey of the time stamp in the corner of the screen.

"The man on the phone with Sean?" Adam asked.

"It seems likely," Dawkins agreed and placed a hand on the tech's shoulder, "Print that out and make several copies, then run a database match and see if this man is in our system."

"Will do," the tech complied and returned his focus on the computer screen.

Twenty-Two

Chavez was becoming increasingly disenchanted with the arrangements of the plan. The risks to make the heist prominent and visible began to weigh heavily on the seasoned mercenary. The stealthy and quick campaigns executes in ill-prepared Central American provinces were more to his liking. He was willing to take on a little more risk, after all, this was to be the motherload of scores, his retirement cash cow. Yet, he was one to hedge his bets. Disappearing from the U. S. government was going to be dangerous and expensive.

It wasn't that his confidence was waning, his greed, however, was taking a stronger hold. His tech-ops man was already sitting at the computer terminal in the corner of the pilothouse, ready to tap into Hasegawa Holdings' tangled web of offshore accounts.

He cast a glare at Hasegawa, "Get up."

Hasegawa stared up at his captor, curious where Chavez was going to take this. Dissatisfied with the shipping heir's slow response, Chavez barked, "Now!"

Hasegawa rose with reluctant indignation and followed Chavez into the NAVCOM station. When the two were away from his crew, shut, the Japanese businessman relaxed his troubled expression. Listening to the rotors of the hovering news helicopter above, he nodded to the ceiling and whispered, "This is good, huh? The whole world sees a robbery."

"Yeah, the attention is great," Chavez muttered and quickly shifted to his intention, "It's time for the codes."

"Sure, set up in the way that we had prescribed?" Hasegawa asked, beginning to feel very unsettled about Chavez' manner. The arrangement he had made with Tug was to allow a portion of his accounts to be "stolen" while the rest of the money would divert to new reports in Hasegawa's name.

Chavez looked across the room at the others, thoughtfully stroking his goatee-covered chin. Without warning, he uncoiled his left arm, striking Hasegawa across the face with a powerful blow.

The freight magnate winced, his right eye twitching with the instinctive rage of being struck. He was beginning to think that his hired thief was carrying out the charade with a little too much zeal. His sizable ego, the cause of most of his problems, was nearing its breaking point.

Hishiro gathered himself, recalling the payoff of the abuse, an end to his rather significant accounting inconsistencies.

"I think we have raised the stakes," Chavez snarled, "I want all the codes."

"What do you mean? What is it you want?"

"Everything."

"What? What the hell is this?" Hasegawa stammered.

"The codes Hishiro. I want you to input the codes," Chavez glared, slamming his fist against the panel.

The sounds of helicopters, news reporters, and the frenzied commands of the various police units filled the parking lot of the Astoria Maritime Museum. Sean Kendall gazed out at the long, high-arching bridge that spanned over the Columbia confluence connecting coastal Washington and Oregon. Several hundred feet below, the mighty river would carry the boatful of hostages, and more importantly, to him - Miranda.

The buzzing of the cell phone at his hip interrupted his thoughts. As he looked down at the screen, his throat tightened as "Miranda" flashed up in the blue ID box. A red light began blinking on top of the communications van alerting the nearby agents to the call.

Sean waited for agent Dawkins to take a few steps closer before he answered. Taking in a deep breath, he hit the "Answer" key. "Hello?"

"Mr. Kendall. I trust you have been behaving yourself?" the gruff voice on the other end of the line sneered.

Unwilling to feed into the man's taunts, Sean tried to keep his voice calm and replied, "The question is, have you?"

A little to Sean's surprise, his retort was met with chuckling on the other end, "It's time to get this show moving. The helicopters hovering overhead should let you know that we are approaching the bridge and heading for the open seas. I am well aware that the Coast Guard has a large cotillion waiting for us. We are going to need safe passage, and since she decided to call you from her little cell phone, you get to be responsible for that."

"And if I don't, another passenger dies...," Sean sighed.

"You're catching on quickly, boy," Chavez grinned into the phone and then paused to ask a question, "Say, why do you suppose she called you instead of say...911?"

"She knew I would believe her, I guess," Sean shrugged and couldn't hold back from adding, "And I would eventually find my way to and kick your ass."

The crowd of agents simultaneously winced at the flippant remark. Montgomery slid his finger across his throat to motion Sean to stop talking.

"Funny, but you shouldn't run your mouth to me, boy. I'll let you slide this once. Next time, your mouth is gonna cost you a life," Chavez snapped and abruptly hung up the phone.

"This is why we can't have a civilian in contact," Montgomery bellowed and turned directly to Sean, "Listen to me hotshot. You could have gotten someone killed. If that maniac does take a life because of anything you do, I will have you arrested as an accessory to murder!"

Before Sean could muster up a response, the mood was broken up with by a field agent waving a thin stack of papers. "Former Mexican Special Forces Ranger Rey Chavez!" the agent blurted out, handing the documents to Montgomery, "Most of his info is classified, it appears he used to perform duties for co-Mexican-American military forces as well as for the CIA. Went rogue a few years ago, turning merc. Landed on the payroll of Columbian drug lords to ambush a U.S. patrol and has since been suspected of countless crimes and terror attacks. He is a bad man."

"Thank you for the report, good work," Montgomery commended his man.

Sean looked anxiously at the group, "So now what do we do? What's the plan?"

"First off, there is no we. You and the wildlife guy stay out of the way. We will try and negotiate and hopefully minimize casualties," Montgomery replied.

"In the meantime, let them get out to open water?"

"Give him a false sense of security," Montgomery reasoned.

"You're gambling with innocent lives!" Sean protested.

"You don't have a say in this, we have procedures to follow," barked Montgomery.

"The procedure is to stand around and wait while a band of terrorists has their way with a boat full of passengers? They've caught the one that was able to reach out and call for help," Sean pleaded.

"Yes, your girlfriend. She was caught talking to you. I'd say whatever happens to her, you can blame yourself," the FBI director scolded.

The emphasis Montgomery placed on 'you' stung Sean. Her phone call might have cost her her life. Glancing up at the large

LCD panel, Sean watched as the Nagaremono sped toward Astoria. He was not convinced waiting for the vessel to reach the Pacific was the right idea. He also was not confident in Montgomery's negotiating abilities. His skin itched from the inside as his brain spun, unable to fight the helpless feeling that overwhelmed him. Sean's eyes streamed together his surroundings - agents and police officers scurried around frantically, a siege of on-lookers stood on the bank of the Columbia. In moments, it would breach the confluence of the chilly waters of the Pacific. All the while, the TV screen followed the path of the yacht as it sped closer to apparent freedom. It seemed to add up to a horrific conclusion with a crowd of spectators merrily watching the events unfold as though they were watching a reality television show.

Sean watched below as the Coast Guard boats peeled back to allow the Nagaremono passage in response to Manning's command. Just downriver, the nose of the Nagaremono pulled into sight. In the corner of his eye, Sean spied a bystander stop by the curb and hop off of his Yamaha sportbike.

Raising his view to the high-arching bridge, Sean fed his compulsion to act. Darting his eyes frantically around the staging area, he found what he needed. Slipping away from the crowd of agents, he stepped quickly to the rear of a rescue truck. Scooping up a coil of rescue rope, he slung it around his neck and sprinted for the parked bike.

Adam's eyes grew large as he saw Sean react. "Oh no...," he groaned, wincing as he looked away.

Montgomery, seeing Adam's reaction, turned to witness Sean run across the parking lot towards the unsuspecting motorcyclist. Stepping away from his bike to ask an attractive young girl in the crowd what was going on. Watching the action, the rider was oblivious to the man making his way towards him. By the time he turned, Sean had already rushed by and had pounced on the seat of the street bike.

"Stop him!" Montgomery screamed.

Sean turned his head, and with the turn of a key and the flick of a wrist, he was gone. The lightweight, powerful machine dodged the surprised crowd as it weaved through the parking lot heading towards Highway 101. Swerving right, Sean swung the motorcycle on to the ramp leading up to the 101 bridge and opened the throttle, launching him up towards the center point of the towering arch.

Over his right shoulder, Sean could see the Nagaremono slipping through the initial Coast Guard boats that lined the banks of the Columbia. Behind him, the sound of the gunning engines of the police cruisers in pursuit relayed to his ears that he didn't have much time.

Reaching the pinnacle of the tall bridge, Sean squeezed the left-hand brake, locking the motorcycle into a sharp, skidding stop. Wasting no time, he tossed the end of the rope he had hung around his neck through the rails of the bridge and began tying a series of knots. Working through the sounds of squealing brakes and shouts from the agents, Sean gave his rope a tug against the nest of knots he had fashioned and tossed the coil over the edge, just as the bow of the boat swept passed.

The footsteps of agents beat mercilessly behind Sean's back as he calmly placed his hands around the rope in rappel fashion. "Stop!" an agent ordered, drawing his weapon. Sean cast a single, nervous glance at the agents' direction and dove over the railing.

The force of the freefall caused Sean to slide thirty feet before his brake hand was able to clamp the line for control. His palms burned in searing pain from the violent friction of gliding over the rope, but his life demanded that he ignore the pain and continue squeezing down on the line.

Looking down, he saw the unmanned flying bridge of the boat - its tallest point - crawl out from under the bridge. Taking a deep breath, he quickly fed the line through his hands, rapidly descending towards the boat. As he neared the end of the line, a good twenty feet from his intended landing site, he let go. Tucking his body in, he hoped his aim was true. In seconds, his body slammed into the canvas top of the flying bridge. The taut canvas covering for the exposed captain's deck acted like a trampoline, sending Sean's slender body skyward once more.

Struggling to regain his breath, Sean stretched his arms out, hoping desperately to connect with the railing of the pilot station as gravity took control and brought him plummeting downward. His arms caught the edge of the canvas awning, and he was able to lock himself in place. He remained motionless as his lungs refilled with oxygen, and his heart rate slowed to normal.

Sean didn't have long to catch his breath before he heard footsteps ascending the teak steps leading to the flying bridge. Heaving himself completely atop the canvas covering, he waited for the owner of the footfalls to reach the bridge. Over the edge of his hiding space, Sean could see the dark hair of a man enter the upper captain's station. Assuming his landing had made enough noise to arouse the ear of a nearby guard, Sean sat on the balls of his feet, ready for action.

Quick footsteps to either side of the small, square roost told Sean the guard was likely looking over the edge of the empty bridge in hopes to see what caused the noise. Soon the footsteps made their way back to the steps leading to the deck below. Suddenly the man paused. Only the sound of the rushing wind broke the silence of the night air. Sean waited, hoping the man would make his way down the steps. His hopes dashed as the barrel of a gun was thrust violently and repeatedly in random patterns into the canvas top. Sean knew he would inevitably be struck by the steel snout and ousted.

Leaving his feet, he leaped backward over the edge of the awning. Catching the aluminum frame with his hands, he swung his body into the bridge. Kicking his feet outward, he slammed into the man below. Allowing momentum to work for him, Sean drove full force into the man, sending both of them and the gun scattering to the deck.

With the mercenary cushioning his fall, Sean recovered quickly and dove for the assault rifle that had landed between them. As he reached the weapon, the other man began to lift himself. Before the assault team member could rise off of his knees, Sean had grasped the muzzle of the assault rifle and swung it at the sentry, landing a blow to the man's head, leaving him motionless against the upper bridge steering console.

Sean paused for a moment, trying to decide what to do with the unconscious man. One thing he knew, he didn't want the mercenary coming back to haunt him. Digging through the storage bins under the console, Sean grinned wickedly as he found the solution to his quandary.

Twenty Three

A dam stood at the handrail of the Highway 101 bridge that spanned across the Columbia River in utter disbelief. Standing amidst a couple of dozen police officers and federal agents, they stared agape at Sean's antics. Below them, the long rope blew in the wind, pointing towards the Nagaremono as if it were a gangly, tattle-tale finger. The Fish and Wildlife officer watched in amazement as Sean clung to life along the awning and then ultimately taking one of the mercenary squad out.

What Sean did next, really shocked the crowd. Scanning the deck below him, Sean hoisted his captive up on his shoulders and carefully descended the ladder. Once on the deck, he squeezed a life-preserver over the mercenary's head and making his way to the stern, tossed the man overboard. Looking up to the bridge and over at the Coast Guard boats lining the mouth of the bay, he seemed satisfied that the captive would be rescued and slipped silently into the bowels of the boat.

"Arrest that man!" a red-faced Dick Beckett screamed, marching over to Adam, "He is an accomplice to that rogue idiot who is going to get himself and everyone on that boat killed!"

"Agent Raines has been with me the entire time, he was surprised as any of us as to Kendall's actions," Agent Dawkins declared.

"I don't give a damn what you think. I want him arrested!"

"My agent is correct, Mr. Beckett, Raines had nothing to do with Kendall's actions. He could be useful to this operation since he knows some of the hostages," Chief Investigating officer Manning said as he approached the scene.

Montgomery shot Manning a look of confused disdain, but gave way to his superior rank.

Before Beckett could respond, a black SUV came to a screeching halt near the crowd and an FBI agent holding a piece of paper jumped out. Running up to Manning, he exclaimed, "Sir, we have the invite list from the Foundation office. You better have a look."

Manning snatched the document from his agent and ran his eyes over the list. Closing his eyes tightly, he sighed as he read the name that had alarmed the agent. Oregon's Governor Roberts and Senator Johnson were listed among the invitees aboard the Nagaremono. "You've checked with his office?"

"Yessir, he's onboard," the agent affirmed Manning's concern.

"Who's onboard?" Beckett growled.

"It appears Governor Roberts and Senator Johnson are among the attendees of the wake for Harrison," Manning informed the Regional Director of the Department of Interior.

Beckett turned to Adam, "If your boy is responsible for the death of a United States Senator..."

"Shut up, Beckett," Adam dismissed the imminent threat from the Director.

As the Nagaremono passed through the mouth of the Columbia River past the Clatsop Spit and into the waters of the Pacific Ocean, Chavez itched to get his exit plan into motion. The first step was convincing the feds that he meant business and that the lives of the hostages were in direct and dire danger.

Hitting the redial button, the embittered mercenary waited for the connection to the foolish civilian that he had made his contact for this exercise. Chavez was shocked, igniting into an immediate rage when the voicemail prompt came on.

Slamming the phone on the desk in front of him, Chavez growled indecipherably. "Troubles?" Don Jenks asked glibly, grinning at his captor.

Chavez swiveled his head and glared at Don. "You think this is funny? A big joke? It's Don, right? From the ballroom?" Chavez snarled and grabbed Don by the collar, "Come with me!"

Shoving a very distraught Don towards the door, the furious mercenary burst out on the deck. Marching to the stern, Chavez pushed Don to the railing and yanking his handgun from his trousers. He stared defiantly at the crowd watching from the high-arched bridge the Nagaremono had passed under minutes before. Lowering the nose of the gun to the back of Don's head, he squeezed the trigger. Using the momentum of Don's slumping body, he flipped Don's legs, allowing the body to tumble over the railing and into the turbulent waters of the confluence.

Chavez returned his glare to the occupants of the bridge as he backed away, slithering inside the yacht's corridors. The sound of the Coast Guard's helicopters swooping to where he dumped the body clapped overhead. The mercenary ignored the commotion. He knew the feds had rules; they wouldn't touch him as long as he had hostages. He would keep the pressure on until it was time for him to disappear. And then, he would leave them with their hands full.

Sean crept along the teak floor of the hallway, trying to remain in the shadows. As he peered out onto the promenade deck, he retreated as footsteps approached his direction. He was mortified as the heavy shoes stopped mere feet from his hiding space. The figure dug in his pocket and produced a pack of cigarettes and a matchbook. As the man struck the match and stamped it out on the deck, inhaling a lung full of smoke, Sean's phone began vibrating wildly at his hip. His heart skipping a beat, he fumbled desperately to reject the call and turn the phone off. A glance at the call screen told Sean that it was Rey Chavez, the leader of the terror squad. Cursing silently, knowing he could not answer, he mashed the silence button on the tiny keypad.

Holding his breath, Sean looked on expectantly, preparing for the smoking man to hear the buzzing and turn to confront him. Letting out a sigh of relief, the retired lobbyist relaxed slightly as the man just outside of his hiding space continued on his patrol.

Sean slumped, not knowing what blowing off a mercenary like Chavez might mean, but he had no choice. If he answered, he would have been found, and Chavez would have known he was aboard.

The crescendo of footsteps slowly faded as the patrolling gunmen continued on his route, allowing Sean to again poke his head out into the open air of the deck. The slowly sinking sun still provided plenty of light, making being invisible a problematic task. Sean spied a utility closet a few paces aft of where he was lurking. Hoping it would be sufficient to stifle the sounds made by a phone conversation, he darted to the dark and twisted the brass handle. Relieved when the handle turned easily, he swung the door open and slipped inside.

The scents that met his nose told him the closet was used for cleaning supplies. Through the glow of his colorful LCD screen, he could see neat rows of solvents lining the shelves as well as a rack full of brooms, mops, and other items the crew would need to keep the boat in its gleaming condition. Punching the keys on his phone, he dialed the last number that called him.

Sean was shocked when the line was not picked up. He studied the screen in dismay as the call time blinked to an end with no response. His contemplation was short-lived as the deck outside his thin door was filled with activity. Sounds of pounding footsteps and scuffling permeated the closet Sean was holed up. As the footfalls passed by, Sean cracked the door carefully as his finger gripped the trigger of the assault weapon he was holding.

Sean was horrified as he saw a man being jostled to the stern and forced to the rail of the yacht. Without even a moment for Sean to react, the gunman squeezed the trigger and effortlessly flipped his victim into the waters below.

A knot the size of a grapefruit seemed to appear in the pit of Sean's stomach. The cold-blooded nature of the killing, the lack of any hint of remorse told him that the man or men that he was up against would not hesitate to kill an intruder, and very likely the hostages aboard. Swallowing hard, he carefully closed the closet door as the killer backed away from the railing.

"Oh, man," Adam exclaimed as he watched the limp body fall through the air and land in the chilly waters in the wake of the Nagaremono.

"If Kendall lives, I'm going to charge him as an accessory to murder! Your boy did nice work, Raines. He killed that man," Beckett barked at the Fish and Wildlife agent.

"Shut up, Beckett! Sean can't be blamed for the actions of a sociopath. That guy was probably looking for an excuse to show his might. Now he has your attention, and no one would dare act in fear of endangering the hostages," Adam defended.

"Now you're an expert in psychology and hostage negotiation? Get out of my face. I am this close to terminating you from the government payroll," Beckett growled, pinching his fingers together.

Placing his ear to the cold wood, Sean listened intently to try and discern if the footsteps would come his way or retreat into the bowels of the boat.

His strained ears failed to pick up any additional movements outside of his door. Sean held his breath as he grabbed the handle, readying himself to crack the door to survey the outer deck. Giving the slightest turn with his wrist, he nearly jumped out of his skin as a wild buzzing erupted from his pocket. Letting go of the doorknob, he leaned back into the little storeroom, trying to collect himself as his racing heart returned to normal.

Taking a deep breath, he answered the phone, "This is Sean."

"Well, hero. How's a little blood on your hands?" Chavez' voice sneered through the phone.

"I'd have to say that was unnecessary. How pathetic are you to have to prove yourself to a guy like me?" Sean blurted, his emotions carrying the message out before his brain could filter it.

"Listen here, you pathetic puke of a nobody. I hold the cards here! When I say move you move. When I call, you had better answer!" Chavez growled and added, "How many more lives would you like to claim by being a smart mouth?"

"Look, I want to help you get through this as clean as possible, okay? I don't want to cause trouble with you," Sean professed, hoping his voice was not carrying out on to the deck.

"Now that's the productive working relationship I am gunning for, if you'll forgive the pun," Chavez mocked glibly, then his voice returned to its cold, down-to-business tone, "Time to go to work. I want a single-manned zodiac to rendezvous at buoy 132. At which point, my team and I will board, and I will provide instructions for a helicopter to land at a location to be disclosed at that time. Got it?"

"Yeah, I got it. One question. Why won't the FBI just take you out once you're away from the Nagaremono?" Sean frowned.

To Sean's surprise, his ears were met with laughter, "I appreciate your concern. Let's just say I will be inviting a passenger that they will not want harmed."

"Who might that be?"

"Enough questions, boy. You have twenty minutes to get that zodiac on its way and procure a helicopter," Chavez snapped and ended the call.

With an ear to the door, Sean listened for intruding footsteps, but the deck was silent. Dialing the number Agent Dawkins had given him, Sean sank back into the corner of the closet.

"Kendall, is that you? Boy, are you in some deep...," Agent Dawkins' voice rang over the earpiece.

"Listen, I don't have a lot of time. Chavez says he wants a one-manned inflatable at buoy 132 in twenty-minutes. He also wants a chopper airborne, waiting for instruction," Sean cut in.

"Standard. We can take him out after the transfer," Dawkins replied as though all were according to FBI textbook.

"He says he is going to be toting a hostage. I don't know who," Sean reported.

"We've reviewed the guest list. It could be bad if he knows who he has on board. Could mean Hasegawa or one of Foundation's supporters," the FBI agent mused.

"Like Miranda," Sean muttered softly.

"I assume it's not safe for me to call you, so why don't you check in at regular intervals. Now sit tight, let us do our job," Dawkins warned, hanging up the phone.

"I don't think I can do that," Sean answered to the dead receiver.

Dawkins turned to fill Adam in as they walked back to the command unit, "I hope your friend knows what he's doing."

"I doubt it, but he's surprisingly resourceful for a little twerp," Adam replied, a faint smile washing across his face.

The scene in the command truck was one of managed chaos. Several agents milled about intent on their tasks, each flowing seamlessly around the other in the tight space. Dawkins found his man at one of the computer terminals.

"Hey Dan, do you have the guestlist for the Nagaremono?" the agent asked, slapping the tech on the shoulder.

"Yeah, sure. You need a copy?" Dan asked, turning to Dawkins and Adam.

"You read my mind, pal," the field agent smiled.

"It's in the tray," the tech said and returned to his work.

Snatching the set of papers ejected from the printer tray, Dawkins motioned for Adam to join him outside. "Here's the list, start going through it, I'll order our boat and chopper," the agent said, handing the print out to the Wildlife Officer.

As the FBI agent ambled off to fill in his superiors, Adam began scanning the guest list. Most of the names meant nothing to the big Fish and Game agent. His eyes stopped at Miranda's entry, and a few names registered with him from some of the Harrison articles he had read. Finally, towards the bottom of the list, one name stood out – Governor Gil Roberts.

"Uhh, Dawkins…," Adam called to the agent.

Covering the mouthpiece of his phone, Dawkins leaned in to read the entry Adam was pointing. The agent's eyes rolled back as he took in the data. Letting out a deep breath, he quickly terminated the phone conversation and motioned for Manning and Montgomery.

Twenty Four

Agent Dawkins' plea for him to remain inconspicuous fell on deaf ears; Sean couldn't sit tucked away in a closet when so many lives were in jeopardy, in particular, the one woman that made him care again. Inching the door open, he peered out on to the deck. The sun had plummeted over the horizon, casting crimson shards through the light evening clouds. The rapidly increasing shadows afforded the young retiree higher confidence in being able to maneuver about the boat without being detected.

Desperately wanting to determine the condition of the hostages and take stock of the band of terrorists, Sean snaked his slender body through the jagged shadows left by the emergence of dusk. Moving towards the bow, activity on the boat took a marked increase. Sean could hear a rumble of voices emanate from behind the closed doors of the ballroom. Edging nearer, he could see a man with a fully-automatic assault weapon standing just outside of the teak encased glass doors.

Reasoning that taking the guard out would raise premature alarm, Sean sunk back into the shadows that concealed him. He had to get to the ballroom to make sure that Miranda and the rest of the passengers were out of harm's way. Once there, he hadn't thought of a game plan. Tactical assaults were more up Adam's alley, and Sean was alone on this one.

Creeping along the dark corridors that stretched across the beltline of the luxurious cruiser, he studied the starboard deck.

Light spilled from a round window of the galley door, illuminating the shade-engulfed side of the boat. Lending a sharp ear to the teak walkway, he found the deck momentarily empty.

Seizing the moment, Sean sprinted to the galley door and pressed his head against the cool brass frame of the window. Peering inside, he found a single guard in the kitchen who was preoccupied with treating himself to a snack out of one of the stainless steel refrigerators. Tightening his grip on the assault weapon, Sean burst through the door, making a bee-line for the snacking terrorist.

The man looked up at Sean wearing an expression very much like the proverbial child caught in the cookie jar. Making an effort to retrieve his weapon slung behind his back, the guard was halted by the steel barrel held at his forehead.

"Not one move. I'll empty your skull right into this fridge!" Sean snarled as his free hand snatched the weapon off of his captive's shoulder and tossed it aside, "Get up nice and easy, if I can't see both of your hands I will shoot you."

Slowly, the mercenary backed away from the appliance and stood up with his back to Sean. Reluctantly, he raised his hands into the air. As he turned to face his captor, the man lunged at Sean, pushing the gun barrel away from his head. In nearly the same motion, he delivered a kick to Sean's stomach.

Reeling back from the kick, Sean fought to stay on his feet. Planting his back foot firmly against the tile floor, he steadied himself in time to prevent the terrorist from recovering the gun Sean had taken from him. Grasping his weapon by the barrel, Sean swung the gun like a baseball bat, connecting with the side of the mercenary's head in a fierce, bone-crunching blow. To Sean's relief, the man fell hard to the floor at Sean's feet, a silent, harmless mass.

Fearful that others might have heard the brief skirmish in the adjacent ballroom, Sean moved quickly to the kitchen door and peered through the window. Surveying the room, Sean counted three guards, none of them looking his direction. Satisfied that he was safe for the moment, he returned to his fallen enemy.

A quick search revealed a small back-up handgun strapped to the unconscious man's ankle and a wireless earpiece that the assault team used for onboard communication. Stuffing the tiny pistol in the waistband of his pants and fitting the receiver into his ear, Sean returned to the ballroom door. His eyes scanned the room, desperately searching for Miranda. With the abrupt end to their phone call, Sean's fears that she had been caught were intensified as his scan froze on Brett and the empty seat next to him.

Pulling away from the door and the view to the ballroom, Sean's head sunk. Not seeing Miranda in the crowd made his pulse quicken its already steady pace. Desperately, he tried to remember the layout of the boat from what he saw from the outside. Thinking from the perspective of the terrorists, he pondered what they might have done with Miranda and the other vital hostages. An unsavory list of possibilities sprang to mind - they may have her locked in a stateroom, Chavez himself might have her held at bay ready to be used as the next 'example', or Sean's least favorite, she may have been eliminated immediately in effort to extinguish a nuisance.

His thoughts shattered by a noise on the other side of the kitchen. Grabbing the assault weapon he had retrieved from the first battle, he strode over to investigate. A heavy storeroom door barred from the outside. Tapping the stock of the automatic weapon against the door, he called out softly, "Hello?"

At first, his feeble call met with silence. As he opened his lips to call out again, he heard rustling within the storage room and then a muffled, "Sean...is that you?"

Hurriedly, Sean began working on the locked bar that secured the door shut. Quickly exhausting any quiet options, Sean wasted no time in slamming the butt of the rifle onto the lock, springing the latch from the bolts that held it to the frame. A final swipe allowed the latch to fall free to the floor. Moments later, a very appreciative Miranda pushed through the door.

Without even thinking, the weary marine biologist flung her arms around Sean, giving him a tight squeeze. Sean gladly accepted the gratitude, but as good as her embrace felt, he knew they could be discovered at any moment. Gently releasing from her hold, he began pulling her towards the door to the deck. "We've got to get you out of here," he said, his exasperated voice telling of his concern.

Miranda stopped him short, "Wait, I can't leave Carrie here!"

Sean paused for a moment, sorting through the brief moral dilemma. Despite his own urgings, somehow, he knew, "Of course we can, don't be silly" - was not a response that Miranda would find agreeable. Relenting, he asked, "Where is she?"

"She's passed out in the storeroom," Miranda replied meekly.

Rolling his eyes, he handed Miranda a weapon, "Keep an eye on the deck side door. I'll go get her."

Hastily, Sean disappeared into the storeroom and quickly reappeared with the limp body of the still snoozing Carrie. "What the…oh, she stinks!" he exclaimed as he carried the over-indulged woman across the floor.

"The coast is clear, what's the plan?" Miranda asked, peering through the window.

Sean looked at her a little confused and shrugged, "I don't know, I kind of figured I would just dump her over and hope the Coast Guard would come along and pick her up."

"That's your plan?" Miranda exclaimed incredulously, "She's passed out, she'll drown!"

"Nah, I heard drunk people float," Sean answered flatly and motioned for her to open the door to the deck.

"Really?" Miranda asked as she pushed through the swinging doors.

Sean burst through behind her and at the rail, released the drunken passenger the thirty feet to the chilly waters below. "I don't know," Sean answered.

"What!" Miranda shrieked as she looked over the edge.

Before Sean could respond, a powerful beam of light flashed along the deck. The beam sweeping along the rail closed in quickly; Sean had only an instant to decide whether they followed Carrie or not. With a mighty tug, he flung himself and Miranda back into the galley.

Landing on the floor, the two stared at each other. Fear and frustration washed over Miranda. With Sean's earpiece crackling to life, he knew they had no time to waste. Whoever was up top shining the beam had instructed one of the ballroom guards to make a sweep along the deck bordering the galley.

Sean jumped up and pulled Miranda to her feet. Handing her his cell phone, he urged her to hide in the storeroom and call in Carrie's position. Running to the ballroom door, he was just in time to see it swing open and a guard storm through.

The man saw his compatriot on the floor first, by the time he turned and saw Sean, the former lobbyist was leveling out his swing with the assault rifle. The blow caught the man on the chin, knocking him backward toward the swinging door. Not wanting to alarm the other ballroom guards, Sean grabbed his foe's shirt, preventing his fall.

Allowed enough time to recover, the mercenary grappled with Sean and drove his lighter assailant to the floor. Sean landed hard on the tile, losing his grip on the assault rifle. The mercenary jumped off Sean and scrambled for the weapon. Seeing Miranda reappear from the storeroom, he called, "Toss me that bag of flour!"

"What?" Miranda shrieked, confusion breaking across her face.

"Just do it!" Sean snapped as his opponent reached the assault weapon.

Miranda snatched the bag of flour and whirled it through the air. Sean whipped the handgun he had stowed in the waistband of the small of his back and raised it as he hooked the sack of flour with his left hand. Capping the sack against the muzzle, he pushed the gun forward, poking through the paper bag, white powder spilling down like a waterfall. Just as the mercenary readied his assault weapon to fire, Sean pulled the trigger on his gun. A muffled pop filled the air along with a shower of white granules. Through the milled wheat haze, Sean could see that he had hit his mark. The guard lay on the floor, a trail of blood streaming from a hole just above the bridge of his nose.

Whirling to Miranda, he asked, "Did you make the call?" The astonished woman managed to nod her head. "Good, let's get out of here!"

Grabbing her hand, he tore for the deck once again, determined to leap overboard. Once again, he was stopped short.

Chavez grinned at the transmission over his earpiece. Turning to the room, he announced, "Seems we have a celebrity among our guests," into the earpiece, he ordered, "Bring our distinguished guests to the Com Room."

Chavez sat in the captain's chair and scratched his chin glaring at Hasegawa, "Looks like you're going to get some company. And I, I get a marvelous new bargaining chip."

In minutes, the door to the bridge opened, and a sharply dressed man with thin, but well-coiffed grey hair was escorted in by a shorter man holding an assault weapon. Yet another gunman prodded a second man, wearing a permanent scowl. Chavez waved for them to enter the communications room and sit next to Hasegawa. Reluctantly, the man complied as his escort gave him a hard poke to the ribs for encouragement.

"Governor Roberts, Senator Johnson...welcome. You two have important roles in this evening's events," Chavez cooed as he poked at the keys of the computer terminal. "Let's see...during your stint as a U. S. Senator prior to your governorship, you voted against the Military Advancement Bill – twice, Governor Roberts. Nay on the proposal for an air attack on Syria 'too costly' you said and instead suggested for a small contingent of ground troops. After approving selling arms to the Syrians in return for a yes vote on the Global Warming Treaty. Ha!" Chavez scoffed, "and I'm sure you view me the animal."

"Is that what this about? Retribution for a difference in politics?" Governor Roberts inquired.

"You gave the enemy the weapons that they used against my squad! You sentenced us to death, you pious piece of crap!" Chavez bellowed, drawing his massive Desert Eagle pistol from its holster and leveling it at the senator, "We went in there with forty troops, with your inferior armor against US-issued weapons at your recommendation - only five of us came home!"

"I am sorry for those losses! Every day, we face difficult decisions. Every day, we have to balance the maximum benefit with least cost using the intelligence we are provided...," Governor Roberts defended.

"You damn politicians wouldn't know 'intelligence' if it bit you on the butt!" Chavez declared and then to Robert's surprise, let out a wicked grin, "Relax, Governor. I am not here for you. I didn't even know you were aboard until a few minutes ago. That said, you are a fine convenience. Your presence will provide a safety blanket and I…I appreciate that."

"I agree with your choice to use the governor and me as bargaining chips. You may gain additional latitude if you let the rest of the mourners go," Senator Johnson suggested.

"Thank you for the words, Senator, I think I have things under control. No, you have arrived just in time to watch Mr. Hasegawa transfer his offshore holdings into my accounts. Isn't that right, Hishiro?" Chavez continued.

"I will do no such thing," Hasegawa scowled.

"Wrong answer Hishiro. You see, with the governor and senator here, I don't have much need for you...," the mercenary smiled briefly, and then his face deteriorated into a scowl, "Now give me those damn codes!"

Hasegawa assumed this still to be part of the mercenaries' overzealous portrayal and remained resolute. Staring blankly ahead, he said nothing.

With a nod, one of Chavez' men slammed Hasegawa's hand to the table and fired a bullet into the back of his palm. Instantly, the freight magnate's screams filled the room.

In horror, Hishiro looked up at the terror squad leader. Chavez tapped on the computer terminal in front of the frightened tycoon demanding compliance. His tech had the offshore bank sign-in page open. Reluctantly, Hishiro's shaky hand began pressing the keys on the keyboard.

Satisfied, Chavez turned away. Hitting the 'speaker' button on his phone, he dialed Sean Kendall. After the third ring, Sean's voice finally offered a meek "hello".

"Mr. Kendall, conference me with one of the G-men. I have business to conduct," Chavez ordered.

"What's going on there?" Sean asked.

"Just do as you are told!" Chavez growled.

A few seconds passed before FBI Field Director Manning's voice came on the line.

"Where's my helicopter?" Chavez asked.

"These things take a little time, Chavez. We'll have it for you," Manning assured.

"I'm not in the mood for playing games agent. Forget about the boatload of whining hippies that could wind up suddenly dead, I have someone else in front of me that you might find quite valuable," the mercenary warned.

"What are you talking about?" Manning asked.

"Ah, being coy...that's what I hate about you government types, you're all so dishonest," Chavez responded, turning to Hasegawa, he chided, "Why don't you tell him, cap'n..."

"Screw you, you bastard!" Hasegawa spat.

"Hmmh!" the mercenary grunted indignantly and raised his eyebrows expectantly to his man at the terminal beside Hishiro. The tech grinned a triumphant nod back at his boss. Without skipping a beat, Chavez raised his pistol and shot Hishiro in the head.

"No!" both Sean and Manning seemed to shout at the same time.

After a pregnant pause, Chavez informed his phone audience, "The unfortunate end to our dear businessman, but I have to tell, it might just as well have been Governor Roberts here. Twelve inches or so to the right and...well, you get the idea, I like to be obeyed. Since you boys are not here, the governor will suffer the consequences should you not comply. Buoy marker 132, that gives you about fifteen minutes!"

Chavez terminated the call and ordered his men to lock the governor in the Com Room.

Twenty Five

As the phone went dead, Sean realized he had to get to Senator Johnson and Governor Roberts. Recalling a skiff stowed off of the stern, he devised a plan that would settle a pair of issues. Urging Miranda to hurry behind him, he sprinted to the back of the boat. Positioning Miranda in a cover position, he hastily began tending to the rigging that held the skiff. Releasing the tie-downs, he began unwinding the crank of the winch. Inch by inch, the small boat began to descend the line.

Close by, Miranda steadied the assault weapon Sean had handed her. Unsure of his intentions, she assumed they would descend the line after the boat and escape the dangerous pirates of the Nagaremono. As Sean worked on lowering the skiff, Miranda eyed the forward deck cautiously.

Miranda's heart fell into her stomach as a shadow appeared from the left, and a guard whistled as he rounded the corner in his circuit of the promenade deck. For a moment, the two locked eyes in surprise. Seemingly in slow motion, the mercenary began raising his gun. "Sean!" a hoarse whisper left Miranda's mouth as she released a torrent of bullets toward the approaching man.

Sean wheeled to see the guard dive to the deck behind a bench used to stow life vests. Scooping Miranda around the waist, he swung her over the rail and let her drop ten feet into the lowering boat. Spinning back around, he fired a random flurry of shots in the direction of the guard. Hearing the alarm through his earpiece, he knew reinforcements were on their way. Pulling a knife from his pocket, he revealed a glistening, sharp blade and sliced the nearest hoist line.

Below, Miranda barely had time to recover from the harsh landing before she scrambled to cling desperately to one of the skiff's seats. Her fingers clutched the edge of the wooden plank as the line that held the bow fell to the water below, causing the boat to swing wildly, dumping most of its contents. Above, she heard a volley of shots traded back and forth as she hung midway down the Nagaremono's stern.

Bullets continued whizzing by Sean's head as the guard recovered from his dive onto the teakwood deck. Abandoning his efforts with the dinghy, Sean darted for cover behind a heavy steel box riveted to the deck of the boat. Leveling his confiscated handgun over the steel box, he fired off several shots toward his adversary. Dropping to the deck, Sean rolled out from behind his protective barrier and positioned himself in front of the terrorist who was firing erratically toward where Sean had been. Biting his lip, Sean ignored the poorly aimed stream of bullets and took his time to line up a clean shot. Squeezing the trigger, Sean saw the first shot knock the mercenary back, momentarily halting the barrage of lead flying back at him. Firing a kill shot, Sean landed a bullet cleanly in the mercenary's forehead, toppling the man backward in a heap on the Nagaremono's deck.

Rushing to the stern rail, Sean looked over to see Miranda dangling from her precarious perch by her fingertips. Hearing the pounding footsteps of the assault team's reinforcements, Sean wasted no more time with the winch, slicing the remaining line, allowing it to fall free toward the waters below.

Miranda and the tiny boat slapped hard into the turbid confluence of Tongue Point Channel and Young's Bay. Sean watched long enough to be sure Miranda was okay and spun to avoid another assault team confrontation. Knowing the speed of the Nagaremono would quickly put distance between the terrorists and the skiff, Sean was satisfied that Miranda would be picked up safely.

Wanting to avoid being overwhelmed by greater numbers, Sean spied the upper deck. Darting for the box that the guard used for cover, Sean used it as a launchpad for him to leap towards the upper deck. Not quite reaching the floor of his intended mark, his hands slid down the high-polished fiberglass wall until they reached a bracket that supported the flag bearing the Hasegawa Corp. moniker. Pulling against the brass hardware, he lunged up to the floor of the upper deck.

With an exhausting heave, Sean vaulted over the edge of the higher deck just as a pair of mercenaries rounded both corners of the stern. He watched silently as the two thugs discovered their dead team member, who lay in a heap, just under his perch. The two gunmen scanned the fallen, knowing Sean could not have gone past them. Rushing to the stern, they saw the boat bobbing in the swells of the Nagaremono's wake. Assuming their prey had slipped over the side with the tiny boat, they abandoned their search and returned to their original assignment as they reported to Chavez that the scourge had fled in the dingy.

A mile away, Adam watched the news footage on the LCD panel of the Communications Van. The federal agent felt very helpless as the video captured Sean in a dangerous gun battle at the rear of the Hasegawa Holdings yacht. He nearly jumped through the screen of when the camera from the news chopper panned in on Sean, dumping Miranda onto the dingy and her eventual violent descent to the waters below. Before he could even flag for help, the Coast Guard had a zodiac and a Jayhawk helicopter tearing across the bay to her aid.

Releasing his tight grip on the rail of the bridge, he watched the Nagaremono, and its terrified occupants slip past the entrance of Baker Bay and closer to international waters. He wasn't sure what his friend had running through his mind, but the burly wildlife officer wished he was on board to help him. Standing by as a spectator, he began to understand his friend's misguided decision to board the yacht as it passed under the bridge. Working through their massive playlist of protocols, the FBI had left all the cards in the hands of the terror squad – hoping a massacre did not take place on board the ill-fated boat before they were finally able to go in and clean up the mess.

As he watched the Nagaremono slip further away, a figure stepped out of the crimson shadows of dusk. Turning, he saw the radiant figure of Rachel York stepping towards him. Even in the turmoil of crisis, she had an air of calm stoicism surrounding her. She always seemed in control and annoyingly calm to Adam, yet he was thrilled to see her. She represented a tremendous ally to his beleaguered friend and offered a voice of authority in his defense.

Casting an even smile, she spoke softly, "He's in deep this time."

"You can say that again," a worried Adam admitted, "He's usually in over his head, but this…"

"I know. I'll do what I can. This thing is pretty big. With the governor and Senator Johnson aboard, there is no room for error," Rachel replied.

"For Sean's life expectancy, there is no room for error," Adam scoffed.

"He'll do alright," Rachel sighed, for the first time showing Adam a chink in her resolute, stonecast emotional armor, "We have to believe that."

"Ms. York!" an angry voice bellowed from behind them. Into the setting light, the scowling visage of Stanley Beckett approached them.

"Hello, Stanley," Rachel responded with a twinge of annoyance in her voice.

"I figured you'd stick your nose in this. Your boy is threatening the life a governor, how do you feel about that?" the Department of Interior Director snarled.

"It feels great, Stanley, what to do you expect? As far as the governor's wellbeing, what exactly have you done to preserve his likelihood of survival?" Rachel quipped.

"Why…there are rules to follow. That fool-headed civilian has no clue of protocol and profiling of a terrorist!" Beckett snapped.

"And you know exactly what this man wants and what he is about to do? You have such sharp insight that you know by sitting on your butt in a command tent that just leaving things be the governor will pull through unharmed, right?" Rachel fired back.

"He's in too deep this time, York. If he somehow manages to live through this, he's going to jail for a very long time. You can't help him out of this one," Beckett barked and spun away before another word could be uttered.

As Adam and Rachel watched the DOI director walk away back into the darkness, Rachel turned to Adam, "He's right, you know, Adam. Sean didn't just stumble into this one. He walked in, right in the middle of a federal crime scene. I can't help him. I can only hope he survives."

Twenty Six

Chavez looked up from the terminal. He was salivating over the massive deposits made to his numbered offshore accounts - each coded with enumerators that only he and his tech were privy. His marveling was put on hold as gunfire erupted on the stern of the Nagaremono.

Frowning, he barked to his two men standing watch over Hasegawa's crew, "Find out what the hell is going on!"

The two men darted out of the pilothouse and down the steps to the main deck. Turning his gaze to the genuine crew of the Nagaremono, Chavez ordered them onto their feet and prodded them into the small communications room that housed Governor Roberts and Senator Johnson. Locking his hostages in, he spun to face his tech that was waiting at the computer terminal.

"Safe and sound, sir," the tech said, gesturing to the screen.

"Yes, Ramirez, I suppose it is," Chavez agreed with a faint smile. His visage never changing, he produced his handgun and brought it to aim at Ramirez' chest. The tech's eyes grew large in fear as his boss pulled the trigger.

As Chavez completed his task, the captain he employed called out, "Buoy 132, sir!"

"Hold her steady. As soon as our transport arrives, load the Governor and the crew and head for the helicopter LZ, whether I am there or not," Chavez ordered. "Senator Johnson will stay with me."

"Sir? You want us to leave without you?" the captain asked, obviously baffled.

"If I am not there," Chavez assured. Getting a nod from the pilot, the mercenary turned his attention to the commotion in the stern. Depressing the transmit button for his earpiece, he asked, "What's going on out there?"

"Sir, there's no one here, but Diggs has been shot, he's dead," Noches responded.

"Probably a trigger happy sniper. Search the deck, and then do a roll call with the rest of the team. I have a task of my own to tend to," Chavez ordered his men and added, "I have ordered the captain to take the governor and board the transport as soon as it arrives and head to the LZ. When you're done, join the others."

Hearing a chorus of 'ayes', he shut down the terminal that had so recently made him a multi-millionaire. Outside, the long-low honks of the buoy told him that the Nagaremono was almost in place. Deciding to keep his own hostage, prodded Senator Johnson ahead of him, "You'll be coming with me, Senator." Turning towards the doorway of the pilothouse, he was surprised to see an unfamiliar figure blocking his path. More to his surprise, the figure pointed one of his own men's assault rifles at his chest.

"Going somewhere, Chavez?"

The mercenary stared hard at the figure, struggling to recognize the voice until a brief smile cracked his lips, "Mr. Kendall. A hero, after all."

"I'm no hero, just doing what I have to do. Now, if you'll have your men drop their weapons and release...," Sean began evenly.

Unwavering, Chavez ordered with a calm in his voice, "Kill the governor!"

The man charged with guarding the revered politician, raised his gun towards the politician.

"No!" Sean yelled as he swung his weapon away from Chavez and towards the guard. A quick pull of the trigger sent two bullets into the side of the guard, knocking him to the ground.

The brief misdirection was all the well-trained mercenary needed to reverse his fortune. In a split second, he had unholstered his Desert Eagle sidearm and delivered a pair of slugs into Sean's chest. The young retiree flew backward through the doorway. Like a rag doll, his body was flung against the brass railing and tumbled limply down the flight of stairs to the deck below.

Satisfied, Chavez turned to the remaining guard and the captain, "Take care of the governor, and get the men off of this boat."

With haste, the lead mercenary left the room and descended the stairs to the main deck. With hardly a glance, Chavez stepped over the crumpled body of Sean Kendall and made his way toward the staterooms in the bow of the Nagaremono as he prodded Senator Johnson forward. Off the port side, the buoy bobbed with the swells alongside the Nagaremono.

Whatever pleasure Chavez had enjoyed in how things were fitting into place, faded as the call came in over his earpiece. "Sir, this is Noches. Raul, Padilla, Diggs, and Ramirez – they're not at their posts…and they're non-responsive."

"What the hell are you talking about? I knew about Diggs and Ramirez, but...damn!" Chavez sighed in exasperation, "Well, who is left?"

"Sir, Valdez in the ballroom, Jenks in the executive stateroom, Smitty guarding Governor Roberts, Captain and myself," Noches replied.

"I'll be damned, Kendall was a busy boy," Chavez muttered to himself.

"What's that, sir?"

"Nothing. Carry out the orders as we drew them up. Get to the helo and take the governor with you. If anyone is not on the zodiac at exactly nine, you leave without 'em," the mercenary lead ordered, "That means me, Captain...whoever."

"Yessir."

At the bottom of the stairs, Sean Kendall's body was slumped into a limp heap. Stifling a groan, he rolled his body over and listened intently to the transmission over the earpiece. His mind bounced erratically from taking a physical inventory of painful body parts, to wondering who was in the executive boardroom, to hoping Miranda made it to safety.

Slowly maneuvering his hands underneath his body, he pushed himself up into sitting position. A stream of blood trailed from his head to the teakwood deck. He raised his hand and found the wet, sticky source on his forehead. Ignoring the gash for a moment, he circled his mouth with his tongue; the taste of blood was profuse, inviting him to take a quick count of his teeth. Satisfied they were all there; he spit the effluence of fluids out of his mouth and quickly crawled into a dark crevice where he could collect himself in relative safety.

In shallow breaths, he tried to regain his composure. His chest ached as though an anvil had crushed it and were pinning him to the ground. Tearing open his shirt, he grasped the Velcro tabs of the Kevlar vest Agent Dawkins insisted he and Adam wore and sprung the vest open. Relief rushed into his throbbing ribs as the pressure alleviated. Gingerly, he poked at his chest, wincing with each touch.

His breathing settled into its normal rate, Sean realized that aside from a wicked headache and a potentially cracked rib, he was otherwise okay. Rising to his feet, his thoughts returned to Senator Johnson and Governor Roberts. He had to find them. He knew the governor was being ushered toward the zodiac. He had to get to him before the craft took off for shore.

Hobbled and weaponless, Sean exercised tremendous caution as he snaked his way through the corridors of the yacht. Off of the starboard side, the incidental rescuer could hear the ocean's swells cut by the vee hull of a semi-inflatable Coast Guard craft. Ignoring his injuries, Sean picked up his pace; he wanted to find the senator before the guards convened at the zodiac. He liked his chances with fewer mercenaries to grapple.

Adam could feel the tension thicken as the news cameras attached to the helicopters overhead followed the zodiac streaking through the Clatsop Spit and out into the open waters of the Pacific. Manned by a single, Coast Guard officer armed simply with his side-arm, the small craft made a bee-line for buoy 132.

In the Maritime Museum parking lot, a small army of agents assembled, each heavily armed in full assault regalia. Slowly, the rotors of the waiting Chinook helicopters began to turn. Breaking off into teams, the agents started filling the helicopters, ready for action.

Despite DOI Director Beckett's protests, Agent Dawkins waved Adam aboard the Bell-Ranger helicopter the agents flew in. A glance over to Rachel York told the Fish and Wildlife officer that the stoic Assistant Regional Director elected to remain onshore to greet and comfort Miranda, who had been picked up by a Coast Guard rescue boat.

Rachel had ensured that Adam's service weapon had been restored to him after initially having been confiscated upon his arrival. Adam chewed nervously at his lip. More shots had been reported aboard the Nagaremono, and twenty minutes had passed without communication from Sean.

Adam would like to have taken comfort in the notion that Sean could take care of himself, but he knew his friend's propensity for getting in way over his head. Adam, himself, had served in the Marines as a Special Forces member and at least been trained in combat situations. Sean had been a paper pusher all his career, hardly a match for a well-trained, well-armed band of mercenaries. The only fighting he had experience in was between accounting and sales departments.

Still, Adam reasoned that his friend had proven himself quite capable during the Seattle affair. Somehow, the wiry Sean Kendall had held his own. Adam was not quite sure how, but he did. Despite keeping himself in excellent shape, Sean was not the most physically imposing man. A solid athlete in his youth, Kendall's thin frame was more adapted for speed than power; Adam feared this disadvantage could prove fatal aboard the Nagaremono. The sinking thought caused Adam to wish that he were aboard the yacht fighting alongside his friend.

Adam's physique was just the opposite of Sean's. At an imposing six-foot, six inches, the muscular Fish and Wildlife agent had become quite used to his brawn neutralizing situations, though he'd prefer to diffuse most with wit and humor. At times, it was that same humor misplaced that created many of the predicaments he encountered.

As Adam climbed in his monochromatic black helicopter, he cleared his mind of concerns and concentrated on the task ahead. The best thing he could do for his friend now was to help take out the terrorists alongside the FBI agents.

Impatiently, they waited inside the helicopter for their cue. "What are we waiting for?" Adam asked, his frustration in waiting on the sidelines boiling out.

Agent Dawkins turned, "We have been informed that the terrorists have Governor Roberts and are taking him with them. If they detect any action on our part, they will kill him."

Adam's face was grim. The mercenaries knew as long as they held an official like the senator, the FBI would be stifled, "Isn't there anything we can do?"

"As long as the governor is used as a shield, not much. We can hope they make a mistake," Dawkins replied grimly, "In the meantime, we position ourselves to take advantage if they do."

Sean tried to ignore the pain screaming through his bones and muscles. If he could keep the senator off of the zodiac and out of harm's way, then the cavalry waiting on shore, on the water and in the air, would have an easier time of apprehending the rogue cadre.

Poking his head carefully around the corner, he found one of the mercenary detail securing a line to a cleat on the deck of the Nagaremono. Presumably, the Coast Guard zodiac was already waiting. Two more men joined as the captain wheeled Governor Roberts around the corner. The captain checked his watch, seemingly unhappy with what it displayed. After some deliberation, he appeared to give the command to board the craft waiting below.

Sean looked on, his mind trying desperately to develop a plan of attack as the first of the terrorists descended the line to the inflatable craft at the water's surface. The remaining three thugs debated about how to get the governor down to the water taxi. Sean wondered where their soulless leader was. Slipping into a dark corner, he kept vigil over the governor until an opportunity to strike and rescue presented itself.

Nudging Senator Johnson forward at the point of his Desert Eagle automatic, Rey Chavez guided them both deep into the bowels of the boat. Finding the engine room, he paused, looking over his shoulder. Confident that he had not been followed, Chavez focused his attention on the senator, who seemed at the mercenary with calm indignation. "I'll give you credit, Senator, you are taking all of this very well," the mercenary sneered, "But, this is as far as I take you." Raising the butt of the handgun, Chavez slammed the pistol hard on the back of the senator's head, rendering him an unconscious ball at the mercenary's feet.

Glibly stepping over the senator, Chavez entered the bay of the engine room. Removing the small pack that he carried, he placed a clay-like brick to the side of the wall. Sliding a charging electrode gingerly into the gray block, and allowed a thin roll of wire to unravel in his hand as he stepped out into the hallway and leaned into the wall. With hardly a moment's hesitation, he pressed the transmitter button.

The Nagaremono was instantly rocked with a violent explosion, causing the craft to list abruptly as the engine room immediately began taking in water. With his usual casual demeanor, Chavez calmly slid down the dive mask over his face and strode into the rapidly flooding room.

Falling into the advancing pool, the mercenary fought the surge of ocean water and allowed himself to submerge. Pressurizing his tank, he bit down on the mouthpiece and swam against the current and out through the open hull that he had just created. Turning on his underwater light, he swam away from the Nagaremono and towards his rendezvous site.

Following the coordinates on the waterproof GPS device strapped to his wrist, Chavez quickly found the submerged vessel waiting for him. A tiny, jet-black submarine about the size of a killer whale, opened up to allow him to swim inside. Once in, the compartment closed, and water drained as the cabin was pressurized.

Chavez worked his jaws to relieve his ear canals and opened the interior hatch to take his place in the vacant passenger seat as the driver was already maneuvering the sub away from the area near buoy 132 and away from the swarm of law enforcement that gathered along Astoria's coastline.

Twenty Seven

Noches had begun to make the crude loop around Governor Roberts with the drop line tied to the stern's high-mounted winch. His efforts were erased by a tremendous explosion ripping through the boat. Dropping the rope, he looked at his compatriots to see if they knew the cause. The looks of surprise washing over each of their faces told him that they, too, were not anticipating any such occurrence.

Before any of them could even comment, the boat listed wildly to the port side, sending the men sprawling on the deck away from the rail. Sean, who had instinctively grasped the first solid object he could reach in front of him, remained on his feet. Instantly recognizing the moment of chaos of the vessel lurching as a momentary advantage, he launched himself down the deck toward the group floundering on the teakwood floor. Grabbing the collar of the governor, Sean dragged him hastily away from his captors.

The first terrorist to recover began firing a spray of hastily aimed shots in pursuit. As the others rose to join him, their ears flooded with the frantic call of the yacht's emergency system, declaring the water that the Nagaremono was taking on. As Sean and the governor disappeared into the swinging doors of the galley, the mercenaries elected to join their partner on the zodiac and take their chances of reaching the helicopter without the governor as their human shield.

In seconds, the boat filled with screams from inside the ballroom as black smoke, and horrific noises joined the complaining groans of the yacht as it pitched towards the waterline. Sean and Governor Roberts scrambled to the ballroom door, fighting the erratic motions of the sinking boat. With a strong kick, the bolted door crashed open, revealing a riotous group of mourners.

Frantically, the passengers flailed around the room, trying to gather their fellow attendees and herd them toward the main doors that had been blasted open with one of the dining chairs. Sean found Miranda's friend Brett trying to urge order and calm, directing escapees to the closet, which held the life jackets before they made their way to the deck. Seeing the bearded man in action, Sean knew that he had found the help that he needed to ditch the governor.

Sean hustled the governor to join the crowd and find a flotation jacket for himself.

"This thing smells funny!" the governor winced as Sean handed him the safety vest.

"Just think how bad you're going to smell if you don't wear it, and we find you onshore all dead and bloated," Sean snapped back, pushing the life jacket further into the governor's grasp, turning to the grizzled Foundation member, "Take care of him, Brett, he's a feisty one."

Satisfied leaving the governor in Brett's hands, the battered and sore Kendall tore down the deck for the stern staterooms searching for where Chavez had taken Senator Johnson. Skidding on the teakwood that now angled steeply with the sinking yacht, he turned down the hallway. As he reached the lower level toward the engine bay, the boat lurched forward as the bow completely dipped below the waterline, sending him sprawling onto the floor.

Looking at the devastation, Sean wondered out loud, "What in the world did Chavez do?"

About to retreat, Sean's eyes widened in horror. Just below the surface of the water, he could just make out a ghostly face. Collecting himself, Sean focused in on the apparition. Recognizing the submerged face as that of Senator Johnson, Sean launched himself off of the stairs and into the water. With two strong kicks, he was able to reach out and grab the senator by his jacket lapels. Heaving backward, Sean pulled Senator Johnson to the surface. Swimming with long, smooth strokes, Sean quickly got the senator to the stairs and out of immediate harm. As he prepared to administer CPR, Sean studied the water. The most recent lurch likely brought in the extra amount of water to cover the senator; he would not have been without air for very long.

Clearing the senator's respiratory pathways, he rolled him on his side, releasing the fluid in the unconscious man's lungs. To Sean's relief, Senator Johnson instantly began to sputter. Suddenly, the senator's mouth opened wide, and a torrent of seawater expelled onto the stairs.

Holding the senator's head up, Sean felt a large bump. Brushing wet hair aside, Sean found a slight cut next to the bump. Chavez had used Senator Johnson as insurance and dumped him outside of the engine room. But where was Chavez?

"Kendall?" Senator Johnson choked.

"Yes, Senator, you're going to be okay. Let's get you out of here. Can you stand?" Sean asked.

"Yes, I…I can stand," the senator replied and allowed Sean to hoist him up. Together, they ascended the stairs, and Sean quickly guided them towards rescue. As they passed the berthing suites on the second level, the two men could hear panicked screams from further down the hallway.

"Let me get you to safety, sir," Sean demanded, cutting the senator off before he could argue.

Within moments, Sean had the senator with the remaining crowd, receiving instructions from the Coast Guard. As Sean handed the senator off and a seaman assisted the senator to safety, Sean turned to find the voices that were calling for help below. Just as Sean reached the steps leading down to the levels below, the yacht let out a menacing groan and tipped radically on end, sending Sean sprawling down the steps, landing in a trough of water. Sean's ears met with invigorated pleas for help and heavy banging from the hall. Fighting his way up the steep pitch, he arrived at a massive, beautifully carved door.

Rising to his feet, he threw his body into the door, ramming it with his shoulder, slamming into the thick mahogany door. Bouncing backward, Sean realized he had only accomplished hurting yet another part on his already tender body. The door loomed before him, unphased by the attempt to free it from its hinges.

Glancing around the hallway, Sean tried to find something he could use for a tool. Remembering an axe affixed to one of the deck boxes on the stern, he sprinted down the hall. Topside, Sean could hear a tremendous amount of activity. The zodiac containing the terrorists screamed toward shore; from the mouth of the Columbia, Coast Guard rescue boats gunned their way to the Nagaremono as passengers flung themselves over the side, away from the rapidly submerging yacht. At the same time, Dolphin and Chinook helicopters roared overhead. Sean's legs wobbled as they contended with the gravity of the boat continuing to slip nose-forward beneath the cold and turbulent waters of the Pacific Ocean.

Carefully finding footholds, Sean crawled forward, the pitch of the yacht nearly making the boat rise vertically from the waterline. Climbing his way to the deck box, Sean retrieved the axe he was seeking. Letting go of his hold, he allowed gravity to send him speeding back to the entrance to the hallway. Bracing his feet against the door jam, Sean was able to steady himself just outside of the boardroom door. Sean quickly went to work, chipping away at the impressive artwork of a solid teak door. Behind the lustrous wood, he could hear the inhabitants urging him on. In a few well-placed strokes, Sean had carved a tight hole around the handle, allowing the heavy door to swing on its hinges, banging to a triumphant end against the interior wall.

Still wielding the axe, Sean hopped into the boardroom where he found several men scrambling to escape the onslaught of furniture sliding along the floor, threatening to pin victims to the down-facing wall, trapping them to continue the ride to the depths of the Pacific as passengers for life. Next to the large picture window, Sean saw one of the trapped men fruitlessly hammering at the ballistic glass with a chair.

"That's obviously not working," Sean said to no one in particular.

"How are we going to get out of here?" one of the sharply dressed men growled.

Sean paused for a moment. The boat's descent completely submerged the bow. He realized that they had to go over the stern, but wasn't sure these men would make it up the steep incline.

"Hey bud, who da hell are you?" one of the men asked. "Are you with the Coast Guard or something?"

Intending to focus on the task of rescue, Sean paused in spite of himself, to study the man. Despite all of the turmoil, the man still wore his suit, which was remarkably unblemished in light of being tossed around a sinking boat. Almost equally remarkable, the man was calmly holding a high ball glass filled with Scotch as he braced his foot against one of the tables to keep from sliding.

"Nope, I'm just here to help," Sean replied.

"Don't get me wrong. I'm glad to see you, pal," the man said and sipping his Scotch, "So where's da rest of your help?"

"I'm all you got. So, if you want to put your glass down, let's find a way to get you out of here," Sean retorted, his voice almost humored by this strange man.

The man responded by slamming the rest of the Scotch down his throat and tossing the highball glass over his shoulder, "I like you, to da point. Most people waste my time kissing my butt. Better to be direct during times of crisis, such as this."

"I'm a bit more concerned about saving our butts, frankly," Sean said and rubbing his chin, he faced the group, "I'll go up top and rig a line, watch for it to drop and use it like a handrail. Can you all swim?"

Most of the men nodded, though each wore an expression of dissatisfaction on their faces. Wasting no time, Sean scrambled to the doorway. The pitch had become such a sharp angle, the weary rescuer hoisted the axe and slammed the blade into the floor as far up the hallway as he could. Using the axe handle as his own rail, he pulled himself along the vertical plane. Pulling his knee up to his chest, he worked his foot over the axe blade and used it as a crude foothold that he pushed off with and launched himself forward, catching his arms in the doorway of the outer deck. Pulling his feet up behind him, he was able to roll against the outer wall, allowing gravity to pin him safely deckside.

Moving quickly, Sean threw himself at the rail nearest to the wall, catching it with his hands. Sliding up the banister, hand over hand, he was able to reach the remnants of the sling that had held the boat he used to help Miranda escape. Snagging the rope, he pulled it through the reel and quickly affixing it to the base of the rail, he cast it down to the men waiting in the boardroom.

Beside the Nagaremono, the Coast Guard crews were busy plinking the wake attendees out of the water. One of the Chinook helicopters swung over to Sean. In seconds, a guardsman in an orange dry suit was being dropped from a winch until he was eye-level with the civilian. Sean quickly related the situation and received a hearty "thumbs up" from the Guardsman.

Soon, the red face of one of the high-rollers popped through the open doorway. Exhausted from heaving himself up Sean's rescue line, he flopped on the deck. Quickly, the rescuer zipped down to assist. In moments, they were harnessed together and were hoisted up to the open bay of the helicopter. One by one, the men were snatched from the clutches of the Nagaremono until Sean, too, was relieved from his station on the boat.

Twenty Eight

The pit in his stomach swelled into a painful knot as Adam watched helplessly as the Nagaremono filled with water and slipped further and further into the sea. As the passengers were retrieved from the water, no reports had come in identifying Sean as one of them.

In the opposite direction, the Fish and Wildlife officer saw the zodiac cutting through the water towards the awaiting Blackhawk helicopter. Each second that ticked by, sped the group of terrorists closer to their escape, while the platoon of agents and federal officers watched helplessly on the sidelines, still assuming the governor was on board, the agents refused to take any action that could endanger the politician.

Grinding his teeth, Adam felt as though he were going to explode. The big man suddenly wished he had boarded the boat as Sean had so rashly done, at least he wouldn't feel like a powerless bystander. Checking his weapon for the sixth time, he was startled to hear Sean's voice over the radio as the cartridge slammed back into place.

"This is Sean Kendall. I am aboard the Coast Guard cutter Faith. I have Governor Roberts with me. He is safe, unharmed, and now secure...I repeat, Governor Roberts is okay!" Sean's weary voice rattled over the airwaves.

Within seconds, the blades of the helicopter picked up speed, and the skids began to lift off the ground. Outside Adam's window, he saw several more tactical helicopters rise to join them.

"Strike teams, you are cleared to go! Team One, on the zodiac crew, pilot take off from rendezvous as soon as contact is made with the boat. Exercise caution, they still have one of our agents piloting that craft. Team Two, head to the Nagaremono, she's underwater, I want divers down there for a search, assist the Coast Guard with rescue and then sweep for body retrieval and evidence," Manning ordered.

In moments, the sky filled with the fast-moving Ranger helicopters joining the rescue Chinook and news choppers. Two of the craft raced to intercept the zodiac as another sped to the site of the submerged luxury yacht.

Adam's stomach lurched from both the rapid movements of the helicopter as well as the anticipation of the impending action. Though his instructions clearly framed for him to observe only, he prepared himself for the forthcoming battle.

As the lead craft closed in on the zodiac, a sharpshooter freed his first bullet, plinking the agent piloting the boat in the chest, sending the unsuspecting agent tumbling into the chilly waters. Adam's stunned face belied his horror.

Agent Dawkins spun to Adam, his face hard and serious. To Adam's relief and surprise, Dawkins cracked a smile, "Rubber bullet, didn't want any of the good guys caught in the crossfire!"

The events began to unfold with incredible speed, the strike teams executing with precision, reminding Adam of his days in Special Forces. Descending upon the zodiac, agents streamed down rappel lines, assault weapons drawn. A brief shootout ensued, but a couple of well-placed shots from the snipers suspended in the open bays of the Ranger helicopters encouraged the remaining members of the terror squad to give up and allow the federal agents and Coast Guard crews closing in on the water to take them into custody.

Agent Dawkins looked back at the wildlife officer and smiled, "Well, that's done."

Across the bay, the remaining passengers and crew of the Nagaremono safely boarded the Coast Guard cutter fleet and Chinook helicopters. Among them, a very irate Frankie Caputo. He cast the Nagaremono a disdainful look as it completed its slow and insidious journey, slipping below the grey surface of the choppy Pacific waters.

As the Coast Guard vessel Faith pulled alongside the dock of the Astoria Maritime Museum, Sean Kendall was already waiting at the gangplank. When the Faith was near enough, he leaped to the wooden pier and panned the awaiting crowd.

Amidst the throngs of policemen, officials, news crews, and curious spectators, a team of EMTs burst through and immediately pulled Sean aside for an assessment. Sean was okay with that, for he knew Lead Agent Manning and DOI regional director Beckett had their own men waiting to process him on countless charges.

As the team of medical technicians went to work, paying particular attention to Sean's cracked ribs, Sean saw a familiar face part through the crowd. Dressed in her usual impeccable style - seamlessly integrating formal elegance with subtle yet undeniable sex appeal - Assistant Western Region Director of the Department of Interior Rachel York strode on a beeline up to Sean Kendall.

Momentarily keeping Manning's agents at bay, she flashed Sean a rare public smile. Relieved to see his friend, Sean waved off the EMTs attending to his injuries. Despite their protesting, the medics collected their gear and moved to assist the first Coast Guard rescue boat that was just pulling up to the dock.

"I'm glad you're okay," Rachel confessed softly, "A boatload of terrorists? This Dudley-Do-Right routine of yours has really gone to your head."

"I guess the 'wait and see' game wasn't working for me," Sean replied evenly.

"Apparently. It looks like since you didn't get yourself killed, you've bought yourself a healthy paid vacation courtesy of the federal government," York retorted. Looking up, she saw the FBI agents step forward, "Even I can't help you out of this one."

"The feds have anything in the Caribbean?" Sean feigned a weak smile.

An agent interrupted the two as he stepped forward with a pair of handcuffs in his hand. Respectfully, he glanced at Rachel, "Excuse me, miss."

With no alternative option, the assistant DOI director stepped aside. The agent with the cuffs approached Sean, "Sean Kendall, I am Agent Thomas with the Federal Bureau of Investigations. I am placing you under arrest for obstruction of justice, assault and manslaughter. We will be taking you to Oregon Health Sciences University Hospital where your wounds will be tended to and then transfer you to a federal prison to await arraignment, is this clear?"

"Yes, it's clear," Sean said softly with a feeble nod of his head.

Placing the handcuffs on Sean's wrists, the agent elected to allow Sean to hold his hands in front of him to avoid aggravating his cracked ribs while his partner finished reading Sean the Miranda Warning script advising him of his legal rights.

"I would like to accompany him," Rachel declared suddenly, almost catching herself by surprise.

The agents began to stammer a response before seeing Agent Manning nod his head in approval. Escorting the agents, Sean and Rachel to the awaiting helicopter, Manning spoke, "You've got stones, Kendall. I suppose I could see why you did what you did, but I can't say the powers that be will see it that way. You're lucky to be alive. You're also lucky that more innocent people didn't get hurt out on that boat."

The lead agent faced Sean, a stern look offered up between tight lips, "I also think you may very well have saved the lives of most of those people on the Nagaremono, not to mention handed us the capture of the entire terror cell. Not sure what I can do, but I can tell you I'll do what I can."

"Thank you. I know you will," Sean replied and allowed the agents on either side of him to lead him into the helicopter. Dawkins jogged over after ensuring Adam would be given a ride back to Portland and hopped into the helicopter.

As Rachel climbed in next to him, Sean looked at the crowd that had gathered to see who was being carted away. Just as the cockpit door shut, he saw Miranda twisting her way through the crowd. Her face did not hide her concern. Her cool blue eyes pierced the dark window of the helicopter, disappointed not to have the opportunity to find out for herself if he was okay. Helpless to respond to her, Sean watched as the helicopter lifted into the air and spun towards the Coast Range and the distant city of Portland.

Twenty Nine

S hedding the thick neoprene wetsuit, Rey Chavez enjoyed the warmth of the SUV that transported him eastward on Highway Twenty-Six. His driver had been waiting for him as instructed, near an inlet between Astoria and Seaside. The narrow channel allowed the small sub to surface with minimal risk of detection. Chavez wasted no time exiting through the hatch and jogging over to the already running Suburban.

"What now, boss?" the driver asked.

"I have a private bird waiting for me at Hillsboro Airport, and then I disappear into anonymity, very wealthy anonymity," Chavez smiled.

"You gonna retire, boss?"

"Yes, I am. I am going out with a very nice pension," the mercenary replied and added, "There'll be a nice bonus for you if I get to the airport without problems, and you watch my back until I'm off the ground."

"You betcha Rey. You'll have no problems today," the man at the wheel promised as he navigated the twists and turns of Highway Twenty-six.

Adam found Miranda as she was turning away from watching Sean's helicopter take off and disappear into the cloudy night air. The expression she wore told of her concern. "He'll be okay," the fish and wildlife officer tried to console her.

Shrugging, Miranda shook her head slowly, "He did it again."

"What's that?" Adam asked.

"Comes rushing in and saves the day," Miranda replied.

"Yeah, he's a genuine boy scout," Adam agreed, a thoughtful grin crossing his face.

"Worse," Miranda sighed, "I think my friend is right...he is Rambo. Only without, you know, all the muscle and military training."

Adam started to laugh, but sensed from her tone that her assessment of his best friend was not intended to be complimentary. "This is a bad thing...."

"It can be a very bad thing. I have lost way too much in my life. I can't...he's going to get himself killed," Miranda fumed.

"So, you do still have feelings for the runt," Adam inquired.

"Of course, I do," Miranda snapped, "Yet, it's just so wrong in so many ways."

"Like, he's responsible for shattering your relatives' lives, especially Jeb's death?" Adam asked bluntly.

"Wow, Mr. Raines. You sure don't pull any punches," Miranda said, obviously taken aback by the straight forward questioning.

"Not when it comes to people I care about getting hurt. Let me tell you, lady, Sean can handle all the crap dished out by those terrorists out there and Beckett's threats of jail a lot easier than the way you left him hanging. He may be a bit impulsive, but I'll be damned if the guy's heart isn't in the right place!" Adam blurted out, a little surprised himself for laying into her so hard.

Miranda opened her mouth to respond, the words in her head seemed to twist into a ball that wouldn't seem to fit into any type of cohesive statement. Taking in a deep breath, she turned away for a moment. As she collected herself, she looked at Adam and tried again, but this time, a voice from the Command Center vehicle stopped her.

"Hey, Raines, we may have got something here!" Agent Manning called out.

Adam and Miranda instantly ceased their conversation and ran over to the FBI field commander.

Manning paused as he looked at Miranda, but in interest of time, decided to continue, "Our divers have not been able to locate Rey Chavez, the presumed leader of the terrorists. Those captured on the zodiac consistently swear that he did not board with them."

The agent waved his cell phone, "We received an interesting report. A man walking his dog called in claiming he saw a tiny submarine submerge in an inlet in Warrenton, about ten minutes south of here."

"You think Chavez had a sub waiting for him?" Adam asked, stunned.

"It's possible. That might explain why he was so adamant about meeting at Buoy 132. It was a rendezvous point," Manning admitted.

"He used his crew as bait!" Adam exclaimed.

"It would seem so," Manning nodded, "We have the Coast Guard scanning with sonar and requested a Portland-based Air Reserve AWACS fly over."

"That might help track down the accomplice, but if the sub was submerging, it had recently surfaced, probably to expel this Chavez guy," Miranda reasoned.

"Yeah, and had another guy waiting to drive him away - south to Mexico, north on 101 to Canada...," Adam added.

"Hmm...You're right. We'll shut down the highways, do a search. They'd only have a twenty-minute head start at best," Manning agreed and spun to enter the command truck, "Thanks, I'll keep you guys informed."

As the FBI commander disappeared to call out his orders, Brett and a woozy Carrie found Miranda and began to browbeat her in accepting a ride home. A fleet of buses had been chartered to transfer the passengers home once the medical staff had cleared them.

"You going to be alright?" Adam asked as Miranda reluctantly allowed herself to be dragged to the waiting transportation.

Looking back, obviously exhausted and conflicted, Miranda responded, "Yeah, I'll be okay. Look, tell Sean...tell him...."

Adam let her mind rest for the time being, "When you're sure of what you really want to say, tell him yourself." His words were rewarded by a nod as Miranda boarded the bus.

He looked on, hoping she would resolve her thoughts, one way or another for the sake of his friend.

Department of the Interior Regional Director Stanley Beckett watched Adam Raines make his way over toward the Command Center. Beckett was determined to impart control over his subordinate. He stretched his legs to intervene. "I think your job is done here, Raines. Your friend is off to jail, and you should feel fortunate that you are not cuffed right alongside him."

"Mr. Beckett, with all due respect, it's a shame you do not value the talent around you," Agent Manning interceded, as he opened the door to the monochromatic black-trimmed truck "Agent Raines, even Kendall - despite his overzealous lack of judgment, have been of great help to my team and I. I would appreciate his continued insight for a little while longer if you don't mind."

"I'm sorry the Bureau is incapable of managing an investigation on their own, nevertheless, if Raines can help you, so be it," Beckett retorted with a wave of his hand to dismiss Adam and then paused, "Raines, I'll want to see you in my office tomorrow morning. We will discuss disciplinary action."

"I told you Beckett, no more spankings, they make me a little uncomfortable," Adam jeered at his boss.

Adam and Agent Manning watched an irate Stanley Beckett stomp off in the direction of the car waiting to take him to the airport. Turning to Adam, Manning whistled, "You two sure don't like each other, do you?"

"Ol' Stanley and me...I don't know. He's a tight sphinctered little dude. I'm pretty sure he whistles when he farts. Not sure he likes anyone, especially those that undermine his authority. Since the whole Seattle thing, he's been breathing down my neck," Adam shrugged.

"I know the type. We've got them in the Bureau. According to them, there are only heroes because they followed the orders of some has-been behind a desk," Manning nodded.

"Maybe. I like to think that they remember the field and how dangerous it can be. They don't want those they are responsible for to come in to harm," Adam replied thoughtfully.

"You're a good man, Raines. You could join my team anytime," Manning smiled.

"Be careful what you ask for," Adam laughed.

A young agent in a dark suit strode hastily towards them, "Sir, the Coast Guard AWACS plane has located the sub. It's heading towards a freighter about five miles offshore. They're sending out an air and sea intercept team."

"Good, hopefully, we can shake some answers out about where Chavez is headed," replied Manning, "Keep me posted, we may have a tiny window to snag him."

"And if we miss him?" Adam asked.

"A mercenary with his experience? He'd be long gone...."

Sean and Rachel watched the Columbia River flow by as they stared out of their respective windows. When they did talk, they had to share their words with the rest of the flight crew over their headsets. Despite the silence, Sean felt comforted by Rachel being there. The Assistant Regional Director of the Department of Interior Western Region was as steadying a figure as she was alluring.

Turning to her side of the helicopter, Sean was met with a slight smile. Knowing her as he did, Sean figured Rachel was already strategizing his defense.

"I will make some calls as soon as we land," Rachel assured Sean, her hand landing on top of his.

As Agent Dawkins' voice called through the thick headphones, Rachel's hand slipped smoothly away, "I have a feeling Manning will put in a good word for you. He didn't care for your involvement at first, but you kind of won him over in the last couple of hours. If you ask me, you need a good psych eval, not a visit in front of a judge!"

Dawkins' laughter rang through the helicopter, giving Sean's thoughts a healthy reprieve.

The laughter was quickly broken up by lead agent Manning's voice ringing through the airwaves, "Agent Dawkins, this is Manning. I have just received word that Chavez might be headed towards the Hillsboro Airport. We have picked up his getaway sub pilot, and he indicates a driver picked him up in Warrenton, and they were headed east on Highway Twenty-Six. He's supposed to have a private jet sitting there waiting for him."

"We are almost due north of the airport. We could be there in ten minutes," Agent Dawkins responded.

The jet-black helicopter tilted abruptly as the pilot swung the nose to the south, leaving the Columbia River basin for

Portland's West Hills. The agent piloting the craft made the necessary communications with the control tower to allow unobstructed air access to land in the parking lot at an Intel plant that sat adjacent to the airport. Receiving the okay, the pilot wrapped around the manufacturing facility in an attempt to avoid a visual line with the airport.

Once on the ground, Agent Dawkins turned to Sean and Rachel, a bit unsure of what to do with them. It was a clear deviation of protocol to divert a prisoner in transit away from their intended destination. "You guys hang tight. I'll leave Agent Hill here while I check things out. The airport is right beyond a fence on the other side of this building. With any luck, Chavez wouldn't have seen us land and I will be able to get the drop on them," turning to the pilot, Dawkins continued, "Local PD is waiting about a quarter of a mile away, I'll call them if I need back up. You get babysitting duty, Hill."

Dawkins flashed a quick grin as he jumped out of the helicopter and made his way around the building towards the airstrip. The Hillsboro Airport was a small facility primarily accommodating small executive jets as well as private planes. Intel and Nike, the two prominent Portland-based businesses utilized the airport frequently to shuttle guests and employees around the country.

Thinking strategically, Dawkins knew it would be a challenge to locate Chavez without being identified himself. Contacting the airport controller, they had narrowed down the hangars that had planes available for departure within the hour. The agent would start with the earliest scheduled departure and work his way forward.

Finding the entrance for the first steel building, Dawkins slid up to the window-less door. Unfastening the loop for his holster, he pushed the door forward. The heavy door exhaled a loud creak as it swung open. Dawkins felt his chest tighten with his entry so rudely announced. Instantly he unholstered his pistol and slipped through the doorway.

In the center of the small hangar, a Gulf Stream V personal jet had just finished being loaded as a half-dozen passengers waited to climb aboard. The flight assistant froze as he saw the man with the gun enter the room. The luggage hatch he had just been loading, swung back on its hydraulic arms behind him.

Responding to the flight crew's reaction and the gasps of the would-be passengers, Dawkins clicked the safety on his pistol and produced his identification. "I'm Agent Dawkins, I'm with the FBI," he declared and quickly launched into his purpose, "I'm looking for a man who would arrive within the last twenty minutes or so, is there anyone aboard the plane or in the hangar?"

The flight assistant was the first to respond, stammering, "N-no, I mean, well...the pilot...he's in the cockpit."

Agent Dawkins followed the attendant's hand, pointing to the cockpit, "Would you call him out here, please?"

"S-sir, could you come out here please?" the assistant called after poking his head into the cabin of the jet, "There's an FBI man that needs to see you."

Dawkins grimaced at the nervous flight assistant's declaration, gripping his handgun, the agent prepared for the worst. Eying the open cabin door intently, he was both relieved and disappointed to see an older Caucasian man in his fifties appear.

"There's no one else here?" Dawkins persisted.

"No, sir, except for the front door you came in, we keep the hangar locked up tight. Who you see is who you have," the assistant answered.

"Very well. There is a dangerous terror suspect that we believe is trying to fly out of here. All flights are grounded; you won't be cleared to leave the hangar until we find him. Please stay inside and lock the door behind me," the federal agent was stern and concise with his notice, knowing he had to move on quickly to catch Chavez.

Without waiting for the hesitant chorus of affirmatives, Dawkins exited the hangar and carefully made his way to the next site on the list of scheduled flights. As he neared the door to Hangar Four, Dawkins could hear the sounds of the pre-flight activities starting. Drawing his gun up tight to his shoulder, he pressed lightly on the door of the hangar. A horrific squeak filled the air as the rusty hinges of the steel door announced his arrival. Rolling back behind the wall, he allowed the door to swing closed. His heart leaped into his throat as the hangar entrance was peppered with bullets. Into the receiver strapped to his left shoulder, he called, "I have found Chavez in Hangar Four! An unknown number of assailants have opened fire, the engines for the jet have been started."

"Roger that, Agent Dawkins, we have ground units closing in, and additional air support is en route," the bureau tech responded.

"What is their ETA? That plane is about to take off!" Dawkins bellowed.

"Ground in three, air in five," came the report.

"That's not soon enough!" Dawkins snapped as he rolled out of his position and began to make his way around to the side of the building. He could hear the jet engines wind up as the plane taxied out onto the tarmac. By the time his support showed, Chavez and his crew would be long gone. "Hill, did you hear that report?"

"Yes, we heard," the pilot replied.

"That is unacceptable. I am going to need back up now!" Dawkins called as he circled the far side of the hangar, cautiously making his way to the front where the jet was waiting revving its engines, "I need your help Hill!"

"What about Kendall?"

Dawkins paused, his pulse-pounding. Backing up to the steel wall of Hangar Four, he slid to the front corner, jet exhaust fumes filling his nostrils, "Uncuff him. He may be of help."

"What?!"

"Just do it! I'll take the heat!" the agent snapped.

"Roger that, we'll join the flank in two," the pilot replied, grabbing his gear, he tossed Rachel a small set of keys, "Uncuff Mr. Kendall, he's coming with me."

Thirty

Chavez impatiently prodded his pilot to get the jet moving towards the runway. "We're ready, sir, had to get the right oil reading first," the pilot replied.

Looking out of the cabin door that had yet to close, the mercenary waited for an assault. He kept his attention on the open hangar bay door, as well as the building's far corner for the agent that pushed his way into the hangar moments before. As the jet rolled forward, an enormous sense of relief washed over him. The highest risk portion of his getaway had now been completed with little difficulty. Surprised that no team of agents was rushing the runway, he closed the cabin door. Whoever entered the hangar door must have been acting alone. His remaining men would dispose of him quickly enough, perhaps they already had.

"Let's get the hell out of here," he called smugly to the pilot.

"Yessir!"

As he settled into his seat and fastened his belt, the wheels of the small jet began rolling forward. As soon as the plane began its taxi, it lurched forward wildly, flinging its passengers sprawling into the seats in front of them. "What's happening?"

"I don't know… it's the front landing gear. I think the tire has blown!"

"What? Get us in the air anyway!" Chavez shouted.

"C-can't, sir. There is no way to get up safely without our nose gear. We can't even get up to speed without tearing this plane apart!" the pilot reported.

"Damn it!" in a blur, Chavez was out of his seat and motioning for his cousin seated across the aisle from him to follow.

Snatching his assault rifle from the overhead bin, he stumbled to the cabin door as the plane skidded to a swerving stop. The door swung open with the mercenary swiftly following it, within an instant, he was on the other side of the ground level nose, using its extended wheel for cover. Pointing his gun in the direction of the hangar, he searched for something to target.

Through the scope, he saw his team stream out of the open hangar door and move to the shadow shrouded side where Chavez assumed the shots that took out the landing gear came from. The lead man in the small team of three tossed a small object in the direction of the corner of the hangar and took cover behind a steel drum. In seconds, a tremendous blast shook the tarmac as a grenade showered chips of asphalt shrapnel through the air.

Following the blast, the team moved quickly around the corner, and a volley of gunfire ensued. Using his time-tooled instincts in combat, Chavez knew this distraction was his best chance to getaway. Motioning to his cousin to follow, he streaked away from the fray and slipped behind a maintenance shed nearest the tall chain-link fence that surrounded the airport. As more gunfire erupted in the alley adjacent to Hangar Four, Chavez and his cousin darted for a small thicket of bushes lining the fence. With a couple of well-placed snips from a wire cutter, the two mercenaries stole away from the airport, leaving the chaos and attention behind.

Agent Hill and Sean ran full speed across the parking lot and around the Intel building. As the Hillsboro Airport came into view, they saw the Gulf Stream jet begin to roll down the tarmac towards the first runway. As the engines began to pick up intensity, a gunshot rang through the air, followed by the horrible sounds of sheet metal grinding against the blacktop.

"Dawkins shot out the front landing gear. May have been our only chance at detaining Chavez!" Hill called out to Sean.

"That means he is going to have a whole bunch of attention coming down on him!" Sean answered, his lean, athletic legs surging with a burst of speed that put him well in front of the pilot. Pushing against the panicked crowd that was trying to exit the airport, Sean leaped up onto the baggage counter and vaulted over and onto the other side. Sliding down the baggage shoot, Sean's guess proved right, as it placed him right on the tarmac. Landing hard on the pavement, Sean tumbled and rolled, but sprang back on his feet quickly. Taking cover so that he could survey the situation, he heard the panting pilot behind land hard on the asphalt as well.

"Ahhh!" the pilot screamed and grabbed his right ankle.

Sean spun to check on him. The pilot cursed at himself and admitted, "My ankle, I think it's broken!"

Sean looked away for a moment as an explosion rang from the row of hangars scarcely a hundred yards away. Turning back to the pilot, "Toss me your gun!"

"What? Hey, it's one thing to have let you loose, but...."

"Your man is going to die out there without some help, now give me your weapon!"

Hesitating for only a moment, the pilot knew Sean was right. Reluctantly, he tossed the Ruger in the air and propped himself up as he watched the fugitive he had been transporting streaked down the tarmac like a track star.

Sean raced up to the first hangar, slamming his back into the wall as he cautiously rolled his body forward to peer down the runway. He saw two men leave the cover of steel drums and make their way to the corner of Hangar Four. Their backs to him, he sprinted to the next line of protection, a service truck parked outside of Hangar Three. Checking his weapon, he found a bullet in the chamber and released the safety.

Dawkins ducked into the shadows lining the hangar wall. He knew that after disabling the aircraft, any men Chavez may have left behind would be on him in moments. No sooner had he slipped into the dark folds of shade, a small pinecone-shaped object came rolling his way from the front of the hangar. Dawkins launched himself towards the rear of the building as a concussive blast filled the alley between Hangars Four and Five. Covering his head, the agent felt the stinging rain of concrete and steel shrapnel from the grenade pelt down on him. Little bits of burning debris melted through his clothing and embedded into his skin. Without time to worry about the pain, he readied himself for the oncoming attack.

Rolling into a defensive firing position, he accepted the meager cover the alley provided him, a discarded propane tank waiting to be hauled away for refilling. From the direction of the grenade's entrance, two shadows emerged from the smoke. Each held fully-automatic assault weapons in front of them. Dawkins knew they would intend on being quick in their elimination of him so that they could commence with their escape.

Checking his clip, he counted six shots left, he would have to target carefully. The men entering the alleyway separated into opposite sides, each taking cover near either hangar. Dawkins tried to find an angle where he could take a shot without losing his protection, but his assailants had superior positions. He would have to wait for them to make a move and hope he could drop them before they got to him. Years of exhaustive training fought to keep his heart rate down as he prepared himself. Diving away from the grenade left him to take cover hastily, and the propane tank was a less than adequate solution.

The first shot hit the steel tank Dawkins huddled behind, the second shot came from another angle. They knew where he was, and they were going to squeeze him to one side or the other.

Shot after shot ricocheted throughout the alley, forcing him to burrow to the very center of his protective screen. He was pinned down, unable to get a shot off against the barrage. Out-positioned, outmanned, and outgunned, he waited for them to move forward, which they would, one at a time, until one of them had a clear target. Desperately, he tried to think of a way out. Suddenly, his thoughts were broken by a new shadow from behind him at the rear of the hangar. As he turned his head, he saw a third gunman wrap around the corner of the building, his gun barrel lined up directly at him. Dawkins swallowed hard, waiting for the inevitable end to his life.

As suddenly as the shadow appeared, the unknown assailant fell before he was able to take a shot. Replacing the gunman was Sean Kendall, who was motioning for the agent to roll to his right and take out the Hangar Four gunman. As Dawkins twisted, he heard a flurry of shots behind him and one of the assault rifles which had had him pinned down, ceased firing. Firing off each of his remaining shots, Dawkins peppered the side of Hangar Four. A volley of bullets exchanged across the alley, as the agent's clip emptied, he felt a metal ball rip its way into his shoulder, immobilizing his right arm. More bullets whizzed over his head as his empty gun dropped uselessly to the concrete floor.

The red glow emanating from the muzzle of the rapidly firing assault weapon was lined up directly at his exposed position. His options exhausted, he tried to roll away, against the pain of his shoulder. Before he could move, a shadowy figure caught his eye as it leaped over the steel dumpster that was shielding the gunman. The spray of bullets left Dawkins' direction and bounced randomly around the alley until after a brief silence, one final shot rang. Gone were the frenzied sounds of bullets echoing off of the steel walls, instead they were replaced by the sounds of footsteps making their way forward.

A single dark figure emerged from the dense shade of Hangar Four. The silhouette was framed by the blinking runway lights behind him, to Dawkins' relief, the assault weapon hung silently pointed to the ground instead of at him. "Kendall?"

"Yeah, you okay?" Sean's voice called back.

"I caught a slug in my shoulder. My whole right side's pretty useless. What about Chavez?" Dawkins asked.

"Not here. Must have used this diversion as his escape route," Sean replied.

Before another word could utter between the two, dozens of policemen and agents swarmed the alley and stripped Sean of his weapons, pinning him to the ground. To Sean's boot-level view, it seemed that armed agents flowed endlessly onto the scene of the once fierce gun battle. Once the alley and adjacent hangars were confirmed clear, Sean was brought to his feet.

Dawkins okayed the agents to allow Sean over as medics tended to his bullet wound. "Thanks, Sean. If you hadn't…man, I was a goner for sure," the agent managed a weak grin.

Before he could respond, Sean's hands were returned to cuffs, and he found himself in front of a verbal firing squad. Several ranking officers from the FBI's Portland contingent joined with Manning and Beckett, who had caught up to them from the coast.

DOI Regional Director Stanley Beckett was incensed when he arrived at the scene. "What the hell is going on here," Beckett screamed after hearing how the events at the airport unfolded, "How could prisoner-in-transport be released and then handed a weapon? I want the agents responsible brought up on charges - aiding and abetting a fugitive, insubordination, interfering with a federal investigation…."

"Now, hold it there, Beckett. I had Kendall released, and he ended up saving my life!" Agent Dawkins interjected from the EMT gurney he was being treated on.

"Good for you, agent!" snapped Beckett, "But where I've been trained, you don't turn prisoners loose and hand them a loaded gun. You're fortunate he didn't shoot you himself. Or run away or…."

"I didn't run, away because I have nothing to run from!" cried Sean.

"You, you shut your mouth. You have the right to remain silent, anything you say...." Beckett spat at Sean.

"Shut up, Stanley!" Rachel York stopped him short. She strode up behind the group, helping the hobbling helicopter pilot to the scene.

"Will you people please quit interrupting me?" Beckett bellowed.

"Maybe if you had anything worthwhile to say," a well-dressed man in a long wool trench coat retorted as he appeared through the crowd.

"Senator Johnson, it figures you would stick your nose in this," Beckett grumbled.

"While admittedly beyond the bounds of civil authority, it appears Mr. Kendall has once again saved lives your men were incapable of saving. Just as he had done earlier today on that ill-fated boat today," the Senator from Oregon declared, "If all citizens were as responsible and patriotic as Kendall, well, maybe this nation would be better off."

"That's real nice Senator Johnson, but save the rhetoric for your next campaign. With all due respect, your power is not going to save this, this criminal this time," Beckett responded defiantly.

"The esteemed senator's opinion indeed won't save Kendall from facing charges, but mine will," Lead Agent Manning approached the group. Beckett stared at the Field Director with his mouth agape. "His actions today may have strayed from stringent legal interpretations, but he intended to assist with my investigation as a key witness. In a time of dire crisis, my agents empowered Mr. Kendall as consistent with the statute for emergency reserve as a Federal Deputy under my command."

"You've got to be kidding me!" fumed Beckett, "This is complete and utter bull, and you know it."

"Not according to my report, so unless your office wants to challenge the Bureau's authority...," Manning cocked his head questioningly.

"I was on the chopper, that's how I saw it," Rachel shrugged, backing the FBI Field Commander.

"He is still under arrest from the matter earlier today," Beckett protested.

"Today's events are my jurisdiction, I revoke the charges against Sean Kendall," Manning replied flatly.

"This is not the end of this!" sneered Beckett as he turned and stormed away from the group.

"I suggest you keep your nose clean, Kendall. I can't promise federal prosecutors won't reinstate the charges, but you will have my full support," Manning said.

"Thanks, Manning," Sean flashed an appreciative smile.

"Off the record," Manning sighed, scanning the group, "Thank you."

The Lead Agent turned his attention to oversee the search of the airport grounds. The hangars and terminal were scoured by an enormous team of local and federal officers, while a square mile grid surrounding the airport was locked down by roadblocks and inspections.

As Sean looked overhead, the skies were filled with the sweeping beams of a flock of helicopters as the coastal town of Astoria had been earlier that day. He worried about the consequences of the massive search not being able to locate Chavez. The mercenary was a lethal virus loose in the city of Portland. He was sure that Chavez would not hesitate to destroy anything that stood between him and freedom at this point.

Thirty One

As the Rose City Cab dropped Rey Chavez off at the front door of the "Bare Necessities" gentleman's club, he was pleased with how quickly and easily he and his cousin were able to slip away. The firefight at the hangar provided the perfect diversion for their hasty retreat.

Reluctant to risk checking into any area hotel or securing alternative transportation until things cooled off, the twenty-four-hour strip club would provide an acceptable - and entertaining shelter to hole up.

Sending Ramon to secure a pitcher of beer and stack of dollar bills, he settled into the vinyl seat of the booth to take in the show. He had just decided which of the three clothing-deprived women to focus his attention on when his secure cellphone began to buzz.

Cursing softly, he reluctantly pressed the "Receive" button on his keypad, "Chavez."

"It's Tug. I assume this line is secure?"

"Of course, what can I do for you?" Chavez asked.

"What the hell is going on out there, Rey? It sounds like you've got quite the cluster going on," Tug's tone was pointed, showing his irritation.

"I've got it handled," Chavez snapped flatly.

"Really. Our employer is dead. You have most of Oregon, Washington, and the feds on your tail...you call that under control?" Tug growled.

"You'll still get your finder's fee, don't worry about it," Chavez responded indifferently.

"Don't worry about it? I still had business with Hasegawa. My name is still attached to that slimy slug. You really cocked things up out there, Rey!" Tug snapped, "If things get ugly for me and you somehow manage to slip out of the country, I will personally end your retirement with a bullet tap to the head!"

"Aw, come on, man. After all we've been through...we're like brothers," Chavez reasoned, while the U.S. government did little to unnerve him, he knew Tug well enough to know his words held no empty threat.

"There is no family in this business, Rey - you know that."

"What do you want me to do, Tug? You want a bigger percentage?" Rey asked, motioning his cousin, who had returned from the bar to take a stack of bills up to the main stage rack.

"Here's what you can do to make this square, Rey. That girl you were supposed to dispose of?"

"Yeah?"

"Complete that job, and take care of her Boy Scout boyfriend. Wire the original fee, and I will wish you a peaceful retirement," Tug requested.

After a brief pause, Chavez relented to one last job as opposed to a lifetime of watching for Tug over his shoulder, "Sure, I guess I could take care of that on my way out of town. Then we'll be square?"

"We'll be square," Tug replied evenly and terminated the call.

Chavez stared blankly at the cellphone. Tug's request would require him to re-enter the danger zone within Portland's city limits – a concept that did not sit well with him. Every law enforcement agency in the region was on the lookout for him. Moving around the town would support abysmal odds of his escape. Still, taking on all of the police forces of Oregon would be a more pleasant task than waiting for the steel blade of Tug's vengeance to find him in the dark of night. With his fingers in the air, he summoned for the waitress.

Adam climbed out of the black SUV Rachel had set him up in and thanked the agents he rode with. Following the flow of personnel to the Hillsboro Airport's conference room, he found Sean and Rachel debriefing Director Manning and Senator Johnson.

As the big Fish and Wildlife officer joined them at the table, he grinned, "Always walking that fine line between stupidity and bravery!"

"So, you heard?" Sean asked, his weary head slumped in his hands.

"Yeah, I heard. We received the report as we descended out of the Coastal Range," Adam admitted, "Sure a lot of confusion over what to do with you, either hang you or give you a medal."

"Well, if Beckett had his choice, it would be the former. Fortunately, Agent Manning and Senator Johnson believe differently. They bought me a stay of execution," Sean replied.

"I wish I could say it will hold, but I really don't know," cautioned Manning.

"Well, I appreciate what you two have done for me. You both went out on a limb," Sean said.

"Boy, I bet Beckett was pissed," the wildlife officer grinned.

"He was about to come unglued. Aside from recommending charges to the federal prosecutor, he can't touch Sean. He'll likely be gunning for you though," Rachel warned.

"Aw, I can handle Stanimal, the Animal. He barks big, but his bite isn't so bad," Adam shrugged.

"Well, folks, I hate to break this up, but I've got one hell of a mess to clean up and a rogue mercenary to find," Manning pushed away from the table, "You fellas have a place to stay?"

"Yeah, we still have a room at the hotel in town," Sean replied.

"Any leads on Chavez?" Adam asked.

"I'm afraid not. We have a large interagency task force assembled. I'd like to say we have a good shot at catching him, but a merc of Chavez' caliber, he could be halfway to Mexico by now," Rachel admitted.

"Very likely," Adam echoed, and seeing in Sean's eyes the toll the day had taken on him suggested they get back to the hotel, "I'd like to get an early start back home tomorrow. Laura's pretty unhappy about our little trip as it is."

With little disagreement, the three broke from the table. As they exchanged their goodbyes, Rachel gave Sean a quick hug and whispering in his ear, assured him that she would talk to the federal prosecutor on his behalf before she called it a night.

Miranda departed the bus and resisted her friends' urges to stay with them. She was exhausted and just wanted her own space to retreat.

She did relent to having them drop her off at her hotel. Thanking them and bidding them an eventless return home, she shuffled into the lobby and to the bank of elevators to go up to her room.

Under a heavy veil of exhaustion, she didn't pay much attention to the man who entered the elevator behind her. It was only after she pushed the button for her floor and the stainless steel doors closed, did she take a conscious look at the other rider. Him not having pushed a button for another floor, her instincts alarmed her to study the man.

The reflection from the doors did not offer a mirror-quality view, but they did provide enough to see that the man was not dressed as she would expect for the hotel she was staying. Clad in grey sweats and a tattered denim jacket, he was out of place, even for the casual persona of the Portland area. Her other senses in tune, she also noticed that the man smelled strongly of cigarette smoke, the stench of hours logged in a seedy bar. What bothered her the most was where the man stood. Instead of standing in the opposite corner, he positioned himself directly behind her. She realized that it was partly her own fault for parking in front of the control panel, but somehow it just didn't seem right.

As the bell declared each passing floor, she tried to get a closer look at the man. A chill danced up her spine, realizing the man bore similar in appearance to Rey Chavez, the man that terrorized the Nagaremono. But this was not that man. She would never be able to cleanse her mind of his image. Still, she inched forward and darted through the doors when they slid open.

Without casting a glance behind her, or even taking the time to see if the man from the elevator exited, she strode quickly down the hallway. Almost to her door, she freed her keycard from her purse and started to let out a sigh of relief as she turned the last corner.

Rounding the hallway nearest her room, she froze in terror. From the shadows, seemingly oozing into the light, the menacing visage of Rey Chavez seeped toward her. Spinning to run back the way she came, she collided with the man from the elevator.

A pair of hands gripped her and spun the frightened woman around to face the mercenary. Before she could utter a shriek, one of the hands moved to her mouth. "Good work Ramon," Chavez congratulated his cousin, "Let's get her inside."

Ramon prodded Miranda forward, the slight man squeezing her tight and keeping his shins clear of her flailing legs.

"I'll take that," Chavez sneered, snatching the keycard that was still in her grasp. Wasting no time, he slid the card into the slot and pushed the door open. Ushering Miranda and Ramon in the room, he allowed the door to close behind them.

With a nod of his head, the mercenary sent his cousin with the fiercely struggling captive towards the back of the room. For a moment, she broke free from Ramon's arms and pulled away from the hand that clamped over her mouth. Before she could let out much more than the "h" of help, Chavez strode forward and struck her hard across the face.

Miranda's body slumped to the floor at the feet of her captors. As her head cleared, Chavez slowly and calmly screwed a silencer onto the barrel of his Ruger pistol and leveled it at Miranda's head.

"You overestimate your value to me. Any further games by you and you will no longer be a problem," Chavez informed his captive.

Miranda glared at him from her sitting position on the floor. Despite the tremendous temptation, she resisted making any comments. Instead, she slowly rose and slid onto the nearby sofa. "So, what do you want?"

"I need to borrow your cell phone," Chavez replied, holding his hand out.

"Didn't you just rob millions of dollars? I'd think you could afford your cell phone," Miranda glared through pursed lips.

"Give me your phone before I have Ramon retrieve it from your dead body," Chavez growled.

"I can't Chavez. You made us all give them to you...," Miranda smiled at reminding Chavez of his actions aboard the dinner cruise.

Failing to see the humor in the situation, Chavez rushed over to where she was sitting and grabbed her by the hair, "Enough games!" Dragging Miranda across the room, he pushed her hard against the hotel desk.

"Use this phone and call your boyfriend!" Chavez shouted.

About to argue the fact that she didn't have a boyfriend, she realized she had probably pushed the angry mercenary as far as she should. Knowing full well he meant Sean, she reached an outside line and punched the numbers for Sean's phone.

Thirty-Two

S ean had just laid down on the soft bed after letting the hot shower relax his aching muscles. Feeling like his weary body would finally get its much-needed rest, he groaned when his phone ring, "Go away."

He stared in dismay at the flashing phone across the room. All he wanted to do was fall asleep after catching up on Sportscenter. "Dang!" he cursed as he rolled out of bed and gave in to the persistent ringing.

Grabbing the phone just as it was emitting its final ring, he called into it, "This is Sean."

Miranda had barely been able to utter Sean's name when Chavez snatched the phone away, "Hero, I am going to keep this brief. I have a gun to Ms. Shaw's head right now. I have no problem pulling the trigger, but I will hold off only if you follow my instructions explicitly. First, she is at the Heathman Hotel downtown. You arrive, alone, and you just might get to see her alive. Call the hotel number and ask for Shaw's room. I'll tell you what to do then." The phone fell silent, and Sean numbly replaced the handset.

Staring at the phone, Sean's mind raced into motion, trying to formulate a game plan. Adrenaline surged through his body, allowing fatigue and achy muscles to be forgotten. Dialing Adam's number, he scrambled around the room, tugging his clothes on.

"What's up?"

"Adam, Chavez has Miranda. They're in a hotel downtown. We've got to go," Sean informed his friend.

"I'll meet you outside," Adam replied, hanging up as he too clambered to get dressed.

In less than a minute, they were traveling at high speed down the dark surface streets towards downtown Portland. From the passenger seat, Sean called Rachel.

"I figured you'd be resting," the Deputy DOI director answered in her traditional business-like tone.

"Can't. I got a call from Chavez," Sean confided.

"What?" Rachel choked.

"Just a few minutes ago. Adam and I are en route now," Sean confirmed.

"What are you going to do?"

"We're not exactly sure yet. It's obviously a trap, but I have to go in," Sean replied.

"Sean, that's suicide!" Rachel gasped.

"I know. They'll kill Miranda if I don't show up, they'll kill us both if I do," Sean admitted, "I want you to call Manning. Have him come in quiet and in the shadows and then hang tight until I can give some kind of signal."

"Sean, you can't give a signal if you're dead."

"I thought about that," Sean replied pensively, "I don't have a choice."

"Let Manning handle it," Rachel pleaded.

"And what survival rate would you give Miranda then?"

"Probably zero, but Sean...," Rachel tried to reason.

"Something's better than nothing," Sean fired back, "Please, call Manning and have him play it cool."

"I will. Sean, please be careful."

"Aren't I always?" Sean grinned through the phone and hung up.

"So, what is the plan?" Adam asked.

Adam parked the SUV a block away from the hotel. He turned to his friend, "You sure you want to do it this way? Rachel's right, this is a suicide mission."

"We have to do something," Sean nodded as he hopped out of the truck.

"Hey!" Adam called, and tossed his friend a holstered handgun. Sean thanked him and wasted no time strapping it on under his jacket as he jogged across the street and down the sidewalk towards the Heathman Hotel.

Trying to think like a mercenary, Sean reasoned that luring him to the hotel was most likely nothing more than a ruse to eliminate a loose end. He figured he would be watched or maybe even killed before he even made it to Miranda's room. Deciding to be cautious, Sean slipped down an alley adjacent to the hotel to find an entrance that might be more discrete.

Midway down the alley, he found what he was looking for, a sundeck leading to the indoor pool sat behind a six-foot-high wall. A section of arborvitae that butted up against an iron gate provided him a peek at the empty patio. Seldom used during the wet months of winter and spring, the sundeck was vacant. The smell of stale cigarettes hung in the air, telling Sean that hotel employees sneak out there to steal a smoke break.

Taking advantage of the desolate spot, Sean grabbed the frame of the wrought iron gate, taking care to clear the decorative spikes lining the top as he vaulted over. Landing softly on the concrete pad of the sundeck, Sean moved quickly into the shadows and found the door to the first-floor hallway. To his relief, the door was wedged open, left ajar by the last smoker who was afraid of being locked out.

Sean wasted no time and entered the building. Slipping along the darkened corners of the hallways, he found the bank of elevators leading to the guestrooms on the upper floors. On a tiny couch beside the elevators, Sean noticed a man reading the newspaper, as though he were waiting for someone. The man tapped his foot subconsciously, quelling his excited nervousness. The well-worn tennis shoes caught Sean's eye.

Playing a hunch, Sean emerged from the shadows. With a purposefully confident stride, he made his way to the elevators and pressed the "up" arrow and waited for the doors to open. Pulling his cellphone from his pocket, he dialed the hotel's number and requested Miranda's room.

"Chavez, I'm here," Sean called out, not minding his volume, "What would you like me to do now?"

"Take the elevator to the fourth floor. Very quickly and quietly come to room four-twenty, we'll be waiting for you," Chavez' voice ordered.

Sean hung up the phone and slid it in his pocket. With his free hand at his side, he flashed four fingers, two and then cupping his thumb and index finger together to complete the sign for "four-twenty". He hoped Adam had been able to see.

As the elevator bell chimed, Sean heard the rustle of newspaper. Ducking inside, he was privy to a figure joining him just as the doors slid shut. The person slid to the back of the elevator and waited for Sean to push the button. Lighting the "four" button, Sean looked up to the reflective brass ceiling and glanced at his fellow elevator rider.

Sean recognized the figure as resembling Chavez. Drifting slowly back, he asked casually, "Which floor?"

"Uh...five thanks," the rider responded, his voice with a hint of a Hispanic accent.

As Sean pressed the button for the fifth floor, he exploded backward, driving his elbow into the Hispanic man's throat. Snapping his head around, Sean saw the man clutching at his neck, gasping for breath. With immediate retrospection, he hoped he was right about his hunch.

"Rey is going to tear you apart!" the man rasped.

The man's threat satisfied Sean's hunch. With a grin, he retorted, "Thanks, I'll look forward to that." With a second flash of his elbow, Sean connected with his would-be captor knocking him to the floor. Having reached the fourth floor, the doors slid wide. Sean knelt next to the groggy mercenary, slapping him in his face, "Come on, time to go meet ol' Rey. Don't want to keep him waiting."

Sean had to support the man who was wobbling through jellied legs. Step by step, he guided himself and Chavez' man down the hall and parked himself in front of room four-twenty. Rapping gently against the door, he waited for it to open. His woozy elevator companion opened his mouth as though he were about to call out, releasing the handgun from its holster, Sean brought it down swiftly against the side of the man's head, knocking him unconscious. Holding him by his collar, Sean pushed the man's face in front of the peephole.

The door swung open, almost causing Sean to drop his hostage to the floor. He felt a surge of adrenaline as he saw Chavez' face in the doorway.

"Good work Ramon, let's take care of this quickly," Chavez snapped.

Sean gave the weary Ramon a shove, "Yeah, let's get this over quick."

Chavez was visibly irritated for assuming that his cousin had Sean in his custody, "What the hell…."

"What the hell, indeed, Chavez. I was going to offer a trade, but now I don't believe that is necessary," Sean mocked noticing Chavez' pistol still in its shoulder holster, "How about you slide that gun out and toss it very nicely aside, or I'll just shoot you both and Miranda. I walk out of here real easy."

Putting his hands up, Chavez carefully made his way to his holster, "Okay, hero. It looks like you got the drop on me. I underestimated you once again, or overestimated my cousin." He let out a scowl to show his disapproval with Ramon. Just as he flipped up the top strap, freeing his handgun, Ramon's limp body suddenly surged, knocking Sean backward. His cousin free from Sean's grasp. Chavez snapped his arm up. His gun leveled evenly at Sean's face.

"Ramon, get your sorry butt up and tend to Ms. Shaw so that hero here doesn't try any other foolish actions," the mercenary held his hand out, and Sean knowing he was beaten, reluctantly gave his gun to the man that would likely kill both him and Miranda.

Across the room, Sean saw Miranda bound and gagged on the sofa. Her eyes were moist with tears, and she was visibly frightened, a sensation that only intensified as Ramon unsheathed a wicked-looking blade and brought it to her throat.

Thirty-Three

Adam hastily gathered his gear as his friend darted across the street. He worried about his friend's hasty exploits, but he did have to admit, Sean had sharp instincts. Still, he was sure this was a trap, and Chavez had only one goal - the elimination of a nuisance, and that nuisance was Sean Kendall. Strapping on the necessary gear, he followed Sean's lead and dashed across the street. Instead of circling to the rear of the building as Sean had, he headed straight for the front. He didn't think Chavez knew his face, but he didn't plan on exactly barging straight in either.

As he reached the entrance, he paused. The only way he was going to be able to help Sean without reinforcements arriving, was by surprise. Surveying the building, he began to hatch an idea. From the back hallway, he saw Sean arrive at the elevator. His friend pushed the call button and flashed his fingers in number format, a four, a two, and a zero. Miranda was in room four-twenty. Another man entered the elevator behind Sean. The man looked out of place for the quality of hotel Miranda was staying in.

Feeling time was now critical, he raced through the front doors, ignoring the front clerk's questioning glance and darted for the stairs. Assembling his gear as he jogged up the steps, Adam pressed as hard his legs would carry him to reach the roof access door, beyond the last floor of guest rooms. A padlock held a bolt shut and a contact alarm secured the door. Wasting no time, Adam slid a razor-thin magnet between the alarm contact points disabling the alarm. Dropping his pack, he extracted a pair of bolt cutters and began squeezing down on the handles until the metal pieces spliced, and the lock fell to the floor.

Swinging the door open, he dashed out onto the gravel roof of the hotel. A quick scan told him his best anchor point was a series of bolts used by window washing scaffolds that lined the roof closest to the side that he hoped was the twenties. Quickly securing a line, he snapped into his harness and bounced off the roof, rappelling towards the fourth floor. As the line slid through his hands, he gently jumped on the brick façade between the rows of windows until, by his count, he reached the correct floor.

Softly landing on the windowpane, he peered between the slits in the drapes. Instead of seeing Chavez and a hopefully alive Miranda, Adam was surprised to see two people intertwined in a mound rolling around the hotel floor. For a moment longer, Adam peered quizzically at the two. As the bodies turned to the side, Adam could see that a third figure came into view, wrapped in hotel bedding. He averted his gaze, trying to focus on anything other than the atrocity that he had just stumbled upon.

"That's why I don't touch the hotel blankets, icky…" he mumbled to himself as this new character was enough to snap Adam out of his voyeuristic trance and back to his task at hand. Realizing he must have misjudged where along the row of windows number four-twenty was, he swung on his line and used his feet to "jog" along the face of the hotel.

One window over, the drapes were drawn tight. He pressed his ear to the glass in time to hear Chavez ordering Sean to drop on his knees and lace his hands behind his head. "Time's up," Adam muttered to himself, pushing away from the window. Drawing his shotgun over his shoulder and leveling it on the large pane window, he let off a blast.

A shower of glass blew into the drapes following the explosion of the shotgun. Cascading on top of the sofa, the curtains covered Miranda and Ramon. Across the floor, Chavez had brought the silenced muzzle of his pistol to the back of Sean's neck. Both men looked to the window, shocked to see Adam strung there glaring in. Seizing the moment, Sean struck back with his hand knocking Chavez' pistol to the side, bullets spraying innocently into the drywall of the room as the mercenary squeezed the trigger a split second too late. As Sean dove away from Chavez, the mercenary tried to re-aim as he fled from the rising barrel of Adam's shotgun.

The blast of the twelve gauge overshadowed the high-pitched report of the silenced gun. Sean's dive took him over an end table peppered with shrapnel from the massive sabot round. Peaking up, he was just able to see the back of Chavez as he fled the room. Looking back to the window, Sean saw Adam shrug as he missed the mercenary, aiming high to ensure he did not accidentally clip Miranda with the shot. Sean swiped away the glass filled drapes from overtop Miranda and Ramon as Adam swung himself into the room, unclipping his carabineer landing neatly in front of the sofa.

Ramon held his blade steady to Miranda's throat, "Back off or the girl gets opened wide!"

Sean and Adam both took a couple of steps back, as Ramon pulled Miranda up from the couch and began to back out of the room. Grabbing the shotgun from Adam, Sean slowly followed the two into the hallway. Ramon dragged Miranda to the emergency stairwell and flung her to the floor as he bolted down the steps. Instantly, Sean was at her side, removing the cloth that Chavez had tied around her mouth.

"Are you okay?" he gasped, looking worriedly at the weary woman next to him.

"Yes, I am now," Miranda choked, her eyes glazed with fatigue, fright, and now relief.

To his surprise, Sean leaned forward and kissed Miranda hard on the mouth. His sense of relief was so great, his mind could think of nothing else. Quickly moving back, he looked to Adam, who was peering down the steps after Ramon. "Here," Adam said, tossing Sean his knife, "I'm going after them!" With a bound, the wildlife officer disappeared down the steps.

Sean quietly went to work freeing Miranda from her bindings, as his ears were met with the sounds of sirens and screeching tires at the front of the hotel. When Miranda was free, he helped her up and supporting her, they walked back to her hotel room, past the shocked and confused faces of the guests that had begun poking their heads into the hallway.

With the sofa in shambles, shards of glass, and splinters of shrapnel coating the cushions, Sean sat Miranda down on the bed in the adjacent sleeping room. He looked into her soft, blue eyes. Miranda's entire visage soaked in fear. Her lips trembled as she spoke, "I was so afraid. More so than on the boat - I knew we were leverage. Here...it was personal. He was going to kill me...and you...you had to know. You came anyway."

"Yeah, I knew. I had to try to stop them from hurting you. I had to try," Sean answered softly.

"What happened here? It...It must have been like the position my cousins put you into," Miranda quizzed, her voice lacking the usual confident demeanor.

"I guess. There's no time to think. You need to react before that trigger is pulled."

Miranda nodded in silence, as though she was processing the information. Suddenly her rigid posture relaxed as she leaned forward and laced her arms tightly around Sean's shoulders. Choked with tears, she sputtered, "I'm sorry, Sean. I'm sorry for not understanding. I'm sorry for placing the burden of Jeb's death on you."

Leaning back, Sean wiped her tears aside with his thumbs. His hands gently framing her face. "I know it was difficult for you, that's why I didn't press. I hoped...," he paused as he fought for the right words, "I hoped...for us."

Miranda's only response was to hold him once again tightly. For Sean, even if it was a moment that was going to pass, it just felt good to hold her.

Their moment was quickly broken up by a crowd of police and emergency services personal. Sean left the room to answer his phone, which had been ringing violently.

"This is Sean."

"Hey, I need your help, bud. I followed the Chavez goons down to the light rail tracks. They just hopped on the Max, and I'm going to follow them in the rear car. I need you to get down here in the truck and follow from the street!" Adam called frantically.

"Yeah, sure. What about the keys?"

"There's a hide-a-key tucked under the driver side fog light. We're heading to the eastside on the train that swings north toward Vancouver. Hurry, buddy," Adam replied.

As Sean burst through the doorway, he ran square into Rachel. "I've got to go. Please tell Miranda I'll be back as soon as I can," Sean rattled off and gently brushed past his friend and scurried down the hallway.

Bounding down the steps of the hotel, he reached the street and sprinted to Adam's SUV. Finding the hidden key as Adam had told him, he started the rig and accelerated hard away from the curb.

Light rain sprinkled on the windshield as Sean meandered through Portland's street before crossing one of the city's numerous bridges. Finding Interstate Street as his friend had instructed, Sean pushed the truck hard to catch up to the commuter train that held a healthy head start. It wasn't long before his headlights caught the reflective lettering of the Max light rail train. Ignoring the red light flashing at the intersection, Sean pressed the accelerator to the floor, catching up to the train. Running alongside, Sean could see Adam's silhouette give him the peace sign, and the two waited for the Chavez cousins to make their move.

At the next light rail platform, Sean brought the truck to a stop and pulled to the side, watching intently to recognize if either Chavez hopped off the train. As the Max train moved forward, he again maintained pursuit. Reaching a busy terminal, the Max stopped again. A scurry of passengers entered and exited the train. Just as the doors were closing, Sean saw Rey Chavez hop onto the platform and quickly mix in with the rest of the crowd. A moment later, Ramon Chavez followed, barely slipping through the automatic doors. Instantly Sean was on his phone with Adam letting him know the movement.

Sean pulled forward, inching the SUV along with the crowd, trying to keep the Chavez' in sight. In the corner of his eye, he saw Adam's arm reach up and grab the train's emergency cord. The squeal of steel brakes pierced the night, and Sean could see the bobbing heads of Rey and Ramon Chavez pick up their pace. As Sean hopped out of the truck, he saw Adam kick his way through the emergency exit and jump out next to the tracks. Together, they raced after Rey Chavez and his cousin.

Feeling the pursuit, Adam saw Chavez motion for his cousin to split up and take a different route. "Take Ramon. I'll get Rey!" Adam called as he sprinted across the street and down the alley that Rey had taken.

Wanting to argue and go after Rey himself, Sean resisted knowing they could not waste time. A former athlete, Sean easily closed the distance Ramon's meager head start had afforded. Sprinting up the hill, the two weaved through cars as Ramon tried to shake his pursuer. As Sean was close enough to tackle Ramon, the fleeing man took a risk, leaping across the tracks as the restarted light rail zipped towards the next station. Ramon jumped, his left foot slipping in the loose gravel that bordered the tracks, significantly shortening his trajectory, landing him in the path of the on-coming train. The Hispanic mercenary looked up in his final moment of life to see his reflection off of the rain-streaked gleam of the train.

Sean froze in horror, covering his face with his arm as he turned away from the gruesome collision. His lungs catching up from the uphill sprint, he called Adam, "Ramon's gone!"

A panting Adam replied, "Did you lose him?"

"He decided to take on the Max, kind of like one of those pennies kids put on the track…," Sean answered.

"Nasty, you mean 'clean up on track four'?" Adam joked.

"You can say that again. Where are you at?"

"Chavez just turned up Russell, he's headed for a busier area," Adam replied, "Why don't you leave ol' spaghetti guts - he's not going anywhere and help me."

"I'm on my way!"

Adam shoved his phone in his pocket and concentrated on keeping Chavez in sight. The conversation afforded his adversary an increase in his lead. With each block, the mercenary got closer to an area that had a history of vibrant nightlife. It also happened to be an area steeped in violence. This trip to the busy street of Highway 99 provided both. As Chavez rounded the corner, he slipped into a crowd consumed with heated discussion. To Adam's eyes, the interruption was not welcomed. A large, African-American man stepped into Chavez' path and with outstretched arms, slammed the mercenary to the concrete sidewalk.

Adam slid to a stop and side-stepped into the shadows. He watched Chavez push himself on his backside away from the group. Before his attacker was able to continue his assault, the arguing factions erupted into a full-scale brawl. Chavez jumped to his feet and darted the opposite direction of the fray only to be close-lined by Adam. Once again, the mercenary bounced on the sidewalk. Knowing Chavez' skills, Adam did not waste time and allow his foe to counter. With a heavy boot, he slammed his foot down on Chavez' face. The impact cracked Rey's head against the sidewalk, a trail of blood trickled down the cracks in the concrete.

Grabbing the mercenary by his collar, he heaved Chavez to his feet. The man wriggled to life, escaping Adam's grasp. Before he could land a blow, Adam kicked Chavez hard in the midsection, sending him reeling. The impact caused Chavez to dance backward, losing his footing and tumbled off of the sidewalk. The sound of screeching brakes was followed instantly by the bright flash of headlights centered directly on Chavez' horror-stricken face. The ordeal ended with the sickening crunch of metal bumper against Chavez' helpless body.

The night grew silent, as even the brawl of the feuding inhabitants of Portland's north-central neighborhood stopped to witness the event. Footsteps behind the wildlife office caused him to turn around. The panting body of Sean Kendall ran up beside him. "Two peas in a pod, those Chavez boys," Adam chided grimly.

"More like pea soup, now."

"Couldn't have happened to two nicer guys," Adam shrugged, "One playing on the train tracks, the other not looking both ways. Not the most honorable way to go, I have to admit. Truly nasty."

"I'm not so sure they were the most honorable of men," Sean just quietly admitted, his stomach turning in tight little knots, recalling the gruesome event.

"I suppose not," Adam agreed. Not sure how Beckett will try to pin these two deaths on us."

"Miranda's safe. You get to go home to your wife. All in all...," Sean said.

Thirty Four

The city of Portland seemed to be in chaos, just as Hillsboro and Astoria had been earlier in the day. Sean Kendall looked solemnly out his window of the police cruiser that sped him towards the federal building where Manning and Beckett were waiting for him. Once again, his exploits were to be debriefed, likely countless times. All the exhausted man wanted was for his head to hit the pillow, and this day to be over. He doubted DOI Director Stanley Beckett had any appreciable level of concern over Sean's weariness.

The transporting officers did grant him an opportunity to call Miranda and find out that her friends Brett and Carrie, had joined her and were going to bring her home with them. She promised him that they would get together in the morning. Hearing her voice and hearing the warm tone having returned, lifted Sean's spirit - almost enough to endure Beckett's tirade when he did arrive at the federal building.

As the police car pulled up, Rachel York was there to greet him, along with a pair of Beckett's agents as well two FBI agents. "You okay, Sean?"

"Yes, I'll be fine. What's Chavez' condition?"

"He' and his cousin are both in critical condition. There were life-flighted to Oregon Health Sciences University. Rey Chavez suffered a severe cranial fraction and was bleeding heavily to go with the rest of his broken bones. Ramon lost his arm and a lot of blood. Both are lucky to be alive," the Assistant DOI Director informed him.

"Lucky for whom?" Sean scoffed.

"Everyone gets their day in court, no matter how despicable their character or actions," Rachel shrugged.

"Well, let's get this over with," Sean sighed and stepped into the marble foyer.

"Is he dead?" Congressman Small bellowed to his staffer as he thumbed his highball glass, watching the ice play around the amber liquid.

"No, sir. While that would have been convenient, he suffered a major concussion, some pretty nasty wounds, but he is going to survive," congressional aid Rhinehart replied.

"Can the bastard talk?" Small asked hopefully, feeling at least for the short term, a coma would suffice just as well.

"Yes, sir. In fact, while he has been hopped on pain medications, it seems he has had rather loose lips," Rhinehart admitted, knowing his bosses reactions he put his hands up to calm him down, "I already have a defense attorney on his way over to nullify the testimony while Chavez is on the meds. I used one of the offshore accounts and channeled it through one of the stupid civil rights defense funds."

"You think that is sufficient?" Small asked.

"I don't know, sir. It could be, unless…" Rhinehart began.

"Unless what?"

"Unless Chavez decides to cut a deal to save his own tail. Even if he does, sir, his implications could only reach as far as Gaskill. Tug is far too smart of a mercenary to be brought in. We have to trust that," Rhinehart conceded, almost pleading.

"Well, we laid that turd with Gaskill, I guess we get to live with the stench," Small sighed.

"I suppose that is one way to look at it, sir. To be safe, I took the liberty of calling in a backup plan," the aide informed Small.

"Oh?"

"Jake deLong. A former covert ops who has been a long term supporter of yours. He is sympathetic to our cause. He's been checked out by the team," Rhinehart concluded, hoping this answer was satisfactory to Small.

The Idaho Congressman mulled this new piece of information for a moment, his hand rubbing his chin thoughtfully, "Good. Keep a close eye on this one, Rinehart. We cannot afford for any bread crumbs to lead their way to our door."

"Of course, sir."

Sean winced at the pounding in his head. He pushed himself deeper and deeper into the darkness, trying to escape. The incessant barrage of thumping just wouldn't cease. Finally, with one eye open, he could see light through the gauze-like haze of sheets. Daylight streamed into the room, and despite what his weary brain was telling him, the banging was not within the confines of his skull, but rather across the hotel room at the front door. A glance at the red lights on the alarm clock told him that it was well after noon.

Rubbing his eyes, he slipped on a pair of pants and stumbled his way to the door. Through the peephole, he saw the grinning face of Adam Raines. Opening the door, Sean grumbled, "What the hell are you so happy about?"

"Aw come on sunshine. We lived to see another day. Now that alone is worthy of good nature," Adam said in a thunderous, very happy voice and then holding up a bag, he added, "I brought bagels...and a guest..."

As Adam brushed past Sean, Miranda stepped forward, a bit tentatively as if to see if it was okay with Sean. "Well, I wasn't exactly expecting guests, let me at least put a shirt on," Sean mumbled, a bit embarrassed as he looked back at his room. A trail of clothes began at the door where he stood and led to the bedroom where he scarcely scraped out a meager few hours of sleep.

For the first time since the last day she spent with him in the Cascades, Miranda responded in a flirtatious manner, "You don't have to get dressed on my account."

"But you do on mine," Adam snorted as he tossed Sean a crumpled shirt he found on the floor.

Oblivious to Adam's jibe, Sean laced the shirt over his head and joined them in the sitting area. Seeing the three large Starbuck's cups in the tray, Miranda was holding, offered Sean hope for shaking off the weary haze the previous day's beating placed him.

"So how was 'downtown'?" Adam asked.

"Oh, you know. Answering the same questions hundreds of times, each time met with scrutiny and some pompous bureaucrat pointing out the different verbiage I used from report number twenty-three. They didn't like it much when I told them I was just trying to keep it fresh," Sean shrugged and then not waiting for one to be offered, he leaned across the table, "Please tell me one, or all three of those are for me."

"Of course, I'm sorry," Miranda slid one of the large cups from its holder and handed it to Sean, "I'm just glad you're okay. No trouble with the feds?"

"Oh, no. I am in trouble. I am facing a few charges of reckless endangerment, interfering with a federal investigation, illegal use of a fire arm…there are a few others. I was just so tired I would have signed just about anything they slid in front of me if they would have handed me a pillow. Of course, Adam should know all about that, since he posted my bail," Sean shared.

"Uh, I would have if you called me. I figured they were going to let you off the hook - hero and all," Adam admitted.

Sean looked over at Miranda, who shook her head, "Not me. I would have if I had known."

"Must have been Rachel, I guess," Sean shrugged.

"Do you really think they will send you to jail?" Miranda asked, visibly concerned.

"Who knows? The fact is, I did break all of those laws. I guess it just depends on context," Sean admitted.

"Don't look to me for conjugals," Adam scoffed, only to be met by two pairs of rolling eyes. "Well, sleepyhead, you probably didn't see the news or hear, Chavez is alive. They saved the evil bastard. We can only hope for some severe brain damage like maybe he pees his pants every time he hears a car horn or something like that."

"Better than that," Miranda added, "According to the reports, he is turning state's evidence. Apparently, there was a bigger player involved in the whole thing."

"No kidding. Did they say who?"

"No, and the reports were not confirmed," Miranda shrugged.

A buzzing from the other room broke up their conversation. Sean got up to retrieve his cell phone from beside his bed. By the time he reached it, it had vibrated to the edge of the nightstand and fell to the floor. Snatching it before it went into voicemail, he answered, "Hello?"

"Sean, its Rachel. Mind if I stop by?"

"Sure. Adam and Miranda are here. They were just bringing me up to speed," Sean said, smoothing the mussed hair on his head.

"Good. I have news for them too. I am going to be bringing someone with me," Rachel warned.

"That seems to be the trend. We'll see you in a few," Sean said, hanging up the phone.

Rejoining his friends in the living space, Sean shared, "That was Rachel. She says she has news for all of us."

"Maybe they finally canned Beckett and all of your charges have been dropped," Adam speculated hopefully.

"That would be nice, but I won't count on that," Sean admitted.

"We're going to have to ugly you up. You are way too pretty for prison," Adam chided his friend, casting a scrutinizing glare across the room.

"I don't know, you think? I mean jumpsuit orange really isn't my color," Sean smiled back. The humor helped settle some of the tension in the pit of his stomach over the issue. Under his casual demeanor, was a genuine fear that a lengthy jail term loomed in the future.

It wasn't long before there was a knock at the hotel door. Sean quickly crossed the room and opened the door to find Rachel - in her usual immaculate appearance and behind her, Senator Johnson, whipping off his sunglasses, giving Sean a warm smile.

"I found this wedged into the doorjamb. It mean anything to you?" Rachel asked, holding up a business card as she and the senator entered the hotel room.

Sean studied the card. It was unadorned, no fancy embossing or design, just the simple text "Frankie C." and the handwritten words "Thank you, we're even." Turning to Rachel, he asked inquisitively, "You didn't post bail for me last night, did you?"

"No. I looked into it. They said it had already been arranged. I assumed Adam beat me to the punch. He didn't?" Rachel shrugged.

"No, but I think I know who did. Anyways, Senator, can I get you a cup of coffee? You, Rachel?" Sean offered, with each declining.

"Senator Johnson had asked if I knew where you were staying, he wanted to get in touch with you. I told him that I had some business to discuss with you and suggested we come together," Rachel said, getting straight to business and continued, "First, I have some great news. Chavez has admitted to killing Harrison. I'm sorry, Miranda, for being so frank. I know you and Harrison were close." Rachel cast a knowing glance Miranda's way before continuing, "We have already secured the release for the Makah boy. We are going to fly him back up to the reservation. I wanted to know if you two would join us, since you two were instrumental in returning his freedom." The Assistant Regional Director studied Sean and Adam.

"I would love to, but aren't I due for arraignment here in Portland at the Federal Building?" Sean asked.

"Actually, that is the news I was coming to you with," Senator Johnson smiled, "I made a deal with the prosecutor on this case. Manning from the FBI was also quite helpful in persuading his decision. The District Attorney agreed to wave most of the charges and avoiding any prison time provided you serve some community service."

"Oh, well, that seems reasonable. What are the terms?" Sean asked.

"Eighteen hundred hours, under my direction," Johnson replied.

"Eighteen hundred hours?" Miranda frowned.

Senator Johnson just smiled and put his hand in the air to quell any concerns, "One hundred and eighty ten-hour days, your typical work year. You would be serving on one of my special project committees for one year. I figured your experience as a corporate negotiator, and your obvious quick thinking could be helpful. So, what do you say?"

"I'd say I'd be insane not to accept your offer, but I'm not sure I know what you think I can do for you, Senator," Sean said gratefully.

"We'll work out those details later," Senator Johnson assured Sean, "By my count, you have saved my life twice. I'm just glad I was able to repay that debt."

"Thank you, sir," Sean eagerly shook Senator Johnson's outstretched hand.

"Let's say you report at my office in three weeks. I assume you have some…recovering to manage," Senator Johnson instructed, looking past Sean's visible bumps and bruises at Miranda sitting on the couch behind him. "Now, if you will all excuse me, I have to rush off to a meeting. I assume that buzzing in my pocket is my driver, letting me know he has arrived. See you in three weeks, Kendall." Waving goodbye to Adam and Miranda, the senator stopped to thank Rachel for bringing him and left for his car.

"That clears up that issue," Rachel smiled glibly, "What do you say, helicopter ride?"

Sean looked at Miranda and then to Adam, "I don't know…"

Adam shrugged, "I've got to drive the truck back."

"You should, Sean. Maybe I can drive up later and meet you if you wouldn't mind?" Miranda smiled.

"I would like that," Sean admitted, and turned to Rachel with a wrinkled nose, "I don't have to be handcuffed this time, do I?"

To everyone's surprise, Rachel slipped from her usual stoic refrain and let out a hearty laugh, "Only if you want to be Kendall."

Realizing the mixed reception for her joke, she faced Miranda and smiled, "Don't worry, Ms. Shaw, Sean will be in excellent hands."

"I have no doubt, Rachel," Miranda grinned in return.

Reaching for the door, Rachel informed Sean that she would have a car pick him up and bring him to the downtown helipad in half an hour. Adam, in turn, quickly excused himself to pack his own room so that he could get on the road for the return trip up Interstate Five.

Sean and Miranda remained in collective silence for a few moments before Sean finally spoke. "Are you sure you want to return to the reservation? I mean after all that's happened...."

"I'm sure," Miranda said softly, taking a step closer, "It's time I start taking on the painful parts of my life directly so that I can return my attention to the good parts."

Without warning, Miranda leaned into Sean, reaching up to deliver a deep kiss. Grabbing the back of his neck, she held him close as her free fingers twirled at his hair. Igniting her veins, Sean's own hands pulled her closer in a warm embrace, bringing the two tighter.

Enveloping her body with his arms, Sean's grasp made Miranda squirm even closer as a shudder slid up her spine.

Sitting Sean onto the couch, she leaned against his shoulder, her hand in his. Her mind reeling. She had surprised even herself with how much she had missed him.

"Oh, Sean. I..." Her own words were cut off by their lips coming together.

Thirty Five

Tug had already wiped down the penthouse and collected his things, as well as what offerings the dead prostitute and Hasegawa had at the apartment that he thought might be of use. Ironically, having only recently arrived in his sanctuary, he knew he had to return to the very place that was hunting him. As he moved along the docks, he searched for the freighter Maboroshi, a Hasegawa Industries ghost ship that did not register on any of Hasegawa's manifests - a boat registered to a chain of shell companies licensed out of Liberia.

As his cell phone buzzed, he hoisted it up, "This is Tug."

"Tug, it's Jerry Rhinehart, and I have Congressman Small with me. I'm sure you have been following the news here, stateside?" Rhinehart asked.

"I have. I understand a mercenary took out Hasegawa and has been placed in custody," Tug replied flatly.

"That is correct. One of your men, I presume?" Rhinehart posed his question with a heavy, disapproving tone.

"If he were one of my men, he would not have strayed from the mission, nor would he have been captured - at least not alive," Tug's answer was terse, not enjoying the indignation in Rhinehart's voice, yet conceded, "I knew him. I vouched for him to Hasegawa.

Had I known he would stray so far from the operation, I would not have allowed it."

"So now, we have a mess to clean up," Rhinehart said.

"Yes, the Seattle operation was messy, and it left strings…" Tug admitted.

"Strings which need to be cut. This Hasegawa disaster brings everything too close. I don't think I have to tell you that the congressman cannot be linked to anything that has happened - in Portland, Seattle, or that damned Indian reservation," Rhinehart stated.

Tiring quickly of the congressional aid's banter and smug demeanor, the mercenary sighed, "What do you propose, Rhinehart?" Tug waited for the response as he daydreamed a dozen ways of exterminating Congressman Small's right-hand man.

"I have someone to take care of Chavez. We may have to use him to take care of that do-gooder boy…what's his name? Kendall?" Rhinehart professed.

"No. You leave Kendall and his girlfriend to me. I am heading back stateside. I will see that it is done," Tug almost shouted in the phone.

"That's fine, Tug, but it must be taken care of," Rhinehart scolded.

"Rhinehart, you remember who you are talking to. Even Small can't protect you from me. Don't piss me off!" Tug warned as he found the vessel with Mabiroshi tattooed on her bow. Before waiting for the response, he ended the call.

Pulling the envelope from his pocket and ensuring the proper amount of bills was stacked inside, he proceeded up the gangplank. Looking over his shoulder, the city of Osaka stood behind him. The road ahead would be an arduous one as his face had quickly ascended the "most wanted" list at all U.S. entry points. The mercenary scoffed to himself, "Then again, it is the U.S. Thousands of drug smugglers, illegal aliens, and terrorists make their way across each year. And none of them are me!"

Dr. Korvath grabbed his coat and ID. He was hoping that he would skate through his on-call shift, but as one of Portland's premier neurologists, he rarely did. His mind had been more on whether or not he locked his Mercedes than on the man who was walking through the parking garage towards the elevators.

Scanning his phone for the preliminary details on the day's caseload, he pushed the call button on the elevator. Cycling through the reports on the tiny device, he didn't notice the light aerosol sprayed in the air behind him. Suddenly, his head felt woozy, and his limbs heavy as his visions plunged down a long, black tunnel.

Jake deLong caught the man before he tumbled to the floor. Sitting him upright in a dark corner of the garage, deLong checked his watch. The physician would be out for roughly fifteen minutes with little more than a headache, and a feeling like he had burnt the candle at both ends a bit too much. Relieving the doctor of his lab coat and ID badge, the mercenary arrived back at the elevator just as the doors opened. Smiling at the nurse who scurried out, her eyes glued to her cellphone, deLong entered and pushed the button for the third floor.

Pulling a small knife out of his pocket, he cut a small slit in the doctor's badge and slipped in a photo of himself. A dab of epoxy smoothed out with his finger, the rough job was sufficiently done in time for the doors to reopen.

Weaving his way through the busy hallway of the ICU, he donned the lab coat and grabbed a small stack of patient folders from a nurse's station. Pausing at the corner of Room 314, he waited for the nurse to make her way down the hall.

deLong pressed forward, flashing Dr. Korvath's badge, bursting into the room like he was on a mission. A quick, satisfied glance around the room told him that he was alone, other than the man on the bed, awaiting his surgeon to arrive. The mercenary walked up to the PICC line and inserted a needle. Depressing a plunger, he inserted a reactant that was lethal for ten percent of the population when added to the standard pool of anesthetics used in the hospital.

Having had access to Ramon Chavez' DNA swab while at a VA over a decade ago, deLong's choice in how to dispense with him was almost made too easy. In seconds, the irreversible process would begin shutting down Chavez' organs. While questionable, the death would never be able to be proven as anything other than an unfortunate medication side effect.

Stepping out of the room, his head in his files, deLong walked past the security detail and towards the nurses' station on the far side of the ICU. Placing the files down, he rounded the corner towards the prep room. Beyond the line of sight of security, he slipped through the door for the stairs and slipped away from the ICU just as one of the nurses received a call from Dr. Korvath calling in sick.

The knock on the door took Sean by surprise. He had been completely lost in the moment holding Miranda close to him. Exhilaration and exhaustion had all but coaxed him to sleep. "Ugh, my ride to the helipad," he cursed.

"I guess you shouldn't keep Rachel waiting," Miranda teased as she watched Sean double check the hotel room to ensure that he had everything. Running to the door, he told the agent that he would be down in a minute. Turning around, he found Miranda beside him.

"I look forward to seeing you at the reservation," the auburn-haired biologist grinned.

"I do too," he replied, leaning to kiss her.

Facing him squarely, Miranda's face grew serious, "I am grateful to have you in my life. I just needed…"

Sean stopped her by placing a single finger to her lips. "I understand."

Returning the kiss, Miranda opened the door and bound down the steps to leave Sean to pack his belongings and meet the agent waiting outside.

Rachel was already on board the Ranger helicopter, reviewing a stack of papers when Sean arrived. Looking up, she smiled, "Good, we're ready to go. The boy is being brought out right now."

Sliding into a seat next to her, Sean noticed the file on top had the name Chavez inscribed on the label. "Has he been a cooperative witness?" Sean asked, nodding towards the enclosed documents.

"Somewhat. He has nothing to lose by coming clean about the events over the last few days, "Rachel admitted, "He refuses to implicate anyone else who might have been involved."

"Oh? You think he was backed by someone?"

"Hard to say. He could very well have been operating solo...I just have a feeling he was being pressured by an outside source. I mean, why stay in town to go after you and Miranda when in all honesty, he could easily have disappeared from Portland and been out of the country instead," Rachel shared her suspicion and grinned, "Let's be sure, you can be a royal pain in the rear, but is that worth throwing away a sure escape?"

"My vote would be on escape. So why kill Harrison in the first place?" Sean asked, getting the subject back on track.

"From a combination of Chavez' testimony and an investigation of Hasegawa's and Harrison's local offices, it seems Harrison had some dirt on Hasegawa, enough information to indict the Japanese magnate for money laundering for the mob. Harrison was trying to extort an agreement for Hasegawa Industries' fishing fleet to abandon their whale harvesting, as well as an initial cash settlement of two million dollars to put in an offshore account Harrison had created."

"Mixing his righteous work with a little personal gain," Sean hummed thoughtfully, "So that explains his nice office."

"Not exactly, we haven't found any evidence that Harrison had ever actually been paid off. He is a trust fund baby, and his family had set him up nicely - not two million lump sum nicely, but he wasn't exactly struggling paycheck to paycheck either," Rachel corrected.

"So Chavez was hired by Hasegawa, why kill him?"

"Chavez just said he wanted it all - a retirement score as he called it. One final job to allow him to buy his own sanctuary and no longer live in the shadows," the DOI assistant regional director reported.

"Pure greed. What happens to him now?" questioned Sean.

"He's probably already escaped the death penalty. We'll see what else we can shake out of him, otherwise, he just grows old at taxpayer expense," Rachel replied. Seeing her agent with the young Makah man in tow, she signaled to the pilot to power up the engine.

The door to the helicopter opened up, and the DOI agent was followed by the smiling face of Sam Riverstone. Eagerly, he reached out and shook Sean's hand, "Mr. Kendall, I cannot thank you enough. I have been told about everything that you have done."

Sean placed his hands up in a humble manner, "I only did what was right, and frankly, I got lucky."

"I know you do not care for the Makah ways, and yet you helped me. You are a good man," Sam pressed.

"Sometimes we need to look at the system we operate in and help it make the wrong things right," Sean told his young flight companion who gripped his seat tightly as the rotors spun quickly, pulling the helicopter into the air.

Thirty Six

The waves lapped upon the shore, pushing ahead of the oncoming mist that frequented the Strait of Juan de Fuqua. After being greeted to a warm reception, Sean spent most of the day relaxing on the beach swapping tales with his hosts. Chief Lanook and a cadre of young Makah girls stole most of Sean's attention, the former expressing gratitude, while the latter giggled and prodded Sean to relate the wild experience he overcame in Portland.

Shooing away the giggling entourage, Lanook excused himself to join a meeting of the tribal council. Left alone to enjoy a cold beer and a quiet moment, he leaned back against a large piece of driftwood. The sliver of sun that fought its way through the cloud layer, joined with the melodic rhythm of the surf to lull him to the doorstep of sleep.

His wary ears picked up the slightest footsteps approaching from behind him. Expecting another Makah visitor, he opened his eyes and waited for them to present in front of him. As the hands suddenly pressed on his shoulders, he jumped, twisting around into a defensive posture. His heart fought to slow down, to his relief, as well as his delight, the figure before him was that of a smiling Miranda Shaw.

The pair burst into laughter at Sean's overreaction. Striding forward, Miranda pressed her hands against Sean's and planted a playful kiss on his lips. "I've been sent to collect you, Mr. Kendall. The Makah Council has an announcement to make, and they want you to be there."

"They sent a messenger I can't seem to resist," Sean smiled, giving her hand a quick squeeze.

When the two reached the beachfront directly in front of the Makah village, they found most of the reservation assembled around the fire pit and stage from the previous week's celebration. Up on the stage, Sean saw the council sitting in a row. Beside them were Sam Riverstone, Adam, Detective Joe Woodfeathers, Rachel York and two empty wooden chairs.

Makah Police Chief Marty Lanook stood in front of the seats and urged Sean to join him with a wave of his hand. As Sean bound up the steps and Miranda paused, Marty called down to the biologist, "You too, Ms. Shaw! Please."

Hesitantly, Miranda followed Sean and accepted the last seat. When everyone settled, Lanook addressed the audience.

"The Makah nation is a proud one. Our culture, even today, is immersed in our rich history. Our ideals and customs have not wavered as our world has continuously been pinched by encroachment and integration. At times, we have defied this encroachment - both in physical terms as well as culturally. This has often created friction, created enemies," Lanook glanced towards Sean and Miranda.

"We have suffered a great tragedy, endured an invasive investigation by a legal entity we don't care to recognize as our rule of justice. Yet, out of the malice, from enemies, we have created friendship," Marty Lanook continued, "Ms. Shaw, we are deeply sorry for your loss. To all of you assembled on the storyteller's stage today, I speak for the reservation when I say we are grateful for your help in righting the wrong and returning Sam to us. Mr. Kendall, you looked for the truth and what was just instead of judging appearances and damning ideals. You are what the Makah call Tsukwak-Laxuk- One Man – a warrior."

The crowd let up an uproarious cheer for Sean. When the applause and commotion settled, the chief excused Lanook and took his place. He stood very still until the very last hint of noise had abated. Even the wind seemed to fall silent in the elder's presence.

"What police chief Lanook says is true. Your assistance to the Makah people was nothing short of heroic. History has a habit of teaching us out of tragedy. This week, we have learned that we can trust outsiders. We have learned that the ideals outside of our nation's boundaries do not differ a great deal from our own. Like the great Sitka Spruce, we must grow, evolve.

Our nation has endured years of abstinence in our practice of whale hunting, and yet we survived. Our ideals, our culture did not crumble. Our celebrations did not cease," Chief Wanah studied the crowd, "For centuries we graciously accepted the gift of our brother from the sea, never yielding to show the proper admiration and respect. In today's world, even in our corner of it, perhaps it is time for the tradition to change."

The crowd let out a gasp and erupted into a confused frenzy, which ceased immediately as Wanah put his hands up, "We will cease the harvesting of whales for celebration, sustenance, or any other matter. Our great hunters will still ride the waves in re-enactment of our historic days with blunt tip spears and humane instruments. When they are finished, they will provide an offering to our sea-bound brothers, allowing them to feast by our hand instead of us on them."

As at the beginning of his speech, he straightened and fell silent. Allowing his words to sink in, the crowd once more broke into a frenzy of chatter.

Marty Lanook leaned forward and whispered to Miranda, "Ms. Shaw, a gift to you, a new light for the creatures we both love."

From the back of the gathering, Rachel York spun away from the council and slipped away into the mist.

"Can you believe the whole dispute with the Makahs is over?" Sean asked as he gently stroked Miranda's arms. The young marine biologist lay nestled in Sean's arms, watching the flames in her fireplace dance their way up to the chimney flue.

"Centuries of tradition cast aside to accommodate the ideals of a society that essentially robbed them of their land and way of life," Miranda marveled at the concept.

"Too bad your friend couldn't witness the change," Sean added sympathetically.

"Jim would've been elated," Miranda agreed and then turned to Sean, "You never did fill me in on the details of the investigation."

"Well, in a nutshell, Harrison was applying some pressure on Hasegawa Industries by using some intelligence against Hasegawa he had acquired. Hasegawa hired Chavez to make it look like the Makah eliminated their old adversary," Sean stated plainly.

"What kind of information?" Miranda asked, still enjoying Sean's feathery touch.

"Apparently Hasegawa has some mob ties and was fattening his empire by laundering money through his myriad of companies. Harrison fought the juggernaut with the giant's own evils," Sean replied.

"Typical, David fighting Goliath, sounds like someone else I know," Miranda smiled, snuggling into Sean's chest. She felt surprisingly comfortable discussing her former fiancé with Sean. It was as if, in some way, the two had teamed up to assist her life's cause.

"Yeah, a hero fallen before his time," Sean said quietly. His mind neatly filed away the knowledge of Harrison's extorting the millions of dollars from the Japanese freighting magnate, a detail he felt Miranda's heart could live without.

"Jim was a good man, but not a hero," Miranda purred into Sean's chest, "You, you're the real thing. An honest American hero. My hero."

Agent Dawkins' emerged from the monochromatic black Suburban. Behind him, Rey Chavez was ushered out by Dawkins' partner. Moving towards the courthouse steps, the procession of federal agents and the mercenary moved quickly through a cleft in the massive crowd of on-lookers, reporters, and Foundation supporters that had assembled.

The case had become the lead story on every news station and taken upfront page residence for every paper in the country. While most of the details were suppressed, there was an air that the mercenary had been very forthright with information and that both he and Hasegawa were two very evil, dangerous men.

The federal prosecutor was pleased with the job that had been done by the DOI and FBI agents. He knew this case would be a fine asterix in his career as he moved up the political ladder. He smiled confidently at the dozens of cameras that captured the scene of Chavez' arrival. The attorney stood on the top stair as the agents and the mercenary approached the courthouse entrance.

The entire scene laid out cleanly for Tug Gaskill. As he adjusted the sights on his Barrett sniper rifle, his body was hidden over a thousand yards away amidst the sea of rooftops visible from Portland's Federal Building.

For just a moment, Chavez' flank was left unprotected, as the trailing agent followed from a step behind. It was more than enough time for Tug Gaskill to pull the trigger and see Rey Chavez' body melt out of sight. Panning up, he allowed himself to be amused for only a moment, taking in the scene of pandemonium as surprised and confused agents scrambled feverishly, trying to determine what had just happened. The federal prosecutor himself, stood with his mouth agape until an alert agent ushered him inside the safety of the courthouse. Chuckling to himself as he watched the smug prosecutor's face morph from an overconfident grin to a blood-stained look of shock and horror.

Effortlessly, Tug disassembled and stowed the weapon in its case before slipping into the shadowy folds of the architecture. He had other matters that required his attention, and the sooner they were completed, the sooner he could return to the sanctum of obscurity that every mercenary called home.

BLOOD
IN THE
SAND

A Sean Kendall Thriller

A diplomatic trip to Mazatlan, Mexico explodes into a multinational manhunt as a dignitary's wife is kidnapped. Tensions along the U.S. and Mexico border rise to a new high. Sean Kendall finds himself in the middle of it all as he is accused as the kidnapper.

Chased by drug lords, Mexican Federales, and a ruthless band of mercenaries, Sean is the unwitting catalyst that ignites a border war.

With agents on either side of the Rio Grande searching for him, Sean has to sneak back into his own country to clear his name and save innocent lives.

www.ingramcontent.com/pod-product-compliance
Lightning Source LLC
Chambersburg PA
CBHW021416110726
47901CB00008B/2186